And Love Was Born...
DEATH FOLLOWED

By
Laura Brown And John Greenburg
Including Poetry By Laura Brown

Acknowledgements

We wish to acknowledge the writers' group at the Dunedin, Florida Public Library. Their constructive criticism and encouragement helped us immensely. We also wish to thank Matt Gould, Laura's daughter Paulina Gould, Janet Moser and Janet Pollak for the hours they spent reviewing the manuscript and their valuable suggestions. Their efforts helped us to take our project to another level.

This story is based upon actual events. Names have been changed for the purpose of privacy, and some of the characters depicted are composites of more than one person.

Vigilante justice still exists in Guatemala. Recently, three young men who lived in a village, one of them twenty one and the other two eighteen, were accused of raping a young woman. No law enforcement authorities were contacted because the people who lived there believed in handling their own problems. They had known the young men and the victim for all their lives. They knew beyond a doubt who was guilty, and they knew what to be done. They lynched them from a tall tree, soaked the bodies in gasoline and set them on fire to eliminate the need for a Mayan burial. It is ironic that such brutality continues to occur in one of the most beautiful places in the world. Guatemala probably has the most perfect climate of all. It always seems to be springtime there.

Guatemala has been a lawless country from the time of its conquest by the Spanish, and this has continued all the way to the present. It is normal for armed guards to be placed on the roof of every bank, as well as having armed security inside. Anyone who visits the country is strongly advised to hire an armed escort. Guatemala is the "youngest" nation in Latin America. Half its population is under nineteen years of age, and the young are fleeing. Tens of thousands of young Guatemalans fled to the United States as undocumented refugees in 2014. Dire problems with health care, education, literacy, malnutrition and public safety fuel this exodus. Things are not likely to change in the near future.

This story took place in 1969. It is about a man and a woman who seemingly had everything, and Guatemala was a big part of their lives. They were very wealthy, physically attractive and possessed high ideals. Like practically all of us, they hoped to find true love, and they were lucky to find each other. In spite of their advantages, they still faced obstacles. Their world was rocked when evil penetrated their golden cocoons, and they found themselves in a life or death struggle.

Prelude

It was Saturday morning. Matt Logan was sitting with his wife Janet in the kitchen of their New Orleans home. Saturdays were always special days for them. They were both busy attorneys with successful practices, and they normally slept in on the sixth morning of each week. This time, he had gotten up very early because his subconscious had been working overtime. He couldn't wait to tell his wife about the monumental conclusions he had arrived at. While enveloped in a blanket of euphoric clarity, he sorted out the harrowing experiences he had been through in recent months that came close to ending his life. Upon awakening, he wondered, "Does cheating the Grim Reaper carry with it the reward of great wisdom?"

Ever since his travails ended, Janet appreciated Matt more than ever. A husband's flirtation with death often has that effect upon his wife. It had dominated her thoughts for months.

She looked at him and said, "You went through a lot, darling, but you have no idea what I went through."

He got out of his chair, went to her, put his arms around her and kissed her. He said, "We are now safe together."

He looked at her with a loving expression and added, "The craziest thoughts kept me awake last night. I had a moment of clarity. I now have a greater understanding of love and of death."

Her ears perked up. He had gotten her attention. She asked, "Tell me."

"All right, here goes. We've heard so many times that love is where you find it. It's impossible to define love, though, and there are no synonyms for the word."

Janet took a moment to think about what her husband said. She then nodded, and he continued.

"Love isn't as uncomplicated as lust, which only lasts in the heat of a moment. Love is next to God and just as mysterious. It can't be methodically examined in detail to determine how it's constituted and structured. It's so personalized that it differs with each individual. It blossoms within a person. From the moment the two people first meet, there's an attraction that can't be explained. They discover that they share values and common interests, but they also respect their differences. They must go slowly to allow enough time for getting to know one another. It's only when they give themselves fully and completely to each other that they begin to really live rather than just survive or exist. Their love is unconditional and unrelenting. They know that they share something beautiful built upon trust and faithfulness."

His eyes began to flash with excitement and he spoke with emotion in his voice. "They're willing to take on the world together. They're so proud of what they have that they want to shout about it from rooftops. Each of them is willing to give their life for the other, if necessary. To live without love is to suffer loneliness, which can be so unbearable that it leads to death. It's been said that the pain and inner turmoil of loneliness could be at the root of all evil. To live a loveless life is to be a lost, empty soul floating through the world."

He continued by saying, "True love is not promised to everyone, and the path a person must take to be with their beloved is never easy. It might be dangerous and could even prove fatal. All lovers face an inevitable parting when their days on this earth are over, but they had their time together, and that is more than the lonely can ever say. The worst tragedies are when a person's life ends before their time is due or they die alone without their loved ones present."

The loving husband paused briefly before adding, "Love and death have a great deal in common. Neither happens the way people expect, and both are mysterious and absolute. Like love, there are no synonyms for the word death. Though some may disagree, I believe it defies being analyzed or described in scientific terms. All that can be said is that death is the absence of life, and it is final. It is not equal to love. True love will never die and only the lucky ones experience it, while no one can escape death. In other words, whenever love is born, death follows."

His wife had listened attentively to every word he said. When he was finished, she asked, "What does that all mean?"

"Well, it proves that the two most powerful things in the world are love and death. Evil doesn't stand a chance against either of them. Evildoers will always self destruct because they are opportunists who feed off each other, and evil isn't found where true love lives."

Janet said, "Your philosophy has taken my breath away." She got up from her chair, went to him and hugged him. She whispered, "Would you like a cup of coffee?"

"Yes, love."

Matt and Janet were two of the lucky ones who had found true love. It was what they were living for, and they constantly nurtured their already strong relationship. They were very much like their friends Nathalie and Alfredo. Both of them were clients of his, and they first met at Matt's office. The experiences Alfredo and Nathalie shared and the remarkable people they encountered made an unforgettable story.

We Fell In Love

Look at the moon,
Hanging from the sky,
Like the brightest lantern,
Cast to us by God.
Moon of such splendor,
That lights our joyous nights,
Our nights of magic,
Nights of tender love.
Charming small Antigua,
In silhouettes of mountains,
Is where our love was sealed,
With a passionate kiss.
And a love was born,
A love unknown by others,
As we came together,
In love's blissfullness.
We fell in love,
In each other's arms,
Under the light of the moon,
Under flickering stars,
Underneath the sky,
Of romantic Antigua.

Book One

Nathalie And Alfredo's Story: Finding True Love

And Love Was Born

Chapter One

Nathalie Ordonez was a beautiful, wealthy woman who lived in New Orleans. She had blonde hair, green eyes and led a very healthy lifestyle. She didn't smoke. She drank wine on occasion and every once in a while, she enjoyed Bailey's Irish Cream. She lived by high ideals and was a true romantic.

At the age of twenty six, she dreamed of true love and was still saving herself for the right man. Until that day came, she had a special hideaway from the harsh reality of everyday life that she could retreat to whenever she wanted. All she had to do was enter the airy unfurnished room in her home with a polished hard wood floor where she practiced her dancing. When she flipped on the sound system, her feet and hands would begin moving gracefully as the melodies and rhythms filled every corner. She was sensational at dancing because, to her, it was more than an art form. As far as she was concerned, to dance was to live.

In the spring of 1969, the petite and stunningly attractive 5' 1" 105 pound diva was rehearsing for a performance at a women's club luncheon. She would be doing a tarantella character dance. The act required the use of a tambourine. She kept time with the music by shaking and tapping the circular instrument and succeeded in making the recorded music sound even better.

Nathalie began studying ballet at the age of eight. Her teacher told her, "If you follow my guidance and work very hard, you could become a true ballerina." Those words of encouragement made her so enthusiastic that she embraced the perform- ing art and poured everything she had into it. She would find that the art of ballet by its very nature stretches a dancer's body to its limits, and sometimes beyond.

She was not in the least dissuaded after suffering permanent damage to her big toes. She endured the pain because she loved ballet so much. She had learned that one must pay a heavy price in striving for excellence. Whenever she was asked about the injuries, she replied, "That's what happens when you get into toe shoes. You're putting your feet into a very tight space and putting all your weight on the tips of your toes." After reaching a certain level, Nathalie decided not to go further. If anyone asked why she was no longer in ballet, she replied, "I'm now going to devote my time to other forms of dance."

Nathalie went into character dancing, which required a different costume for each type of dance. She found great enjoyment in designing her costumes, some- thing which ballet didn't offer. She performed tarantellas, flamenco dances with castanets and Indian dances using cymbals on her fingers and bells on her ankles.

She never performed professionally because it was not the sort of thing a woman who came from wealth and high social class would do. Show business was full of questionable people, and the idea of dancing for money would have been disrespectful to her family's traditional values. Rather than perform for the mass- es, she put her talents on display for women's clubs and charitable organizations. To Nathalie, dancing was not only artistic expression but a form of philanthropy.

And Love Was Born

And Love Was Born

Chapter Two

Nathalie's family had a long history which extended all the way back to the time Spain ruled the world. Her father, Pedro, was the son and only child of Mario Ordonez. Mario was a workaholic who became wealthy by building a baking empire in his native Ecuador. His bakery operated twenty four hours a day and provided many hard working people with opportunities to make good livings. He lived in a magnificent mansion in Cuenca and became the most prominent citizen of that southern Ecuador town.

Mario married a lovely woman named Sarah who was from England. She was most attracted to him by what she called his "beautiful mind." She considered him a genius, and she was so in love with him that she embraced his Castilian Spanish heritage. She even took classes which enabled her to become fluent in his native language.

At the age of sixty, Mario Ordonez closed his bakery, left his magnificent mansion, uprooted his family and migrated to New Orleans. He left his native country in hopes of increasing his wealth. This was in 1930, when America was in the grip of the Great Depression. Mario said to Sarah, "*Necesitamos hacer dinero*. Stock prices on solid companies are far too low. Those stocks will come back, and I want to buy as many of them as I can." He was right, and his bold decision resulted in a vast increase in his holdings. Rather than heading for New York where he would have been close to Wall Street, Mario chose to settle in the Big Easy because he liked the people and the French influence.

Even though he was pleased with his new surroundings, he always carried his homeland in his heart. He insisted that only Castilian Spanish be spoken in his house. The patriarch also saw to it that his son retained the traditions of the father's culture. The father's point of view was later enunciated by the great South American filmmaker, songwriter and singer Leonardo Favio. "If you forget traditions, you won't know who you came from or where you are going." Mario did not want that for his son.

The son turned out to be very different from his father. Mario devoted his leisure hours to reading newspapers from all over the world. He prided himself on being very knowledgeable about business and politics in every corner of the globe. Pedro had a passion for classical music, and he played the accordion in his spare time.

Pedro was born in 1919 while his family was still living in Ecuador. He had green eyes and chestnut hair and grew to be 5' 11" and 160 pounds. He had good size and a rugged physique, but he was never attracted to athletics. He kept in shape by performing the daily chores his *papa* assigned him from the time he was tall enough to place his hand on a work bench. If he made the mistake of letting his father know that he absolutely detested doing something, Mario would order him to do that very thing. He would say to his son, "You may not like it, but doing it will make you stronger." The boy was never allowed to sleep late, and he excelled in the classroom because his dad would not tolerate mediocrity. He never got into trouble because his father kept him busy and repeatedly warned him, "No one has ever put one over on me, so do not think you will ever get away with anything." Papa Ordonez often said, "No matter how much money a man has, he must work hard each and every day. It is the price you pay for the air you breathe."

Mario hoped that his male heir would follow in his footsteps and become a giant in some form of commerce. The son loved and respected the father, but he wanted to take a different path. He wanted to become a physician so that he could treat those needing the most help and do it for free, if possible. Pedro modeled his life after the great Nobel Prize winning humanitarian Albert Schweitzer, who viewed the practice of medicine as a calling to help those less fortunate. When the son told his father of his dreams, Mario was not pleased. He said, "No one can take care of the entire world." His father's displeasure did not deter Pedro from pursuing his vision. When America entered World War II in December, 1941, Pedro Ordonez was a dean's list medical student at Tulane University.

While attending there, he met his wife Kathleen, who was not Hispanic. She was blue eyed, blonde, had been born and raised in the United States, was a real Irish colleen and a devout Catholic. Nathalie, their only child, was born in New Orleans in 1942.

And Love Was Born

Chapter Three

At the end of the war, Mario and Sarah Ordonez looked forward to spending time with their son and his young family. Where they came from, upper class families were close knit, affectionate and usually lived in close proximity to each other. When Pedro and Kathleen married, Mario mentioned to his daughter in law, "There's only one bumble bee to a nest, and only one female can run a household." He wanted the couple to get a house close to his mansion, and they did that.

Dr, Ordonez spent a few years on the staff of a New Orleans hospital, and he and his wife enjoyed an easy, comfortable life during America's post war boom. He grew restless, though, because he wanted to do something more fulfilling. He was open and truthful with his spouse, and he shared his dreams with her. Whenever he brought up leaving New Orleans, she would say, "Darling, I love you, and I love everything about you. You will be successful wherever you go, and the only place I want to be is right by your side."

"What if it's a remote place in a foreign country, far from all the comforts you've become used to?"

Kathleen Ordonez looked at her husband with a loving expression. She said, "Wherever you choose to be, I'll be there with you. We will do it together."

During the late 1950's, Dr. Ordonez heard about a remote section of Guatemala 6,600 feet above sea level that was desperately in need of a clinic and a doctor. It was in the Huehuetenango Province along the Mexican Border and near the Cuchumatanes Mountains. The remote area had only winding dirt roads. It was a primitive land of illness and troubles, much like the dangerous days of America's western frontier.

Most people would have regarded it as a place better forgotten, but it appealed to Pedro because he believed he could do a great deal for those who lived there. The physician who was about to enter his peak earning years carefully considered the possibility of practicing medicine in that Central American location. Once he made his decision, he met with his father to tell him of his plans. This was a bold act for the doctor because even though he had just turned forty, he was still intimidated by his papa. Mario Ordonez' eyes could chill a person. Pedro had candidly admitted to his wife that, "One look from him and I'm ready to hide under a table."

Pedro was seated on a sofa in the living room of his father's mansion on St. Charles Avenue. He was wearing a summer weight suit, a white shirt and a tie. Mario wore a white long sleeved *guataberas* shirt and white slacks. He sat in his favorite living room chair. It was his vantage point for ruling over his domain.

Pedro spoke first. "Papa, Guatemala has been on my mind. I've read a great deal about its history."

"I have never heard you talk about that country before. *Que sabes de ese pais?*"

"I know enough to realize that the people need me. They have the same dreaded diseases we have in the U.S., but the quality of care is nothing compared to what it is here. I will be able to change this for them."

His father answered, "*Trata de ser fuerte!* You cannot take on the world's problems. People will never pay you back, and you know that is the truth. You have a wife to take care of and a daughter to raise. Focus on your family."

The father and the son did not agree, but they were not about to engage in a heated argument. Their family culture did not condone solving disputes by raising their voices or shaking fists at each other. It was much better to write down their opposing points of view, exchange their papers and talk it over after reading each other's written statement. This method maintained the respect which existed between parents and their offspring.

Mario and Pedro sat down at the dining room table. Pedro went first. He wrote,

I want to go to Guatemala because the people there need me. To me, the physician's oath means carrying the weight of humanity upon my shoulders. True love is based on service. I love my wife and daughter, I love you and my mother and I also love my fellow man.

He put down his pen and handed his statement to his father.

Mario Ordonez read it and then looked at his only child for a couple of moments with the electrifying gaze Pedro had seen so many times. The father then took a sheet of paper and a pen and wrote out his response.

I do not like your answer. But I expected it. From the time you were a little boy, you have been softhearted. That is no way to be if you have a family to take care of. You are a grown man. I cannot stop you from going, but I can wish you the best of luck in your endeavor. God knows you will need it.

Despite all the risks involved, Dr. Ordonez persisted in following his dream. The setting he chose offered the exuberant beauty of deep green hills, canyons shrouded with clouds and floral bursts of purple and yellow. The beauty was in stark contrast to the extreme poverty in the area. When the doctor and his wife first arrived, water came from open streams and there was no indoor plumbing. Outhouses and pit toilets were used. Native women made all the clothing. Women wore colorful embroidered tops, woven skirts and belts of different colors. They even made their own hair pieces. Men normally wore white long sleeved shirts, ponchos, woven trousers in either white or black which only went to mid-calf and woven cloth belts. They were used to living on tortillas, wheat *atole* (an oatmeal drink), black beans, corn and the pigs and chickens they raised.

Clusters of homes made of wood and palm thatch roofs dotted the landscape, but were accessible only by foot. Women were often seen carrying bundles of wood on their backs or baskets of fruits or vegetables upon their heads. The inhabitants would have to walk nearly a mile along rocky and often muddy paths through the canyons in order to get to what few stores and schools there were. Telephones were not to be found were not to be found, and the only means of communication was by short wave radio. The natives felt comfortable living this way because no one bothered them. Illnesses and accidents were their dreaded enemies. and they had a life expectancy of only thirty eight years, Dr. Ordonez was determined to help them battle their biggest threats.

He was a driven man who finally prevailed over all the adversity he faced. By the early 1960's, he established Heart to Heart Hospital. When asked why he chose the name, the doctor replied, "It symbolizes my desire to give my heart to people who have shown so much heart in their constant striving and struggle." Mario Ordonez was still alive and attended the opening of the medical facility. The father said to his son, "I'm proud of you. You have honored your family with your compassion and generosity. It took me a while to become used to your point of view, but now I understand. There is too much unhappiness in the world, and you are trying to bring some joy into it." The moment was captured by a photo taken of the doctor with his father, mother, wife and daughter. It was displayed on a wall and could be seen by anyone entering the hospital.

Mario was so impressed by what his son had accomplished that he committed millions to the expansion of Heart to Heart Hospital. It soon became the finest health care facility for the poor in Guatemala. The doctor and his wife also established a coffee plantation close by the hospital which provided a major part of its funding. In addition, they were able to attract substantial donations from all over the world. Dr. Ordonez was able to assemble a very good staff of physicians because he could pay them in American dollars.

Once the plantation and hospital were in full operation, Pedro and his wife made regular trips to Guatemala, but spent most of their time in New Orleans. The doctor was fortunate to find a trusted assistant in Efrain Cordova. He proved capable of handling things whenever the Ordonez' were absent. It wasn't until their daughter Nathalie was high school age and attending a boarding school that they moved to Guatemala permanently.

After high school, Nathalie attended a college in Rome, Italy, graduated with honors and returned to New Orleans. Rather than embark on a job search, she chose to work with her parents. It only took a couple of trips to Guatemala for her to become as enthusiastic about the mission of Heart to Heart Hospital as they were. It "ran in the blood," as the saying goes. She diligently kept many of the books and records and performed other administrative tasks while living in her grandfather's mansion on St. Charles Avenue. Sadly, both grandparents had passed away by then.

She made periodic trips to Guatemala and on every occasion, found the country's natural beauty fascinating. She also fell in love with the descendants of Mayan Indians who lived in the village near the hospital. Their ethnic group constituted a huge portion of the Guatemalan population. It amazed her to see them bring her mother and father food they had prepared. When the villagers presented her with flowers, she was even more amazed. They were tokens of appreciation for all her father had done. Even though the natives had little in the way of money or material possessions, they were happy, upbeat people who liked to laugh.

They avoided trauma and drama and they would often get together for parties. Nathalie never laughed as much as she did whenever she went to Guatemala. Her parents were fortunate to have found a special place in a beautiful country away from the stress of modern civilization.

And Love Was Born

Chapter Four

The early and middle parts of the 1960's were good years for the Ordonez family, but a painful change occurred early in 1968. Nathalie received an unexpected phone call. Rodrigo Ramos, the middle aged manager of her parents' coffee plantation, was on the line. He was calling from the hospital because it had one of the few phones in the area.

Ramos did a poor job of trying to tell her something very important. Even though he was a man who had experienced some harsh things in his time, it was hard for him to say the words. This caused her even more anxiety than if he had come right out with it. He finally said, "*Patrona, tengo algo mal para decirle.* I hate to give bad news. Your mother and father were killed in an auto accident. The car blew up and there was nothing left to bury."

Nathalie felt ice cold. She said, "It just can't be possible. Are you sure?"

"*Si, Senorita.* It happened just like I say. I hate to tell you."

"I'm taking the first plane down there. I'll make the funeral arrangements." She began to sob as she said, "I'll let you know about my flight so you can pick me up. Thank you for calling me, Rodrigo."

Her world was coming apart. She thought, "You're never prepared for this."

She began to shake as she put the receiver back into its cradle. She had been standing while on the phone, but her legs were giving out. They felt like rubber bands. She had to get to a chair because she suddenly had difficulty breathing, her head was spinning and she felt like she was about to pass out. It was only by holding onto various pieces of furniture that she made it to her favorite chair. After falling into it, she covered her face with her hands and began to cry. She said aloud, "Now, I am left alone. I no longer have my wonderful parents."

A feeling of guilt came to her. She thought, "Maybe if I had stayed in Guatemala none of this would have happened." She suddenly felt as though she had stuck her finger in an electrical outlet and the current was invading her body. She became nauseous and barely made it to the bathroom on her wobbly legs before she threw up. She collapsed on her bed. The room began to twirl and she felt lifeless.

After a half hour, she was able to get herself together enough to arrange a flight. For days afterwards, she was barely able to eat, and she found herself in a stupor. She experienced the downside of having loved her parents so much.

Rodrigo met her at the airport in Guatemala City and drove her to the plantation. Along the way, Nathalie questioned him about the circumstances of her parents' death. He answered, "Their car went off the side of a mountain road. It rolled over and over, and then it blew up. There was nothing left but metal."

She could have simply had stone crosses erected in memory of her parents, but she chose to embark on a search for their ashes. Unfortunately, the search proved futile.

In addition to her grieving, the tragedy placed a great burden upon Nathalie. As the only surviving member of the Ordonez clan, she had the enormous responsibilities of overseeing a coffee plantation, a hospital and a vast estate.

And Love Was Born

Chapter Five

Nathalie relied on Efrain Cordova and Rodrigo Ramos to keep things running smoothly. Both of them had been so trusted by her parents that they had been given signature rights for the Guatemalan business account. She saw no reason to change things.

Everything went well for a year. A check from a bank in Guatemala arrived at her bank in New Orleans on the third of every month, just like clockwork. Both Cordova and Ramos were very prompt in submitting monthly expense reports.

Early in the spring of 1969, no check arrived. It was as if a faucet had been shut off. She immediately made a phone call to the Guatemalan bank. The banker couldn't tell her anything more than there was no money in the account. "Where did it go?" she asked.

"Rodrigo Ramos withdrew all of it. He closed the account. I thought it was strange, but he had every right to do so. He said he was ordered to do it, so I presumed you knew about it."

She made another overseas call to the hospital. Efrain Cordova told her that he hadn't seen or heard from Ramos or any of his family members for several days. She asked him to go over to the plantation and find out what was going on. "I'll be at home all day tomorrow. If I don't hear from you by evening, I'll call you."

Efrain called her early the following afternoon. He said, "*Madre mia!* The plantation has been taken over by *bandidos* with guns! It is too dangerous to even try to get close. Lord knows what has happened to poor Rodrigo, his family and the rest of the workers."

She was in a state of shock. Her world was coming to an end. She thought, "People will say I'm crazy not to walk away from the hopeless mess. They'll tell me how corrupt Guatemala is, and that the authorities will give me no help. I know that squatters down there can get away with taking property that belonging to others. Since I wasn't around, they'll try to say it was idle. If armed bandits took it, that's even worse. I don't care what they say. I'll fight for my family's legacy."

Nathalie decided to call her best friend, Tisha Miller. They were so close that they spoke almost every day, and it was natural for Nathalie to turn to her when a crisis occurred. Tisha was four years older. She was 5' 4", 123 pounds, had raven black hair and brown eyes. She was not as buxom, but had longer legs than Nathalie and enjoyed a cocktail every once in a while.

Tisha had a boyfriend named John Meyer, a handsome man who was six feet tall and had black hair and dark eyes. Both of them were Jewish, but practiced their religion only when their families gathered to celebrate the holidays. Meyer had recently graduated from Tulane's law school and was waiting to take the bar exam. His future was all mapped out for him. A lucrative position with his cousin's law firm was awaiting him once he was licensed.

And Love Was Born

John happened to be at Tisha's when Nathalie called. He got on the line and recommended Matt Logan's law firm, Logan, Silverstein and Tyson. He said, "Leon Silverstein has a fantastic mind when it comes to international law, and he's one of Matt's partners. His fees are high, but he's the best in the business."

The thought of going to an attorney made Nathalie cringe. Her mother had often said, "Attorneys are the most dishonest people in the world, but they are everywhere. They run the country, and they are in the government and the White House. You never really know how honest their billings are or how much work they actually put in on your case. You have to watch your back whenever you're around them and you have to count your fingers after you've shaken their hands. They're very bad, and they will steal anything when you least expect it."

With her mother's warnings echoing in her ears, she made an afternoon appointment to see Matt Logan. She coped with the stress she was feeling by working out in her dance studio. Peak years for dancers were between the ages of seventeen and nineteen, but at the age of twenty six, she still had the rhythm, fluidity, grace and almost as much stamina as when she was in her prime.

At the end of her strenuous workout on that March morning, she was soaked in perspiration and went to take a shower. She happened to catch a glimpse of her green eyes and long blonde hair in a mirror as she toweled off. She decided to gather her hair up into a bun for the visit to the attorney's office.

And Love Was Born

Chapter Six

Matt Logan was the senior partner of Logan, Silverstein and Tyson. He had inherited the firm from his father, who had been a very successful sole practitioner. Matt joined the firm after he had graduated from Tulane's law school. He took over when his father died, brought in partners and made it even more successful.

Matt was ruggedly handsome, tall and athletic. He had attended college as a war vet after seeing action in the Pacific during World War II. The years of military service had been a very unpleasant experience that produced battle fatigue and haunting nightmares.

Much of his problem stemmed from his first close range engagement with a Japanese soldier. It happened on a day when his platoon spotted a little hut perched atop a rise overlooking the ocean. It seemed like an ordinary fisherman's shack, but Matt suddenly heard the sound of gunfire and saw two men in his company drop to the ground. They had been shot in the center of their chests and were dead. It was the work of a sniper.

From the angle of their fall, he knew the firing had to come from a window on the other side of the hut. He was all alone in his fox hole, and he would have been unprotected if the Japanese sniper decided to fire from the window on his side. According to his upbringing, aggression connected with the taking of life was unacceptable and prohibited. In war, however, "the worth of two thousand dollars of education and upbringing drops to ten cents."

The first option would have been to lob some hand grenades into the fisherman's shack, but there were none around. There always seemed to be a chronic grenade shortage. Matt only had an automatic pistol, but he knew he had to do something. He decided to sneak up on the sniper by running as fast as he could toward the hut. By moving in little bounds, zigzagging, dropping to the ground every dozen steps and remembering to tumble and roll each time he dropped, he was able to cover twenty five yards in practically no time. In his haste, he had forgotten his steel helmet and was wearing a cloth cap. Fortunately, no shots were fired at him.

He jolted to a stop when he reached the threshold of the shack. The tension was overwhelming. It made him feel a twitching in his jaw, turmoil in his stomach, dryness in his mouth, sweat born of fear and shakiness in his legs. His eyes became out of focus but just as suddenly, his vision cleared. He unlocked the safety of his Colt automatic, kicked the door to the hut open with his right foot and leaped inside.

He was surprised to find himself in an empty room. There was another door opposite from the one he had unhinged. Whoever was behind that door had surely heard the noise and was warned. Matt chose to immediately smash through the second door.

Just as he burst through, he saw a blur to his right. It turned out to be the first Japanese soldier Matt had ever seen up close. The sniper was a fat, moon faced, roly-poly little man with thick, stubby, trunk like legs sheathed in faded khaki puttees and squeezed into a uniform that was much too tight. He was armed with a bolt action Arisaka rifle known for its harsh recoil. In order to steady the weapon, he had used the rifle's sling like a harness and strapped it tightly to his upper body. This improved his accuracy, but restricted his movements. He was trying with all his might to turn toward Matt, but he couldn't disentangle himself. When he realized he couldn't get his arms free, his eyes rolled in panic and he backed toward a corner in a curious crab like motion.

Matt wheeled in the direction of the enemy, crouched, gripped his pistol with both hands and fired. He missed, and his bullet became embedded in a wall that appeared to be made from straw. Logan's second shot went into the Japanese sniper's left thigh. It blossomed and then swiftly turned to mush. A geyser of blood from a main artery pulsed out, soaking his legs and pooling on the earthen floor. The enemy soldier was silent. His shoulders gave a little spasmodic jerk, as though someone had whacked him on his back. He then slumped down and died. Matt was so emotionally over the edge that he kept firing at the ground until his pistol was empty.

Logan stood there staring at the man he had killed. He began to tremble and was soon shaking all over. He sobbed and said aloud in a mournful voice, "I'm sorry." Immediately after he got the words out, he threw up all over himself and peed in his pants. Just then, Sergeant Sal Cardinale burst in, ready to fire his M 1 carbine. The sergeant's predatory eyes quickly took in the entire scene. He noticed the dead Japanese soldier and the vomit on Logan's uniform. He looked Matt in the eye and said, "You're pathetic. If you can't kill like a man, you're a disgrace to your uniform. That Jap wouldn't have thrown up if he'd killed you. Besides, you should have put a bullet in the back of his head before he could turn toward you."

Killing the Japanese sniper fueled nightmares which plagued Logan for years after the war. Another engagement which caused bad dreams took place when Matt's platoon encountered a Japanese stronghold where Chinese "comfort women" were being used as human shields. Matt froze and couldn't bring himself to shoot any of the women. Trigger happy "Sergeant Sal" shoved Logan out of the way and fired without hesitation, killing seven women and the four Japanese soldiers hiding behind them. Capturing the stronghold was a great strategic coup, and the ruthless sergeant not only was awarded a medal for the bloodshed he had committed but received a bump in rank.

Matt made the mistake of drinking to escape the horrible memories of the atrocities of war, and especially Sergeant Sal Cardinale. That didn't solve his problem. It only made things worse.

He was confronted with more adversity when he was finally brought back to the States. He contracted the mumps and when he recovered, a doctor at the Army hospital told him something very disturbing. The physician looked Logan in the eye and said, "I'm sorry, but you'll never be able to have any children."

And Love Was Born

It was only by the grace of Janet Trattenberg coming into his life that he was able to get back on track. They met while both were attending Tulane's law school. She was the most brilliant student in their class. They made an attractive couple. She was 5' 8" and 140 pounds. At six feet, he was tall enough to make her feel comfortable about wearing heels whenever they went out. She was always there to listen to every problem he had, no matter what. It took him a while to work up the courage to tell her about his being unable to father children. Her response was, "That doesn't make any difference to me. I love you, and I want to be with you."

"I love you so much for accepting me as I am," he replied.

They married immediately following graduation. She became his rock, and he made sure to tell her how much he loved her each and every day.

And Love Was Born

And Love Was Born

Chapter Seven

The first person Nathalie encountered in Matt Logan's office was his forty five year old secretary, Louise Duncan, who was neatly dressed in a conservative navy blue suit. The secretary also had a yellow and black scarf tied around her neck, a small bracelet on her right wrist, a tiny gold wrist watch on the left wrist and wore two inconspicuous rings. Louise was a disciplined secretary. Nothing was ever out of place on her desk, and she always knew exactly where to find anything. Her most outstanding asset was her personality. She was gracious and made her boss' visitors feel welcome. Nathalie thought, "She certainly represents her employers well."

When Louise escorted her into Matt's office, the innocence and vulnerability Nathalie projected hit him at his core. His immediate thought was, "She needs someone to watch over her." He had always wanted to be a father, and she fueled a desire in him to be her protector.

After listening to her problem, he said, "My partner, Leon Silverstein, is the best man to handle your case." Matt leveled with her and told her that even Silverstein might not be enough. "I have to be honest with you. Leon has had some bad experiences with cases in Guatemala. I'll have to do a selling job on him in order to get him to handle your matter. That might take a few days."

Logan then brought up the issue of money. He said, "For a case involving travel to a foreign country, we would require a retainer of fifteen thousand dollars. Will that be a problem?"

Nathalie answered, "I have no problem paying that amount. Just let me know when you want it."

Matt said, "First let me get Leon to agree to it."

Leon Silverstein was soft and pudgy in contrast to Logan's lean, athletic build. Matt had boxed as an amateur and still worked out by running, jumping rope and punching both heavy and speed bags. Leon's hobby was going on cruises. Outside the office, his wife Judy called the shots, and she picked the places they traveled to.

Matt knew that Guatemala was the one country in the world his partner never wanted to go to. Leon had been there several times and often complained about all the "*manana* and corruption" that went on. Once, after returning from a trip to that country, he said to Matt, "The way they do business, it takes them too long to get to the point. As far as I'm concerned, they're procrastinators, they're insincere and they lack direction. They also disrupt things with their *siesta*, which is a midday nap. They'll stop everything at noon to go home, eat a heavy meal and then go to sleep. They don't return to the office for two hours. Could you imagine pulling that stunt here in New Orleans? We'd be out of business in no time."

Memories of the unintentionally funny comments Leon had made about a country where time isn't money brought a smile to Matt's face. Since it happened in the middle of his meeting with his new client, it brought a quizzical expression to Nathalie. She wondered if her lawyer somehow found her predicament hilarious. Matt noticed her look and considered sharing his heavy set partner's comments with her, then decided against it. He gracefully extricated himself from a sticky situation by saying, "Excuse me. I just remembered something funny that our dog did this morning. Her name is Gigi, and she's a Maltese." One of the qualities which made him a successful attorney was his ability to think on his feet.

Nathalie replied, "I've seen some of them. They're very affectionate and make excellent house pets."

Their business had been concluded, so Matt stood up, offered his hand and told her that he would get back to her as soon as he persuaded the international law expert to handle her case. He said, "Leon will come around. He enjoys taking on challenges."

The moment Nathalie stepped out of Matt Logan's office, she saw a very handsome man in his early thirties rush up to Louise's desk and say, "Sorry I'm late. The traffic is horrendous." A sixth sense told him to turn around at that very moment. He saw Nathalie, and there was instant electricity as their eyes met. A warm sensation enveloped her body, while he couldn't take his eyes off her. He approached her and introduced himself by saying, "I'm Alfredo Milla. Matt is very good. He has been handling my affairs for years. Do you come here often?"

"No. It's my first time."

"Do you live here in New Orleans? I have a home on St. Charles Avenue. I also have a villa in Guatemala."

She replied, "What a coincidence. I also live on that street, and I have visited Guatemala."

"May I ask what your name is?"

"Nathalie Ordonez."

He handed her his business card and said, "Perhaps we can meet at the Court of Two Sisters for lunch sometime, if that would be okay with you." He gave her a warm smile, then turned and walked toward Matt Logan's office.

She was intrigued by him. She asked Louise what she knew about Alfredo. The secretary replied, "He's nothing less than an absolute gentleman. He's been a client of this firm for a number of years. As a matter of fact, he has sent me flowers or boxes of chocolates every so often to say 'Thank you.'"

Nathalie was impressed by Louise's candid remark. She tucked away Alfredo's card in her purse and thought, "I just might call him. He interests me."

Driving back to her mansion in her white Mercedes Benz sports coupe, she thought, "I've met many handsome men, but Alfredo Milla has something very special about him. I can't put my finger on it yet. He seems like a gentleman, he dresses impeccably and his manners are polished. I hope he had a similar upbringing to mine. That would definitely help."

And Love Was Born

Chapter Eight

Nathalie would not be disappointed with Alfredo's upbringing. He was born in Guatemala, was of Spanish and German descent and was of the upper class. His father was a pharmacist who became wealthy by owning a chain of pharmacies and a pharmaceutical firm. His family was loving but strict. Like Nathalie, his parents sent him to Catholic schools.

Integrity, responsibility, sympathy and the ability to forgive were instilled in him at an early age. He learned that the way you treat yourself is the way others will treat you. He was taught to keep his commitments, be honest and make as few excuses as possible. He also learned to avoid telling little white lies, to show sympathy and respect others. He practiced acceptance, learned to be patient and showed tolerance for the shortcomings of other people.

Like most Guatemalan males, Alfredo did not sign his name in long hand. His full name was stylized into a *rubrica*. It was a distortion of letters that he wrote the same way every time. Bank tellers in Guatemala did not read names. They recognized or matched *rubricas*. He followed the tradition of developing and practicing his *rubrica* when he was an adolescent and continued using it for the rest of his life. It became his symbol, somewhat like a coat of arms.

As a Latin American male who was by nature romantic, Alfredo would often make gestures with his hands in order to add emphasis to what he was saying. Sometimes he would also use his head to do this.

He was very bright, studied abroad, graduated with honors from Tulane and also obtained a master's in business administration from that university. He worked very hard in school and continued to do so during his entire life because he believed "You will reap what you put into your work."

Once he was out of school, he displayed an innate talent for business. Whatever he touched turned to gold. He had a sixth sense when it came to the art of the deal. He was a multimillionaire before he turned thirty.

He was not driven to become wealthy merely for the sake of acquiring possessions or indulging in vices, traps which too many young millionaires fell into. He was a man of honor, but was also committed to living in an elegant way. He liked the better things in life and always said, "There is a cheaper way to live, but it's not worth it."

Alfredo had no problem attracting members of the opposite sex because he was charming, soft spoken and never used foul language. In addition to being extremely bright, he was also very stylish. He was 5' 11" and a rock solid 170 pounds, and he kept in shape by swimming and playing tennis. He also enjoyed the theater, boating, riding horses and country clubs.

He wore colored shirts, suits and sport coats and was always color coordinated. With his dark brown hair and kind mahogany eyes, he was a refreshing figure to be seen whenever he entered a room. During the time he spent in New Orleans, he drove a brand new midnight blue Cadillac Coupe De Ville with a blue interior. It had speakers both in front and back, which was state of the art in those days. When in Guatemala, he used a black Mercedes Benz diesel driven by his trusted chauffeur, Pablo.

He could be playful at times, and this side of his persona almost got him in trouble. He met a bank teller in Antigua, Guatemala who was not at his social level. Alfredo was interested in her only for having a good time. Their encounter lasted less than two weeks, but it was a fiery, drama filled period. Once he learned that she was known as the "Antigua Telegram," he sensed impending disaster and ended their rendezvous. The experience left him with a sour feeling, but it taught him a lesson.

Alfredo seemingly had everything, but he was missing the key ingredient in his life. He always wanted to marry, raise a family and grow old with one woman. He decided it was time to find the right lady. Could it be that the beautiful green eyed blonde he had met at Matt Logan's office would be the one?

Chapter Nine

When he arrived at work, Leon Silverstein thought it was going to be a great day. The way he had decorated his office always gave him a reassuring feeling. Some men adorned their offices with mounted heads of game they had shot or photos from their days as athletes. Leon's trophies were photos and prints of places he and his wife Judy had visited. They had been up late the night before planning a cruise to Antarctica. They loved to go where few had ventured, then invite their friends over and show them slides of their travels.

He was surprised to see Matt Logan knocking on his open door the first thing in the morning. Matt had a certain look in his eye that Silverstein had seen before. It always meant that the senior partner was about to ask him for a difficult favor.

"How are things going, Leon?" asked Logan. "How's Judy and your daughter?"

"They're fine. What's up, Matt."

"How would you like to take a trip on behalf of a client? You'll fly first class and stay in a five star hotel. There's a big retainer involved, and the client is willing to be billed for any amount it takes to get the job done."

"What's the catch? Where do I have to go?"

Delivering the bitter pill was the hard part for Matt. He lowered his voice slightly when he said, "Guatemala."

"I knew there was a catch! That's asking me to go to the biggest cesspool in the world."

"What do you have against that country? Many people say it's the most beautiful place of all, and the climate is supposed to be ideal."

"There are beautiful women who have a kiss of death. Since it's early in the day and you have time on your hands, would you like me to give you a brief history of that hell hole?"

"Go ahead," said Matt.

"Listen closely. I'll try to be brief, but I may have to give you a roster so you can keep track of all the names involved." Matt chuckled at his partner's joke.

Leon said, "Guatemala has been one of the most exploited countries in the world. The Spanish were the first to do it. I heard a story about a Spanish priest who burned ten thousand Mayan texts in a single day. "

"That's interesting," said Matt.

Leon continued by saying, "The Spaniards at least honored claims to land the Mayan Indians inherited from their ancestors but in the 1870's, a dictator named Justo Rufino Barrios abolished hundreds of Mayan land titles. He also forced seasonal laborers to work for huge coffee plantations for little or no pay. Many of them were given only food and a place to sleep. By the 1920's, the growing demand for coffee in North America and Europe created the first millionaire fortunes there. Soft palmed landowners posing as frontiersmen barb wired their properties off and put the country's leaders into their pockets. During the 1930's, the country was ruled by Jorge Ubico, who continued to take advantage of farm workers. FDR inaugurated a Good Neighbor Policy with Latin America a couple of years later, but I don't think many upstanding people would want someone like Ubico living next to them. Two years later, in 1934, he passed vagrancy laws that forced anyone owning less than two and a half acres to give a hundred days a year of manual labor to one of the large plantations. They were paid nothing and received only food and a place to sleep. Men were also forced to join the Guatemalan army where they were paid less than fifty cents a day, given hand me down uniforms to wear and looked like ragamuffins. This Ubico character ruled with an iron fist, and he got away with it because of all the military aid and money he received from the U.S.A. There's no telling how much of it he put in his own pocket."

"You really know your history," Logan responded.

He thought he might be boring his partner, but Matt was paying close attention, so Leon continued. "Everything changed when there was a double cross and some younger men in his army overthrew him. That's the way it always seems to go in those countries. Coyotes feed on coyotes."

His partner's wry remark made Matt smile.

Leon moved along in his rant. "They established what they claimed would be a democratic government, headed by Jacobo Arbenz Guzman, and promised free elections. Democracy wasn't going to happen. It later came out that Che Guevara was running the government for Guzman. I'd have to admit that some social reform took place, but only up to a point. Schools sprouted up all over the country, but it was reported that many of them were started in places where there weren't enough students to fill the schools. I also heard that the teacher training was nothing more than whirlwind six week programs. A high percentage of the population remained illiterate, and this group was exploited by the Arbenz Guzman regime. I found it interesting that he was supported by university professors and students, union leaders, liberal lawyers and white collar workers. You would think that they would be the most intelligent classes in Guatemala, but I wonder about that. There was also his land reform idea. The government sold bonds and used the money to buy idle and unproductive land from extremely wealthy Guatemalans and American monopolies such as United Fruit. The problem was that the government set the prices, and then peasants and workers in cities were placed on those lands as tenants. It was similar to eminent domain in this country. All it added up to was more control by the government. It was no surprise that United Fruit despised Arbenz Guzman and wanted him out of office."

"There were other problems," added Silverstein. "Let me give you another interesting tidbit. In 1946, a Dr. John Cutler was ordered to cease infecting Alabama black males with syphilis in order to test drugs on them. He didn't stop using human guinea pigs, but transferred his operation to Guatemala. He injected soldiers, prostitutes, prisoners, inmates in mental asylums and children in orphanages with diseases. They were rewarded with a cigarette each time they were injected. When they questioned him about this, he said, 'The syphilis vaccine we develop will save millions of lives. Those who suffer and die are just part of the price of progress.'"

The international law expert then said, "It's no secret that there are people in our government whose only concern is to get rid of every Communist in the world. Guatemala is controlled by the United Fruit Company. The people down there call United Fruit *El Pulpo,* which means "The Octopus." If you don't know who they are, just think about all their ships at the New Orleans docks and the banana you eat every day. They have hundreds of miles of plantations, and they own the railroads and power lines. Well, United Fruit and all the others who hated Communism had their way. Do you recall what happened down there in 1954?"

"I can't recall," said Matt. "Please refresh my memory."

"American taxpayer money was spent attacking Guatemala without a formal declaration of war. It all resulted in Jacobo Arbenz Guzman being overthrown by Colonel Carlos Castillo Armas and his rag tag army of three hundred that was armed and equipped by the CIA. Armas was pro American, but no one living in Guatemala liked him. Right away, he abolished all labor unions and returned the land to United Fruit. So, the pendulum swung again. Have you had your belly full yet?"

Matt shook his head, so Leon continued. "When I think of Guatemala I see a place where they like *gringos* who spend money, but they hate the American government. So, why would we want to get involved in any dealings in such a black hole? Whatever the client is paying, it still wouldn't be worth it."

"I didn't mention the size of the retainer," replied Logan.

"How much are we talking about?"

"Fifteen thousand."

"Wow!" said Silverstein. "You could buy a decent house with that."

"I thought that would get your attention. With your share, you and Judy can go on a nice long trip."

"What sort of case is it?"

"It involves some squatters who are unlawfully occupying a coffee plantation."

"How big is the plantation?"

"From what I understand, it's twenty thousand acres."

"How soon will I have to leave for that God forsaken place?"

"I'll ask the client for all the pertinent information and a check for the retainer today. Would you be able to leave by the end of the week?"

"I'll clear my desk and be down there by Friday."

"Thanks, Leo. You're a real mensch."

"Let's be honest, Matt. We're talking about some serious money, and I've got a strong stomach."

And Love Was Born

Chapter Ten

When Matt came out of his meeting with Leon, Louise asked him, "How did it go with Mr. Silverstein?"

"It went nothing less than perfect, Louise. I'll have good news for that girl. Leon agreed to help her."

"Faan-tastic!"

Matt could hardly wait to give Nathalie the good news. He went into his office, sat down at his phone and dialed her number. She answered, "Hello."

"Nathalie, this is Matt Logan. I hope you can come in at ten tomorrow. Leon has agreed to take your case."

He could hear her swallow hard. She said, "I've lived with a frog in my throat ever since my problems in Guatemala began. I'm so happy that I can have some of my life back. I feel like thanking you a million times over."

"You're welcome, pretty lady. Bring any important documents and the fifteen thousand dollar retainer. See you tomorrow at ten."

When Nathalie arrived at the firm the next morning, Matt greeted her in the hallway. "Hello, Nathalie, follow me," and they walked into his office.

Once inside, she said, "I don't know how to thank you. I didn't know where to turn to." She began to tear up. Matt noticed she was about to cry, and said, "There's no need for tears."

"But these are happy tears." She gave him a big smile and said, "I'm appreciative for anything your expert can do for me."

After she gave him the documents and the check, he asked, "Would you like some refreshment before you go? You've been going through a lot of stress."

"An orange juice would be fine. I'll go to the waiting room. I feel like I've been a total pain. Please forgive me."

"Not at all," said Matt. He called out to his secretary, "Louise, please bring a glass of orange juice to Nathalie. She'll be in the waiting room."

Even though Leon was given the case, Matt didn't relinquish full control. He had become determined to do everything he could for Nathalie because once again, he was beginning to feel like a father towards her. He had the best of intentions, but was becoming very protective. Not everyone in his life shared his level of commitment to the young woman's well-being.

And Love Was Born

And Love Was Born

Chapter Eleven

For nearly twenty five years, Janet Logan had not only worked hard at her domestic law practice but was also very supportive of her husband Matt. She was always there for him, and she would call him twice a day to see how he was doing. Recently, she had become tired of hearing so much about Nathalie Ordonez. He was showing an inordinate amount of attention to her. She wondered if Matt had become fascinated with the rich young woman, or even something more.

God gave women intuition, which could be thought of as special radar amazingly effective at detecting positive or negative vibes. Matt's actions had triggered an alert, so Janet decided to confront him after breakfast. It was the ideal time because it was Saturday and neither of them had any commitments.

Matt walked into the kitchen. He had come down from their bedroom and was still wearing his pajamas. She greeted him with a cup of coffee.

"Thanks, Dear," he said as he took the cup from her. He sat down on his favorite kitchen chair that had a view of their expansive back yard.

Janet was already on her second cup. She said, "I made pancakes for you."

"Great, honey. That's what I love about Saturdays. During the week, I only have time for a bowl of cereal."

Janet placed a plate of pancakes in front of him and said, "Enjoy." She said it in a tone that he sensed meant trouble was on the horizon.

"Thanks, I know they'll be delicious." He wondered, "What's wrong? Why is she acting this way?"

Despite his wife's pleasant words and great hot cakes, he could see that she was not herself. She was quiet, distant and not as talkative as usual. It was a sign that something was brewing in her head. He knew she was upset, but he couldn't think of anything he had done to displease her.

When they both finished eating, Janet said coldly, "Let's go to the living room. I want to talk to you."

Matt got up and followed his wife. They sat on the sofa sideways to face each other. She spoke first.

"I know what the war did to you, Matt. I was there for you, and I helped you get away from the heavy drinking. I also helped you with all the other problems you had readjusting to everyday life."

"Janet, my love, I don't know what I would be without you. You've done so much for me."

"I have two worries," she said. "For the last few days, all you've talked about is Nathalie Ordonez. I think you should walk away from this huge problem that she has brought into this house. Let Leon take charge of all that's going on. After all, he's the top attorney for those matters overseas."

"But Janet, the girl needs everyone's help."

"Matt, you've become obsessed with her. You talk about her every day. You bring her up in every conversation we have. This is bothering me because I think there's something going on between you two. If you're infatuated with her, at least be man enough to admit it."

"Why are you accusing me? For Pete's sake, I've never thought of her that way! Just remember, the girl is all by herself. Look, Janet, look into my eyes. I love only you. You are my world." Matt moved closer to his wife, took her into his arms and kissed her.

"I love you," she said, "but I want you to make any calls to her from your office. That will make me feel better."

"My love, I won't be talking as much about her. You're right. Leon should handle her problem."

"Thanks for being thoughtful. Now that we understand things better, let's forget this conversation ever took place."

And Love Was Born

Chapter Twelve

A few weeks after Nathalie had retained Logan, Silverstein and Tyson, she happened to walk over by the desk in her library and notice Alfredo Milla's business card. It was still where she had set it. She dialed his number, hoping he would answer. His phone rang three times before he picked up.

"Hello."

"This is Nathalie Ordonez. I met you at Logan, Silverstein and Tyson a few days ago."

"Of course I remember you. How could I have forgotten such a beautiful woman?"

"Thanks for the compliment."

"I would like to take you to dinner, Nathalie. Would you like that?"

"No, I don't believe that would be appropriate. Since it's only the first time we will be going out, I'd prefer we make it lunch"

"That is perfectly fine with me. Shall I pick you up at your house?"

"Let's meet at Logan, Silverstein and Tyson."

"When should we meet there?'

"Thursday at noon."

"Great," said Alfredo. "Would the Court of Two Sisters be all right?"

"Yes, I love the Court of Two Sisters. I'll see you then."

"Thank you for calling me, Nathalie. I am really looking forward to our first date."

After they met at the law firm, Alfredo and Nathalie drove to the restaurant in his midnight blue Cadillac. Her face had a special glow. She did not have to worry about the land in Guatemala, since Leon and Matt were in charge.

When they were seated, they were each handed a menu. Alfredo asked her, "How about a glass of pinot noir red wine before lunch?"

"I'd love one," replied Nathalie. "What are you having?"

"I think I'll order a brandy old fashioned."

He ordered the drinks, and then said, "Tell me about yourself, Nathalie."

"Well, I was born here in New Orleans. I'm Spanish and Irish. My father was born in Ecuador. His ancestors can be traced back to El Grand Capitan, a military leader from Granada. His exploits earned our family a coat of arms. I saw it every day because it was mounted on a wall in our home. It was a shield with red horizontal stripes against a gold background. A knight's helmet with three red feathers was placed on top of the shield. My grandmother told me an interesting story about it. She said, 'El Grand Capitan had been accused of flirting with the Queen of Spain. Anyone else would have been executed immediately for such an offense but because of his military triumphs, he was given a choice to either leave Spain or die. He chose to settle in Ecuador.' She often told me that story to remind me that making bad choices leads to bad consequences."

He replied, "That is so true, Nathalie. Life has a way of catching up with those who do bad things. What do you like to do in your spare time?"

"I enjoy eating Creole food. I love to travel. I like to read ghost stories, even though they frighten me. I believe there's some truth in those writings. I think I've talked enough about me. Tell me about you, Alfredo."

Nathalie intrigued him. He thought, "She has an aura of innocence. She is also sweet, bright and has a pleasing personality."

In answer to her question, he briefly went over the high points of his background, which seemed to impress her. In closing, he said, "I have been looking for a woman just like you, and I am so fortunate that I have found her. I cannot take my eyes off you. I do not say that to just anyone, Nathalie."

She blushed and smiled sweetly. She could not believe what he had just told her. After taking a deep breath, she said, "Thank you. It's nice of you to say that."

The waiter had hesitated to come to their table because he could see they were deeply involved in their conversation. After a few minutes, he approached them and asked, "Are you ready to place your orders?"

"Yes," said Alfredo. "What appeals to you, Nathalie?"

"The Chicken Tarragon sounds tasty."

Alfredo took a moment before deciding. "Hmmm," he mused, "I will order Steak Diane."

The waiter turned and was about to leave when Alfredo looked up and winked at him, saying, "Please do not place our orders yet. Give us half an hour."

"Certainly, sir." The waiter smiled and left the couple alone.

Alfredo said to his lunch companion, "I am glad you like this restaurant. I have always liked coming here. Tell me more about yourself, Nathalie. Where do your parents live?"

"Both of them have passed away. I'm by myself."

Alfredo took her hand and said, "I am sorry."

"I went to Europe with my girlfriend Tisha last year. It was such a nice trip. I wish we had stayed longer. We were in Paris, England and Spain."

"How long was the trip?"

"We were gone for three weeks."

"Let us toast," he said. "I drink to Nathalie. I am so happy to have met someone like you." He looked into her light emerald eyes.

She reciprocated. "And I salute you, Alfredo, a true gentleman." Her eyes feasted on his manly countenance.

They clicked their glasses, and then looked lovingly at each other. Once more, total silence born of fascination fell between them. Alfredo broke the silence when he said, "I have also traveled. Europe has such interesting history." He was so hypnotized by her that the spell wasn't broken until he spotted the waiter bringing the food. He said, "How time has passed. I see our lunch coming." Nathalie smiled sweetly.

The waiter asked, "Can I bring anything else?"

"Would you like anything else, Nathalie?" asked Alfredo.

"No, everything is fine."

During their meal, they were constantly glancing at each other. It was obvious to the waiter and the people sitting around them that there was a strong attraction between the two. When they finished eating and the busboy had picked up their plates, they resumed their conversation, oblivious to their surroundings.

"Do you have any hobbies?" he asked.

"I like dancing, interior decorating and painting. Since my parents' death, I haven't done any painting. I like to paint dogs, especially the Maltese. I find that breed to be smart and elegant. I believe they are the most beautiful dogs of all. How about you, Alfredo?"

"I like the world of finance. I guess that would be my hobby. I like numbers, and I get all I want and more in my business. I also like boating and horseback riding. The theater intrigues me. Do you like the theater?"

"Yes," she replied. "There is so much stage talent these days, and I appreciate good acting. I also love horses and boating."

"Great. It seems we have a lot in common." He playfully winked at her when he said that. He then asked, "Would you like some dessert or coffee?"

"A cup of cappuccino would be wonderful." She added, "Alfredo, it's been a total pleasure meeting you. You're so interesting and nice. I can tell you have a European education. You know how to behave as a gentleman."

"I did study in Europe. I have a couple of degrees in business administration."

Nathalie said, "After high school, I was given no say in picking a college. I was sent to a women's school that my father, Papi, chose. He selected one in Rome because a female cousin of his lived there with her husband, who was in the diplomatic corps. They lived on an upper floor of an apartment building with an old fashioned elevator that had wrought iron doors. I was driven to and from school by their maid so that I would not be exposed to the Italian men. They were very handsome and well dressed, but were known for pinching the bottoms of attractive women who passed by. They also whistled at them or walked up to them to say how beautiful they were. I became fluent in Italian and understood every word they said. They'd say things like 'You look like a princess. I could eat you alive. What a meal and what a dessert!' I admit that I would flirt a little bit but the minute that started, the maid would get upset and say, 'Hurry up! We have to go to class.' After a while, I was allowed to take the bus, but the maid had to always be with me."

Alfredo said, "I can understand why those men said things to you. You are very beautiful."

Since he seemed interested in her college days, she decided to tell him more. "I majored in business and in addition to economics and other academic courses, I took typing, short hand and bookkeeping. I worked hard because I had few distractions. Papi often reminded me that I was there for an education, not to party or play. He would say, 'You may party after you graduate.' My only social life was attending receptions at embassies with the cousin and her husband. One time, I met Pope Pius XII. By this time, I was a weak Catholic, but I showed him respect by curtsying. I also toured the Sistine Chapel and attended a concert in the Vatican. All of these restrictions weren't easy for me. One time, I went to the fountain mentioned in the song Three Coins in the Fountain. I threw in three coins and made three wishes, 'To get out of here, to get out of here, to get out of here fast.'"

Nathalie added, "I learned from a friend's unfortunate experience. She was one of my classmates. She became involved with a married man. She never wanted to take part in such a thing, but the man had lied to her and told her he was single. She was devastated when she learned the truth. The humiliation was too much for her. She wound up drinking heavily and because of her guilt, she got hooked on heroin."

Alfredo said, "Women have to be very careful. Both men and women must take their time so that their real selves eventually come out. No one can keep up a façade forever."

Nathalie then directed the conversation to Alfredo's background. She said, "Where were you born? I detect a slight accent."

"I was born in Antigua, Guatemala."

Nathalie froze. His answer hit too close to home. She didn't think it was the right time to tell him about her problems. She took a moment to compose herself before saying anything more.

Her pause concerned him. He asked, "Is anything wrong, Nathalie?"

"No, I guess I'm a little too full. Tell me about Antigua."

"It is a place with mountains and flowers of every color. When I am there, I feel as though I am in a rainbow. The weather is like spring all year round. We have different tribes of Indians who dress in colorful attire."

"I love flowers and spring weather."

"Nathalie, Lake Atitlan is known throughout the world for its beauty. It sits between mountains. The local food is very good and naturally grown. It has a different taste than the food here in the States. You must come to visit. I know you will like my country."

"It sounds so inviting."

And Love Was Born

"I am inviting you to come. I have a villa with a view of the mountains near Antigua. It has a huge courtyard with a large fountain. Everywhere you look, you will see bougainvilleas in pink, white, purple, red, orange and lavender. I live by myself, so there would be plenty of room for you. I have hired an Indian family to care for my place on a full time basis. They live on the premises, but in a separate house. This family has been with me for a number of years. I hope you decide to visit someday."

"I may do that, Alfredo. It sounds great. I could learn Spanish while I'm there."

"My ancestors were Europeans," said Alfredo. "They migrated to Guatemala in the early eighteenth century. I am Spaniard and German."

"How interesting that we both descended from Europeans," said Nathalie. She looked at her watch and then said, "Oh Alfredo, it's three already. It only feels like I've been here a few minutes. I've enjoyed you so much."

"And you have charmed me. When can I see you again?"

"I have to make a brief stop at Logan, Silverstein and Tyson tomorrow at ten to drop off more papers."

"Can I call you tomorrow?"

"Yes."

"When?"

"At one."

"Your number please." He handed her a small address book. She wrote her name, address and number in it. While she was writing, she could not stop thinking about how happy she was. She had found him to be delightful. She returned the book to him.

He said, "Nathalie, I have truly enjoyed this afternoon and want to get to really know you. I have bought a home on St. Charles Avenue. It is very big. For the moment, my sister Maria Louisa is staying with me."

"I also live on St. Charles Avenue," she said. "I'm close to Jackson Street. Where are you?"

"I live close to Tulane University. It is not too far from where you live. Our living so close together seems like Kismet." He smiled with a flirtatious look as his eyes locked onto hers.

After Alfredo paid the bill, he took Nathalie's hand and held it gently, admiring her. When his Cadillac was brought to the front of the restaurant, they got in and he drove her to the law firm where her Mercedes was parked. After he parked his car, he opened his passenger door, helped her get out and then walked her to her vehicle. He helped her get in on the driver's side and then made sure her door was securely closed. After he shut the door, Alfredo said, "I will follow you to your home to make sure you get there safely."

And Love Was Born

Once he saw that Nathalie was home, safe and secure, he headed to his house. As he drove, he thought, "Nathalie is quite different from all the other ladies I have dated. She is warm, feminine, smart and well mannered." He had an intense feeling about her that he had never experienced before. He was falling for her. He asked a question aloud. "Will she be the piece in the puzzle of my life that has been missing?"

And Love Was Born

Chapter Thirteen

Nathalie was excited because she had met a man who might be "Mr. Right." She said under her breath, "Yes, I want to keep going out with Alfredo Milla! He is such a gentleman." After returning home from her second date with him, she knew he was the love she had longed for. Even though they had only been out together twice, he had made her so comfortable that she felt as though she had known him forever. He had a strange effect on her. She thought, "When I'm with him, I feel like a marionette held together by strings. It would be fine with me if he were the puppet master."

She said out loud, "I feel hypnotized. My heart yearns and throbs for him. Maybe Alfredo has put a spell on me." She thought, "I hope I don't make a fool of myself. Love has a strange way of touching you suddenly."

She walked toward the kitchen in a semi daze. Time had flown by. It was already six in the evening. She thought, "Tisha's a woman. She's also my best friend, and she can understand my inner feelings." She picked up the phone and dialed her friend's number. There was no answer.

She went to her bedroom, bathed, then slipped on her lavender baby doll negligee. Looking in her bathroom mirror, she said aloud, "I am not the same Nathalie."

She returned to her kitchen and sat next to a window that looked out on the back yard. She gazed skyward and saw the beginning of a stunning sunset in which the sun and clouds were turning a crimson gold. She let out a sigh and said, "I want this feeling I have for Alfredo to last for eternity." She felt relaxed. Her stomach pains from all the Guatemala stress had vanished.

She looked at the clock and saw that it was seven thirty. Time had passed quickly while her thoughts were on Alfredo. She picked up the phone again and tried Tisha. This time her best friend answered, "Hello."

"Oh Tisha, I'm so glad you're home. I met a man named Alfredo Milla at Matt Logan's law firm."

"Slow down, Nathalie, you're too excited."

"There was instant electricity between us. He invited me to lunch."

"Did you go to lunch with him?"

"Yes, we've gone to lunch twice, and we've had great times together. I think I'm falling in love, Tisha. I've never felt this way about any other man."

"Love strikes when least expected. Take your time. Time gives love a reason to blossom. If it happens, it's meant to be."

Nathalie replied, "I know what you're saying. Both my grandmother and my mother were always reminding me to save myself for the man I will truly fall in love with and marry. Grandma often said to me, 'If you are free with your affections, you will end up being some man's toilet.' My mom used to tell me, 'No real man wants used merchandise.' My father told me to, 'Stay away from any man who tries to take you to bed.' Alfredo is not like that. He's a gentleman. He treated me with respect, and we connected."

"This sounds like love to me."

"It is true love. Time disappears when I'm with him."

"It sounds as though happiness has made its way to you. John and I were worried about you because you acted like your dates were grains of salt. You went out with them and enjoyed their company, but that was it. They were not important to you. I'm happy for you. Keep me updated on your love life."

"Thanks, Tisha. I'll talk to you later."

When Nathalie hung up, her phone immediately rang. She thought it might be an old boyfriend whom she had not talked to recently but to her surprise, it was Alfredo. "I just wanted to check and make sure you are all right," he said. He had really called just to hear her voice again.

"I'm fine, thanks. I want to thank you for the lovely lunch."

"It was my pleasure. I was thinking about tomorrow. What are you doing? You mentioned that you were going to Matt Logan's law office."

"Yes, but it's only for a brief visit to check up on how things are going with the case they're handling for me and drop off more papers."

"I do not want to impose," said Alfredo, "but would you like to go to the Audubon Zoo? Animals are interesting creatures. A baby elephant has just been born. Can you come?"

"I would love to."

"Where can I pick you up, at the firm or at your home?"

"At the firm will be fine. I'll be finished by ten thirty."

"I also want to tell you how beautiful you looked today. *Que linda te ves.* I really enjoyed being with you."

"Thanks, Alfredo. I consider you a gentleman. I'm looking forward to tomorrow."

"Have a restful night. I will see you at Matt's office."

This was all too much excitement for one day. She loved hearing his compliments. It turned her on. It was only a little past nine, but it felt like midnight. She wanted to get to bed early. Tomorrow, she would be seeing Alfredo, the man who had not only entered into her life, but had suddenly and without warning gone into the center of her heart.

And Love Was Born

Chapter Fourteen

Matt Logan arrived at his office just before nine. He stopped to tell his secretary, Louise, "Nathalie Ordonez will be here at ten. She said she wanted to bring me additional documents and other information she just found. I think something is brewing between her and Alfredo Milla. They make a cute couple."

"I have the same feeling," said Louise. "Mr. Milla has inquired several times about Nathalie. Ever since he placed his eyes on her, he has often called to find out if she happened to be at our firm. Each time he did, it sounded as though he was ready to drive over if she were here. I think they're using our office as a meeting place. He seems smitten by her. Who could blame him? She's a good looking, classy lady."

"I agree with you," said Logan. "Alfredo is also a class act. He's a total gentleman, and he rates triple A with me."

"We don't usually have excitement like this at our firm," said Louise, smiling.

"I hope it works out," said Matt. "They're both excellent people. I better get back to my paper work. Please bring me a cup of coffee when you can. I have a lot of work to do."

Nathalie arrived early for her appointment. She was carrying a small briefcase. She said to Matt's secretary, "Good morning, Louise."

"Good morning, Miss Ordonez."

"Alfredo is coming here. We're going to the zoo after I finish with Matt. They have a new baby elephant. Louise, I really like Alfredo."

The secretary replied, "It's wonderful that you have that feeling. I wish you the best. He seems to be crazy about you."

Just then, Matt Logan came out of his office. He went up to Nathalie and said, "I'm ready for you. Let me carry your briefcase."

"Thanks, Matt."

Matt placed the briefcase on his desk and said, "You have the very best attorney New Orleans has to offer for your case. Leon is a lion. He'll eat anyone who gets in his way. He's very aggressive."

"Thank you for all you've done," she said. "I hope my case will be resolved without complications."

As Matt opened the door to his office for her to leave, he heard Alfredo's voice in the waiting area. Nathalie also heard it, and she quickly made her way to him. He smiled charmingly when he saw her.

"Hello, Alfredo," said Matt. "What brings you here?"

"I am taking Nathalie to the zoo. I thought it would be convenient to pick her up here."

"Both of you have fun," said the lawyer with a smile.

Alfredo and Nathalie left holding hands. Matt watched them and thought, "I see a strong love connection. How happy they look. If they can be as happy as my wife and I, they will be blessed. Love is definitely in the air."

And Love Was Born

Chapter Fifteen

After their outing at the zoo, Alfredo took Nathalie to an oyster bar that offered fresh seafood and Dixieland jazz. They sat down and each ordered beer with a dozen oysters. A man was playing a saxophone, and people had gathered around him like bees. He captivated them not only with his talent but because he played with his heart and soul.

Nathalie said, "That sax player is incredible. He makes his instrument talk."

"It is an imposing instrument, Nathalie. He is very good. I am glad I brought you here."

He took her right hand and kissed it. This made Nathalie blush.

"Would you like anything else?" he asked.

"I'm fine." She smiled and winked.

He was receptive to her flirting. He leaned over and gave her a kiss on the cheek.

She said, "That felt wonderful."

"You are like a soft *munequita*."

"What's a *munequita?*"

"It is a Spanish word for a doll. You are like a perfectly sculptured porcelain doll. I will always call you by that name."

"Thank you. I love the name. I really want to become fluent in Spanish."

"I will make a deal with you. You correct my English, and I will correct your Spanish. Repeat after me, '*Alfredo le gusta a Nathalie.*'"

She repeated, "*Alfredo le gusta a Nathalie,*" then asked, "What do those words mean?"

"It means that Alfredo likes Nathalie." He was gazing into her sparkling green eyes.

"Oh Alfredo, you are doing something to me!"

He moved closer to her and put his arms around her. His touch felt electrifying on her skin. She reached over and caressed his face. He gave her another kiss on her cheek, but this time it was closer to her lips. It made Nathalie wish he had kissed her lips instead.

He said, "I made reservations for seven at Brennan's. Would you be my date?"

"I accept your invitation, Mr. Milla." She smiled at the formal way he had presented the question.

"I will take you over to your car and will again follow you home. I will pick you up at six, *Munequita.*"

"Thank you for making this day so memorable. I love being with you, Alfredo."

And Love Was Born

As they left the oyster bar, Alfredo held her close to him, so close that he could sense her heart beating. When they arrived at Logan, Silverstein and Tyson, Alfredo took her in his arms and kissed her many times on the lips. He savored her, and she returned his kisses while breathing in his manly scent. The next day Nathalie sent him a poem she wrote.

And Love Was Born

Mysterious Love

I feel a mysterious love,

That comes and goes,

Like a shadow in the night.

It travels toward you,

Capturing your love,

So it can bring to me

In its golden wings,

Your love then settles,

Peacefully inside my soul,

And inside my heart.

He had returned from a short business trip when he went through his mail and found her poem. In response Alfredo mailed a note to her. It read, "My skin hurts for you. It yearns to have you close to me. To be without you is to be without me."

And Love Was Born

And Love Was Born

Chapter Sixteen

It was Monday afternoon and Alfredo was back at work after having spent most of the weekend going on dates with Nathalie. He decided to have lunch at the Court of Two Sisters. As he entered the restaurant, he saw his good friend Rodolfo Munez waving his hand at him. He wanted Alfredo to join him at his table.

"I have news for you, *amigo*," said Rodolfo.

"What is it?"

"Carmen Fernandez de Cordova is back in town. She was working in Europe after getting her degree, but is now staying with her mother. Carmen has really matured into a beautiful woman. I remember when you used to follow her around with your tongue hanging out like a little puppy dog."

Alfredo instantly formed a picture in his mind of his beautiful high school sweetheart, with her black hair, dark almond eyes and perfect white skin. Her family had come from Grenada, and she was one hundred percent Spaniard. He thought, "Rodolfo knows about Nathalie. I cannot let him know how much I would like to see Carmen again. He is a gossip spreader."

He changed the topic of the conversation. He and his friend didn't mention Carmen during the rest of their lunch, but Alfredo's curiosity had gotten the best of him.

After leaving the restaurant, Alfredo went back to the office he had set up in his mansion. He closed the door to make sure his sister Maria Louisa could not eavesdrop and then he looked up the number for Carmen's mother in the phone book. He nervously dialed and a black maid answered. After he asked for his old girlfriend, the maid went to her and said, "There's a call for you, Miss Carmen."

"Who is it?"

"I don't know. It's a man. He didn't say what his name was." Carmen normally didn't take calls from strange men, but her antennae urged her to talk to the mysterious caller. She picked up the receiver and cautiously said, "Hello. Who is this?"

"This is Al." Carmen was the only one who ever called Alfredo "Al."

"Al! What a wonderful surprise. I've only been back a couple of days. How did you know I was here?"

"My friend Rodolfo told me, and I just had to call you. I still remember our wonderful times together in high school. I still carry the beautiful picture you gave me in my wallet. You must have become even more stunning."

"Thank you, Al. That's most kind. I thought of you many times during the years I was away. What a gentleman you were! I can never forget you."

"Carmen, I would love to take you out so we can talk about our great times in high school. Let us meet at Pontchartain Beach tomorrow."

"That would be perfect. It holds so many memories of what we once had." He detected the same flirtatious quality to her voice which he remembered from years before.

"We'll meet at eleven tomorrow morning, and then go to lunch," he said. "It will be a good way to catch up."

Alfredo was so nervous that he showed up a half hour early. When Carmen walked up to him, he was astounded at how much more beautiful she had become. She was 5' 5" and had filled out to a tantalizing 130 pounds. He couldn't help putting his arms around her and kissing her on the cheek. As she responded to his embrace, she gushed, "Oh, Al, you look so manly!"

"I remember how much you love seafood," he said. "I know a good place close to here. We will go in my car."

Alfredo found Carmen more charming and feminine than she had been in high school. He couldn't take his eyes off her. They held hands as they walked to his Cadillac. Many pleasant memories flashed through his head. He felt like a teenager again.

When they arrived at the West End Seafood restaurant, Alfredo requested a table far in the corner so they could talk. As he pulled her chair out for her, he had butterflies in his stomach from the excitement of being with his first love again. They spent two hours reliving their old times together.

When it was time to go, he said, "I am planning a business trip to Baton Rouge this Friday. I would love for you to come with me. We could stay for the weekend."

"I would love to join you," she replied. "We have so much to talk about. I have a cousin who lives there, and I can stay with her. I'll call her tonight."

Later that evening, she called him and said, "Everything is set." They made arrangements to meet in a parking lot early Friday morning and leave in his car. Both of them wanted to keep things quiet until they had enough time to see what would happen after being apart for so long. She had mentioned an old boyfriend who was madly in love with her, but he didn't say a word about Nathalie.

They spent most of the drive to Baton Rouge laughing and talking about their teenage episodes. As they neared her cousin's home, Carmen said, "I have never forgotten you. You have always been in the back of my mind. Maybe we can get to know each other more."

Alfredo froze. He had gotten more than he bargained for. It was fun to feel like a teenager again, but she had let the door open for his becoming serious about her once more. After a momentary pause, he replied, "Maybe we can go back to what we had between us." The way he said it lacked conviction. It wasn't a "yes" or a "no," just a weak, noncommittal "maybe." Carmen didn't pick up on it because she was beginning to fall for him again.

They had dinner Friday night and spent ten hours Saturday seeing the sights, dining and dancing. It was late when he returned to his hotel room but when he crawled into bed, he was unable to sleep. Guilt was eating away at him, and he needed something to drown his torturous thoughts. He threw some clothes on and headed for the hotel bar. He ordered a double shot of bourbon, quickly downed it and then ordered another just before the bar closed. The alcohol failed to relax him and he was still unable to sleep.

He was fully clothed as he sat on the side of the bed and thought, "What am I doing with Carmen? Nathalie is the one I love. I must get back to her tomorrow." He became overwhelmed with guilt for having lied to her about his reason for going to Baton Rouge. He had told her, "I must check on some properties." All the while, he was having a grand time with an old girlfriend. He began to sob and as a tear rolled down his cheek, he said aloud, "I am lower than a cockroach!"

After regaining his composure, he thought, "I cannot be this way. I must clean up the mess I made and never let it happen again."

Even though he had not slept, he sat wide awake until a reasonable hour to call Carmen. When she was on the line, he said, "Something has come up and I must get back to New Orleans. We will have to leave as soon as possible." She sensed that she was losing him, but she said nothing.

As they drove past the Baton Rouge city limits, he turned to her and said, "Carmen, I must be truthful with you. I am dating someone I truly love. You are intelligent and beautiful. You will find someone perfect for you. Let us stay with just the memories of our teenage years."

Carmen started to cry. She sobbed as she said, "They are only memories. They aren't you."

Neither spoke the rest of the way to the Crescent City. Carmen was sad, but Alfredo was relieved at having put an end to her thinking of getting back together with him. After they arrived where she had parked her car, he put her suitcase in the trunk for her and helped her get in. Before starting her car, she looked into his eyes and said, "If things don't work out between you and your girlfriend, you have my phone number."

Alfredo replied, "I wish you all the best."

She pulled away. It was the last time they ever communicated.

He still felt guilty for overstepping the boundaries as he drove back to his home. He had a look of sorrow on his face as he said under his breath, "As God is my witness, I will never do this to Nathalie again."

And Love Was Born

And Love Was Born

Chapter Seventeen

It was a warm spring day in the Crescent City when Leon Silverstein walked to his car in the long term parking area of the New Orleans International Airport. He was happy to be home, but he was frustrated after having been on such an unsuccessful business trip. He had failed to accomplish anything of importance in Guatemala. He had never liked that country because he never got used to the procrastination and blasé attitudes common among so many government leaders and businessmen. The authorities with whom he had discussed Nathalie Ordonez' problem didn't seem at all interested. They listened to what he had to say, but the looks in their eyes told him that the issue was not going to be a priority any time soon. He would have been able to get a judge to sign an eviction order, but the location of Nathalie's property was too remote to expect any help from local law enforcement in making judicial decrees stick. He thought, "I've never seen so many lazy people in one country." Since the authorities couldn't be bothered, the rules in the Guatemalan highlands were made by those with guns who were willing to use them.

He pulled out of the parking lot and headed home. It was early in the evening. He looked forward to seeing his wife and having his favorite home cooked meal. Judy would get his mind off the bad news he would have to deliver to Matt Logan in the morning. She was probably planning another trip for them to take. They shared a love of traveling, and they had almost as much fun planning their trips as going on them. The thought of going somewhere always excited him, as long as it wasn't Guatemala. He would rather go to Siberia than that Central American arm pit.

The next day he told Matt that nothing could be done for Nathalie. Logan immediately called her and set up an appointment for that afternoon. He didn't tell her anything over the phone. He would give her the disappointing news in person.

When Nathalie met with Matt and Leon and had been told about the hopelessness of the situation in Guatemala, she said, "There has to be something that can be done. I'll have to go down there and see what I can do myself."

"I strongly advise you against doing that," said Logan.

"Matt, you don't understand. The plantation makes the money to pay for the hospital that my father and mother gave their lives for. No matter what, it has to be saved. I can't lose it."

Matt felt very sad for Nathalie. She wasn't going to give up, even though her cause was hopeless. He paused to decide what would be best to say, and then replied, "I don't know what else to tell you other than you must take care of yourself and not try anything dangerous. Without you, your family will no longer have a legacy."

Her response was, "I want to thank you and Leon for all you have done. I promise I won't do anything foolish, but you must understand that I will never let the matter drop."

She was very agitated as she drove home from the attorneys' office. She thought, "I don't have the slightest idea of what I'm going to do next." She needed to do something right away, but there were too many barriers, too many spineless attorneys and too many weak governments. A thought came to her. "Maybe it would help to talk to someone who operates outside the law." She quickly dismissed that idea as foolishness. The answer would not come easily. She needed to be patient.

And Love Was Born

Chapter Eighteen

Shopping was one of Nathalie's favorite diversions. She was known for being well dressed and color coordinated. Tisha called Nathalie to remind her of the coat sale they had planned on attending. "Hi. It's Tisha. The coats are sixty percent off, so we should leave early."

"I agree. The nicer ones will disappear quickly."

"I'll pick you up at ten."

"I'll be ready."

When Tisha pulled into Nathalie's driveway, the blonde with the emerald green eyes was locking her front door. Tisha greeted her by saying, "Good morning. I'm happy you could come with me. When are you going to introduce me to the famous Alfredo?"

"I think I'll do that after we've gotten to know each other a little better. You know how it is at the beginning. Couples like to be by themselves. I can tell you one thing about him. He has manners not often seen in men."

"I'm glad for you, Nathalie."

"You know, Tisha, I've often wondered why I enjoy shopping so much. I think it has to do with all the restrictions I had during high school. Did I ever tell you about the Ursuline Academy?"

"Not that I recall."

"It's a boarding school here in New Orleans run by an order of Ursuline nuns. The only time I had any moments to myself was when I went home on weekends. If my conduct had not been satisfactory during the week, I would be denied permission to leave the campus. We wore uniforms which consisted of navy blue skirts with hemlines past our knee caps and starched white blouses. We also had to have white caps that we used to cover our heads whenever we entered a church. Labels had to be sewn into the clothes to help them sort out the laundry."

Tisha seemed interested, so Nathalie told her more. "They assigned me to a large circular dormitory room with nineteen other girls. We were all the same age. We had to make our beds perfectly each morning. A nun inspected all the beds while we were in class by bouncing a coin off the bed spreads. If it didn't bounce, she'd pull all the bedding off and pile it on the center of the bed. If that happened to you, you'd have to spend your play time remaking your bed."

"Did that ever happen to you?"

"It happened to me once, and I made sure it never happened again."

"That school sounds like a prison. What else went on there?"

"There was a small cubicle behind the head of each bed. It had in it a sink, three drawers and a bar for clothes hangers. There was also a little desk in front of the cubicle. The closets had to be kept in order and the sinks kept clean. We had to make sure our shoes were shined. The nuns would go into all of our dresser drawers whenever they felt like it to make sure every item was folded correctly."

"Did they let you watch any television?"

"Absolutely not. Each dorm room was supplied with a couple of radios, but we could only listen to approved stations. No phonographs or records were allowed. Magazines had to be approved, otherwise they would be confiscated. We had to ask permission to use the phone, and we could only call our parents. My parents were in Guatemala most of the time, so there wasn't anybody for me to call. They called me. I didn't call them. We couldn't wear frilly nightgowns or negligees. Each of us had to wear pajama tops and pajama pants. When a nun rang a hand held bell at eight o'clock, we all had to be in bed and reciting the rosary out loud. Our hands and rosary beads had to be held on our chests so that a nun could walk from bed to bed and make sure all the girls' fingers were on the same bead. Lights went out at nine. At six thirty in the morning, a nun rang a bell to awaken us. We had forty five minutes to get dressed and make our beds, since we had taken our showers the night before. Then we had to pass inspection by a nun standing in the doorway. We waited in single file as she looked each of us over. If you met her approval, she'd say, 'You're groomed.' After inspecting all of us, she'd say, 'Follow me to church, and cover your heads. Don't disrespect the Lord.'"

Tisha said, "I couldn't have handled that. Why didn't you run away?"

"Because they kept every door locked. There were many times when the thought of running away went through my mind, but we were on the second floor. It was too high for me to jump out of a window."

Tisha said, "Well, here's Holmes. We've arrived."

After Tisha parked her car, they both got out and walked toward the D. H. Holmes store, one of the finest in the Deep South. In addition to quality merchandise, it also offered a nice dining room. They quickly went through the front entrance and headed straight to the women's coat department. A crowd of customers were already there frantically searching through the racks. They joined in the melee.

After examining many coats, Nathalie found three to try on, while Tisha found five. All of the dressing rooms were occupied and the female customers were milling around while they waited for a room to vacate. Tisha said, "I'm not going to wait in line. Let's go over to that open space next to the dressing rooms and try them on there. Otherwise we'll be here for hours. We can watch each other's purses." Nathalie agreed that was the smart thing to do.

They each put a coat on. Nathalie said, "Tisha, how does this look on me?"

"Great, Nathalie, how about mine?"

"It fits you very well, Tisha." They tried on all of the coats they had selected, and each one fit them well. Nathalie said, "Well, we found what we came for. Let's leave this mob."

Tisha replied, "I agree. Sales can be awful because they draw so many people. Let's pay for our garments and get going. We need a cocktail to wind down. How does the Court of Two Sisters sound to you, Nathalie?"

"Good pick, Tisha."

When they arrived at the restaurant, Tisha gave her car keys to the valet. They walked in and Tisha asked for a table for two. They didn't have to wait long. To Nathalie's surprise, she spotted Alfredo and Matt sitting at a table. She turned to her friend and softly whispered, "You won't believe this, Tisha. Alfredo is sitting over there with Matt Logan. They're at the table by the big plant."

"I can see them. Hmmmm, he's good looking, Nathalie."

"They haven't seen us because they're completely involved in a serious conversation."

A waiter led the two women to a table close to where the two men were seated. Nathalie looked at Alfredo, but he was too involved in conversation to notice her. All of a sudden, Matt waved at her. This caused Alfredo to wonder who his lawyer saw. He turned slightly around in his chair and spotted Nathalie. He immediately got up and went to her table. "What a great surprise, *Munequita Linda*. I received your poem. You are very talented. Thank you very much."

"Alfredo," she said, "this is my best friend Tisha Miller. Tisha, this is Alfredo Milla."

"It is nice to meet you, Tisha," he said, shaking her hand. He turned toward Nathalie and said, "I had a morning meeting with Matt. We decided to come to this restaurant. It holds so many memories for me." As he spoke, Alfredo was looking at Nathalie with loving eyes.

"I've heard nice things about you," said Tisha. "It's nice to meet you, Alfredo."

"The same, Tisha. Unfortunately I must leave. Matt and I have to go back to his office to finish our meeting. I'll see you later, *Munequita Linda*."

Nathalie said, "See you later, Alfredo."

Before he left the two women, Alfredo leaned towards Nathalie and gave her a kiss on the cheek. He then joined Matt. As the men walked out of the restaurant, they both waved at the two women.

Nathalie turned to her friend and asked, "Well, what do you think, Tisha?"

"He has incredible manners, he's handsome and really nice. He makes a terrific first impression. I could fall for a man like that. There were a couple of words he said that I didn't understand. What does *Munequita Linda* mean?"

"The word *munequita* means doll and *linda* means pretty, so *Munequita Linda* means pretty doll. It's a nickname Alfredo has given me. Now you know why I have fallen for him. Enough about romance, I'm hungry. I'm going to order Alfredo Fettucini." Nathalie said this with a glow on her face. She giggled at her own joke.

"Oh, Nathalie, you *are* in love."

"I admit it. I was just joking about the Alfredo Fettucini. I'm actually going to order gumbo."

Tisha said, "I'll have the special crawfish with Cajun sauce. Let's order mimosas. After meeting handsome Alfredo, we need to make a toast to him."

Nathalie said, "Champagne and orange juice would be fine. Just don't ask me to order a martini. Did I ever tell you about my bad experience with a martini?"

"No. Tell me about it."

"I went home to New Orleans for summer vacation after my freshman year in college. A man who had just graduated from Tulane's medical school asked me out on a date. He was tall, slim, had brown hair and personality plus. I was eighteen years old, and I was allowed to go out with him because his family knew my family. He took me to the Blue Room. I don't know if you've been there, but they have floor shows. After we were seated close to the performers, he asked me if I would like something to drink. I asked him, 'What are you having?' He said he was having a martini, so I decided to have one too. That was a big mistake, because the drink went to my head and the room started to twirl. He immediately ordered strong black coffee. That didn't sober me up. He wanted me to eat something before taking me home, so he ordered for both of us. Right after eating, we left. I was still woozy when he finally got me home. That was the last I saw of him, and the last time I ordered a martini."

Tisha said, "Well, you learned a lesson."

Nathalie replied with a chuckle, "Yeah, I did."

The two friends had an enjoyable lunch. After Tisha drove Nathalie home, she helped her take her purchases inside and then she went back to her place. Nathalie picked up her mail and found the note Alfredo had sent her. She held it close to her heart and decided to put it under her pillow so she could read it again in the morning when the sunlight first penetrated her bedroom window.

And Love Was Born

Chapter Nineteen

It was early the next morning and daylight had just arrived in New Orleans. Nathalie was outside on her patio, preoccupied with the pleasant memory of the kisses Alfredo had placed on her lips during their most recent date. The telephone interrupted her daydream. She quickly answered it and was pleasantly surprised to find that it was the man whom she was falling in love with. "Oh, Alfredo! You're already awake. What made you get up so early?"

"Nathalie, my *munequita*, I don't know what you have done to me. I could not sleep. I woke up at one, at three and finally at seven. All I can think of is you. You were my dream before I met you and when I saw you, I knew I loved you."

She replied, "Is it true that I could have such an effect on you?"

"Yes it is. It is as true as the new light outside my window. I dream about you, *Munequita*. I cherish our times together because I remember our kisses. I enjoy being with you so much."

She said, "Your kisses were so warm and tender, my love. Can you come over this evening? I'll fix crepe suzettes."

"Of course I will. I cannot wait to taste your dessert. What time should I be there?"

"Seven would be perfect."

"I will be there. I know they will be delicious, Nathalie. I have to tell you that I feel your presence all the time. You are becoming an important part of my life."

"I feel the same way about you, Alfredo."

"Nathalie, you have just made me the happiest man alive. See you at seven."

"See you soon," she replied sweetly.

After hanging up, she stood up, spun around and shouted, "WE FEEL THE SAME WAY!"

She had vivid thoughts of their most recent date. She remembered his kisses, his embrace and the way he looked at her. They produced an electric feeling in her. She felt a strange but pleasant kind of heat whenever she was close to him, and she wanted to have that feeling forever. She couldn't imagine those feelings happening to a person more than once in a lifetime. From the first time they met, Alfredo had ignited a burning desire inside her. At first, she tried to make it go away, but the more she tried, the more she lost her battle.

Nathalie could not wait to see him again. The hours did not pass fast enough to suit her. It seemed like a very long day, and the excitement and anticipation made her a little tired. Her living room sofa suddenly seemed inviting. She stretched out on it and fell asleep. A strange noise awakened her. It turned out to be two squirrels fighting. She glanced at a clock and realized that Alfredo would be arriving in only a couple of hours. It was time for her to get up. She went upstairs to freshen up, and then she made her way to the kitchen to start preparing the crepes. She finished by making the orange sauce. All that was left was waiting for Alfredo's arrival.

She hurried upstairs to add some final touches. After spraying expensive perfume on her neck and arms, she was ready for him.

She went into her living room, took some records out of a cabinet and placed them on a table so that Alfredo could pick his favorite songs. Just as she finished doing that, she heard his Cadillac pull into her driveway. She looked out the living room window and saw him carrying a bouquet of yellow roses. He rang her doorbell, and she opened the door.

"*Munequita Linda*," he said, "these yellow roses are for you." After he handed them to her, he kissed her lips.

"Thank you so much. They're beautiful. I love yellow roses. I'll put them in a vase."

"It is customary in my country to give yellow roses to ladies with blonde hair."

"I love the customs of your country."

"Is there anything I can do to help you?"

"You can make the coffee, if you like. I'll be warming the crepes."

He said, "What a surprise when I saw you that day at the Court of Two Sisters. It is incredible that we would pick the same place to have lunch."

"It's called mental telepathy, Alfredo. What did you think of Tisha?"

"She is very pretty and she seems nice."

"She's a loyal friend."

"Coffee is made," he announced.

She said, "The crepes are almost ready. Please have a seat at the dining room table."

Alfredo went into the dining room and took a seat at the head of the table. Nathalie followed him in with the crepes. The pleasing aroma of the orange sauce she had drizzled over the tops of the delicate French pancakes awakened Alfredo's taste buds. "Eat them in good health, Alfredo," she said as she served him.

After a few bites, he said, "These are really good. You are a master chef."

"Thanks," she answered shyly.

When they finished eating, Nathalie suggested that they go to the living room and listen to music. He walked over to the long play records she had stacked on the table next to her phonograph and said, "Let me see what you have. Here is a good Perry Como song, And I Love You So." He looked into her green eyes with intensity and said, "I dedicate this song to you, *Munequita Linda*. Listen to every word."

And Love Was Born

After laying the vinyl disk on the turntable and gently placing the phonograph needle, he put his arms around her and held her close. He kissed her lips passionately. She returned his feverish kisses. The music had become entwined with the love they felt for each other. He looked into her eyes and spoke to her while the song played softly in the background.

"I love you. I am in love with you. I want you for the rest of my life. I will make you happy, you will see. I am a man who falls in love only once. I am not young and foolish. I know what I want, and it is you."

Nathalie was speechless. His words had taken her breath away. Her heart was beating fast.

"I hope I haven't shocked you," he said. "I am speaking the truth to you."

"No, no," she replied. "I have deep feelings for you also."

Alfredo kissed her again. She was melting in his arms. She did not want the evening to end. Suddenly the music stopped.

"Nathalie," he said, "play that same song again. From now on, it is our song."

Nathalie was holding him and caressing him. She said, "I love you. No one has ever touched my heart the way you have."

"I want you so badly," he replied. "I will restrain myself, though, because I respect you and love you."

Alfredo got up and went to the kitchen. He had to get away from her or else things might have gone too far. He was only human, and his love for Nathalie had become uncontrollable. She followed him into the kitchen, went up to him and whispered in his ear, "I understand. I also love you with all my heart."

He looked into her eyes and said, "I want us to express our love for each other at just the right time. It will be when you understand the immense love I have for you. I want our love making to be a beautiful moment that we will cherish for the rest of our lives."

And Love Was Born

And Love Was Born

Chapter Twenty

Nathalie's phone rang at ten in the morning. She ran to it, hoping that it was Alfredo. She was disappointed when a voice came on the line saying, "This is a survey on breakfast cereals. Would you like to participate?"

"No thanks. I'm busy." Nathalie hung up and said under her breath, "They get you every time you least expect their call."

She went upstairs to her bedroom, got dressed and left for her favorite nursery. She wanted to add more plants to her back yard. After purchasing four crepe myrtles in pink and purples and one yellow rose bush, she made her way back home.

When she arrived home, she carried her new plants to the back yard and placed them where they could be seen from the kitchen window. She then went upstairs to her bedroom and changed into gardening clothes. She thought, "I'm going to get nice and dirty this morning." She took along a small radio so she could listen to her favorite station as she toiled.

She removed the old plants and dumped them in the garbage. As she began to dig holes for the new arrivals, she looked at the yellow rose bush and thought, "I love the yellow roses Alfredo gave me. I want to be able to look out my kitchen window and see the same type of flower to remind me of him."

She heard the phone ring just as she filled in the soil around the last plant. As she rushed inside to answer it, she thought, "I hope it isn't another survey." She blushed with pleasure when she heard Alfredo's voice on the line.

"*Munequita Linda*, I want to invite you to dinner tonight at my home. My sister Maria Louisa is going to fix Guatemalan food. Will you be able to come?"

"I'd love to. At what time?"

"I will pick you up at six. You will have a chance to taste our cuisine. Maria Louisa cooks *delicioso*."

"Thank you for the invitation, Alfredo. I'll be ready."

She went upstairs, filled her bathtub and poured in bubble bath. She took off her soiled gardening clothes, put them in the hamper and stepped into the tub. She luxuriated in the fragrant water surrounded by bubbles. She began to daydream about what it would be like to be married to Alfredo. She suddenly realized she would have to hurry if she was going to be ready when he arrived.

She got out of the tub, dried off and applied her makeup. She chose a green dress from her closet that would be perfect for the occasion. She carefully applied a discreet amount of perfume around her neck and behind her ears. As she passed a tall mirror mounted in a hallway, she took one last glance at herself. She wanted to look perfect not only for Alfredo, but also his sister. She would be meeting his family for the first time.

She still had a few minutes before Alfredo was expected to show up, so she called Tisha. "Hi. I'll be seeing Alfredo's home and meeting his sister this evening. What do you think?"

"That's great, Nathalie. When he starts introducing his relatives to you, it means he's serious."

"He'll be here any minute."

"Have fun! I'll call you tomorrow."

It wasn't long after Nathalie hung up that Alfredo rang her doorbell. She opened it right away. He said, "How are you? I missed you, my darling." He kissed her lips and gave her one yellow rose. She accepted the flower and passionately returned his kiss. She replied, "I missed you too. Let me put it in a vase so it won't wilt." After she tended to the flower, they left. Once she had locked the front door, he put an arm around her waist and guided her to his midnight blue Cadillac. He opened the passenger door, helped her get seated, closed it, then went to the other side to get behind the wheel. He looked over at her, saying, "You will like my sister. She's sweet and speaks English as well as I do. She went to college in Boston. She is in her early fifties, but very perky." It was reassuring for Nathalie to hear that the sister spoke English.

It was beginning to get dark when Alfredo pulled into his driveway. Fancy lighting illuminated his mansion. It was three stories high, made of stone and had a four car garage. Nathalie was impressed at the sight. While he helped her out of the car, the sister came out to greet them.

Alfredo said proudly, "Meet Nathalie, Maria Louisa."

The sister gave her a hug and said, "How nice to meet you, Nathalie." The green eyed blonde found the warm reception comforting. It reminded her of the way the people in her mother and father's village had welcomed her. She thought, "This is something we don't often see here in the U.S." Nathalie returned Maria Louisa's hug.

Alfredo said, "We are a people that like to hug. We like the warmth associated with hugging. Latins always greet people that way."

Nathalie replied, "I like your custom. It makes me feel very welcome."

Alfredo said, "Let us go inside."

They entered the mansion through massive double wooden doors that had flowers elegantly carved into them and then passed through a foyer with marble floors. A living room was to the right of the foyer, and a dining room was on the left. The ceilings were fifteen feet high. Large windows looked out on St. Charles Avenue.

As they entered the dining room, Nathalie noticed a handmade table cloth and candle holders carved with faces of Indians and animals. Maria Louisa spoke first and said, "I hope you like the decorations. They are all from my country. I will be playing recordings of Guatemalan music as we dine. I think it will provide the same ambience as if we were in Antigua."

"It looks colorful and beautiful," said Nathalie.

Alfredo said, "Shall we go to the living room, *Munequita Linda*?"

Once they were in the living room, Maria Louisa asked Nathalie, "What would you like to drink?"

"A glass of red wine, thank you."

"I will serve, sister," said Alfredo. He poured three glasses, gave one to Nathalie, one to his sister and then picked up the last glass.

Maria Louisa said, "A toast to you, Nathalie. I am so happy you were able to come tonight. I think you will like our food."

Alfredo said, "A toast to *Munequita Linda*, the woman who has stolen my heart." He raised his glass in salute.

It was Nathalie's turn. She said, "I drink to having met you, Alfredo, and your sister, Maria Louisa."

With that out of the way, the sister said, "Let's go back to the dining room for our meal." She led Alfredo and Nathalie there.

Within minutes, Maria Louisa brought in serving dishes filled with tortillas, baked chicken, black beans and rice. She placed them on the dining room table. She turned on the stereo system and Guatemalan music began playing softly. Nathalie thought, "This is so different. It's good to get away from the same routine."

She found the food delicious. Alfredo noticed how much she liked it. When everyone had finished, Nathalie said, "It was wonderful, Maria Louisa. You are a very good cook."

"Thank you, Nathalie," replied Alfredo's sister. "You are sweet. Can I get anything else for you?"

"No thank you. The food was wonderful. Can I help you with the dishes?"

"Thanks for offering, but I will take care of them."

While Maria Louisa was busy clearing the table, Alfredo took Nathalie back to the living room. They sat down on a sofa. His face revealed how attracted he was to her. He was thinking, "She seems to be my perfect match." He said to her, "I hope this has been enjoyable."

"It was because it was so different. All the things your sister told me were so interesting. I had forgotten some of the history and culture of Guatemala."

Alfredo replied, "*Munequita Linda*, I see that it is late. I will take you home. You have to get your beauty rest." He kissed her on the forehead and said, "I would love to see you again. I will call tomorrow. Think about lunch at the club. We have an excellent chef."

"I don't have anything to do tomorrow. I'd love to be with you, Alfredo."

"I will call you in the morning," he said as he got up and helped her off the sofa.

And Love Was Born

Just then, Maria Louisa came into the room holding a little statue of a Guatemalan Indian. She handed it to Nathalie and said, "This is a little token for you. It was hand carved by a Mayan Indian."

"Thank you. I will cherish it."

Alfredo said, "Well, sister, I have to get this princess home. I will see you shortly."

As he walked Nathalie to the front door, Maria Louisa walked behind them. She winked at Alfredo. It was a signal that she approved of Nathalie. The sister hugged her and said, "You are always welcome. I hope I will see you again soon."

Nathalie returned the hug and said, "We will get together again. Thank you for the tasty meal."

As she watched Alfredo and Nathalie walk toward his Cadillac, Maria Louisa thought, "Nathalie is lovely. I can see why my brother fell head over heels for her. He has to be careful. I still don't know if she can adjust to our Guatemalan culture."

And Love Was Born

Chapter Twenty One

Nathalie and Alfredo learned more and more about each other as the days went by. They did this by talking about things that had happened to them in the past. Nathalie told him about her parents. She said, "My father, who I called Papi, was my hero, my protector and my comforter. When I was little, he would always tuck me in at night, kiss me and hug me."

She added, "Papi was very protective of me when it came to men. One time when I was fifteen and visiting in Antigua, a twenty one year old man from another wealthy family became so infatuated with me that he hired three musicians to stand outside my bedroom window. They were going to serenade me while I was getting ready for bed. The musicians played beautifully, and I flung the window open to hear them better. Suddenly, I heard Papi shout, 'GET OFF MY PROPERTY OR I'LL FINISH YOU ALL!' He was cradling a rifle in his arms and had two German shepherd guard dogs at his side. I heard him say to the young man, 'Don't ever come here again. You're not to have anything to do with my daughter.' That was the last I saw of him."

Alfredo said in response, "Your father loved you and was trying to protect you. After all, he did not know the man who wanted to serenade you. In fact, when we have our daughter, I will act the same way."

Nathalie then told Alfredo about another occasion when her father stepped in to protect her. She said, "About a year after he ran off the man in Antigua, a twenty two year old friend of my grandmother called me and asked me out. He wanted to take me to a matinee at a movie theater here in New Orleans. I accepted his invitation because his family had been friends of my grandparents for years. I didn't bother telling my father because I thought it was a safe date. We drove to the theater and just as my date parked his car, Papi appeared. I couldn't believe it. It took my breath away, and I almost fainted. I was so embarrassed. Before I had a chance to explain anything, Papi grasped my right arm firmly, ushered me into the back seat of his car, closed the door and locked it. He then went up to my date and warned him, 'Don't you ever try to have anything to do with my daughter!' As we drove back home, I kept saying, 'Mommy and Grandma know him. It was only a little movie at four o'clock in the afternoon. Why would you do that to me?' All he said was, 'We will talk at home.' After we got there, I was told not to make plans unless my parents knew about it."

Alfredo responded by saying, "You had a very tough father. When we have a daughter, I will not do that to her."

She also told him a story from her years at the Ursuline Academy. "I was approached by a nun who had a unique physical trait. She had a blue eye and a brown eye. I tried not to stare at her because she might have taken offense, and I didn't want to cause any trouble for myself. The sister said, 'I think you would make an excellent nun. I can arrange for you to enter a novitiate.' The thought of that sent chills up my back. I couldn't just ignore her and try to keep out of her sight because she had a remarkable ability to find me whenever she wanted. So, I took a deep breath and said in a calm voice, 'But Sister, I've always thought about someday getting married and having children.' That didn't solve anything. She said, 'You will be a bride of Christ, my dear. That's the highest honor any woman can achieve in this world.' I then said, 'I'm going to think about it and pray for guidance.' That seemed to satisfy her. Lucky for me, the Ursulines sent that nun to a new assignment at a different location."

She added, "My experiences at the Ursuline Academy led to my falling away and no longer being a devout Catholic. I believe, however, that the strict discipline benefits young people. It teaches them that marriage is forever."

Alfredo said, "All these experiences have made you into a lady. Look how you turned out to be. I am proud of your family and of you."

They grew closer and closer. Anyone who saw Alfredo and Nathalie together could tell how much in love they were. It was as if rays of sunshine constantly surrounded them. Nathalie's good friend Tisha wondered what it was like to be that way. She had a conversation with them about it after Alfredo returned from a business trip to Guatemala. She asked him, "I've never seen a love like yours and Nathalie's. What's the secret behind so much bliss."

"Let me try to explain love to you, Tisha. Nathalie is like a rose and I am a carnation. When we met, we had to be willing to peel away each of the petals from our flowers. After we had peeled away all the petals, only the hearts of the flowers remained. We realized that we had become vulnerable. We are totally open to one another and have given each other our hearts, and this is the only way two people can love. My carnation and her rose became entwined as one."

Alfredo added, "The ability to love is within each of us, but few are willing to seek it. Many people live in a tunnel that is dark, lonesome and empty because they are afraid to give their hearts and to love without limits. Those who understand this can attain the greatest treasures in life."

Nathalie spoke up and said, "Tisha, you have seen the happiness that I carry since Alfredo and I have given each other our hearts. True happiness comes with true love. Any other man I happen to look at is no more than a piece of stone to me. My heart has only enough space for one, and that space belongs to Alfredo. He is the man I will always love."

She added, "If you love from within your heart, love gives back a gift. It gives the gift of living rather than merely existing. Our love is a nectar found within us. We always have a thirst for each other, and we tap into the nectar whenever we want to drink. Love must be nourished every single day. We respect each other and treat each other with kindness and understanding. We focus on each other and are sensitive to each other's needs. I must love him just as he is and be his loyal friend to the very end, and he must do the same for me. I believe that to truly love is to be close to God."

When Nathalie finished speaking, she and Alfredo showed Tisha a rose and a carnation that had been entwined. It was a symbol of their undying love for each other. She also read a poem she had written.

Carnation

You are a male carnation,

Aromatic to my senses,

To my brain a fascination,

To my body a sensation.

Wilted I found you.

I picked you up.

With tender care,

I watered you.

I touched you,

Then I held you.

I also loved you,

My carnation.

As I loved you,

And embraced you,

Signs of life,

Invaded you.

Male carnation,

Now you've opened,

Your precious petals,

So we can love.

Like the whiteness,

And the pureness,

Of two white doves,

Born was our love.

And Love Was Born

And Love Was Born

Chapter Twenty Two

Nathalie's phone rang early in the morning. She picked it up on the first ring because she thought it was the love of her life. She was surprised to hear a strange husky voice on the line. The caller said, "You and I need to talk business, Nathalie. It's about your coffee plantation."

"Who are you? Where are you calling from?"

"The name's Bill Sanders. I'm here in New Orleans. Do you know Murphy's Restaurant on St. Charles Avenue, not far from Canal Street?"

"I'm familiar with it."

"I'll be wearing a red carnation and sitting in one of the booths. Meet me at one o'clock and make sure you come alone." He hung up before she could say another word.

Murphy's occupied space in an older building and was strictly a place where locals went to eat, but it did a booming lunch trade because of its tasty home-made food. The front of the restaurant consisted of large glass windows and a glass door.

When she opened the door and went in, she saw a dining area that was long, but somewhat narrow. On her right was a cashier. All the way back and to her left was a row of brown booths. It didn't take her long to find Sanders. He was seated by himself in the very last booth and was smoking an unfiltered Camel. He had an unusual presence that set him apart from all the other men in the place.

He wore a navy blue suit, a blue turtle neck and had a red carnation in his lapel. His hair was cut extremely short in military burr head style, but he had high cheek-bones and finely chiseled features that seemed somewhat delicate for a man. She could only see his upper torso. He didn't appear to be muscular, but he had broad shoulders and his hands were big. As she approached his booth, he spoke in the husky voice she recognized from his phone call. "Well, we meet at last. You're even more attractive than your photos. Have a seat." She wondered how he had seen pictures of her.

As she stood next to the table, his piercing dark eyes moved up and down her body as if he were undressing her. This made her stomach turn sour. His attention quickly shifted to the waitress who brought them menus, and he ogled the server as he gave her his order. Bill appeared ready for a heavy meal. He said, "The food's great here. I really like their catfish." She didn't want to eat with anyone who repelled her but because of the way she had been brought up, she considered it impolite not to order anything at a lunch meeting. She spent a few minutes with the menu before deciding on a bowl of gumbo.

When their food arrived, he smothered his fish in hot sauce, which repelled her even more. She drank tea, but he was drinking beer. She was in a situation she wished she wasn't, but she felt she had no choice. She had to sit there for the better part of an hour and a half and watch him stuff his face with food, wolf down his meal, consume three Jax beers and finish three cigarettes. The smoke and ashes nauseated her. He could tell she was very uncomfortable at his horrific table manners, but he didn't care. He picked his teeth before he finally started speaking.

"What happened to your coffee plantation is a shame. If you don't already know, it was taken by Solomon Garcia and his gang of Mayan Indians. His father was a thief and a murderer who was executed in public. Solomon is a chip off the old block. You're lucky that I have a lot of influence with Garcia. He really doesn't want your place. All he wants is money."

"How do I know you're telling the truth?"

"I go to Guatemala quite often. I was down to your plantation recently. I picked up some interesting souvenirs."

Sanders reached into a briefcase he had placed under the table. He pulled out two framed photographs. One was of Nathalie with her parents and Rodrigo Ramos, the manager of the plantation. The other was the family photo displayed at the entrance to Heart to Heart Hospital. She immediately recognized the items, and her heart stopped. She thought, "I have violent evil schemers working against me." She asked him, "How did you get these?"

"It was easy. I just took them off the walls."

At this point, Nathalie could see that not only the plantation but also the hospital was under the complete control of Garcia, and probably Sanders too. She had no option but to give in to their demands. She asked, "What do you want from me?"

"You can buy him off with $100,000. Since there are ten Quetzales to a dollar, he'll think it's all the money in the world. The price for my personal guarantee that you'll never be bothered again is $200,000. So, for three hundred grand, your troubles are over."

"How do I know he'll leave if he gets the money?"

"Do you have a passport?"

"Yes."

"I can arrange it so that you can meet with him face to face in Guatemala. If you want, you can be at the plantation to watch him leave. You won't pay until he's finally out of there and you have your own people take over."

"Can you guarantee my safety?"

"Absolutely."

"When do I pay you?"

"We'll meet when you return from Guatemala and everything has happened the way it's supposed to. That's when we'll open a joint bank account. You'll deposit it in there, and then you'll sign a promissory note to me for $300,000. That way, I can freeze the account so you can't touch it."

"What happens if I don't go along with this?"

"I hate to tell such a pretty woman like you, but Garcia is about ready to take over both your plantation and your hospital. He won't stop until he has it all. I am your only hope."

Nathalie's rosy cheeks turned to chalk. She didn't want to give this Sanders creep a dime, but what else could she do to save her family's legacy? Her lawyers had told her that the law in that country was useless. Her only option appeared to be paying them off. After a couple of moments, she nodded her head and said, "Okay."

"Fine. You'll be leaving within five days. Just so there's no misunderstanding, don't even think about going to the cops. The New Orleans PD can't help you. If there's any funny business, you'll lose everything, including your life."

She couldn't stand being with Bill Sanders a minute longer. She got up to leave and he said, "Don't go away mad, sweetheart. Lunch is on me."

Nathalie thought, "It was the most disgusting meal I ever had, and it's going to be very expensive. I hope he chokes on a fishbone."

Bill Sanders gathered up his briefcase after she had left Murphy's. He looked forward to working off the calories by getting some exercise between the sheets at a brothel in Gretna, a town just across the Mississippi River. The bordello was run by Matt Logan's old sergeant, Sal Cardinale.

And Love Was Born

And Love Was Born

Chapter Twenty Three

At first, Nathalie was so anxious that she thought, "I can't tell Alfredo anything about the trip. I'll have to make up a story." After she became a little calmer, she considered things very carefully and decided she wouldn't do that. She knew that they would have to be completely honest with each other for their true love to be nurtured. She immediately called him and said, "I must see you as soon as possible. Something very important has come up. Can you come to my house at two?"

"What is it about? You sound different. There is a strain in your voice. What is troubling you?"

"I'd rather talk about it when you come over."

After he arrived at her home, she said, "I don't want you to be upset, but I have to go to Guatemala by myself. It's urgent that I do this."

"Why do you have to take this trip?"

"I have to save my family's plantation and hospital by meeting with bandits who have possession of the plantation." She began to cry as she said, "They also want to take the hospital from me."

He took her arms and said, "This is a man's job. I will help you."

She stopped crying as he held her, then she said, "You can't be involved with this. If you breathe a word of it or the police find out, I'll lose the plantation and the hospital. Everything my parents worked for will be gone."

For the first time in their relationship, he raised his voice to her. He adamantly said, "*Amorcita Linda*, you cannot go by yourself! You will not get on that plane! Let the plantation and hospital go! I will build others for you." As he spoke, he gestured with upturned palms.

She was non-confrontational by nature and didn't raise her voice, but she was very intense when she said, "How heartless can you be to say that to me. What's wrong with you that you can't understand?" She began to cry again and said in a sobbing voice, "I must take care of this alone. Go easy with me. We're talking about the things built by my father. I must protect them. Please don't talk about them as though they're easy to discard and walk away from. These things have far more than sentimental value to me. They were my parents' dreams, and they are my dreams too. I am emotionally attached to all of it."

He had no idea of what to say. He just looked at her and wondered, "What can I possibly do to keep my *munequita* safe?" After a momentary pause, he said, "*Amorcita Linda*, are you sure you have to do it that way."

"Yes. It is what it is. I am the architect of my own destiny."

And Love Was Born

Chapter Twenty Four

Bill Sanders called Nathalie two days after their meeting at Murphy's. He told her she would be leaving in three days, gave her the departure time for her flight and said, "A woman named Gina will meet you at the airport an hour and a half before the plane leaves. She'll have your tickets, and she'll be traveling with you. You should be able to recognize her. She's blonde and has blue eyes. She's 5' 1" and weighs 115 pounds. She'll be wearing a black dress and a black and yellow scarf. By the way, she's going to college and knows nothing about why you're going there, so don't say anything about it."

Meanwhile, Alfredo had acted quickly to protect his *munequita*. On the day before she left, he sat down with Nathalie and told her about arrangements he and his cousin Marcel had made to assure her safety. The two cousins were part of a handful of families who controlled the vast majority of the land, wealth and power in that country. The cousin had made use of his close contacts within Guatemala's secret police, and they devised a distress signal for the green eyed blonde to use. The code word was *suquita*. All Nathalie had to do was make a phone call or short wave transmission to her Guatemalan bank. Her call for help would be immediately forwarded to the authorities.

After a restless night, Nathalie left her Mercedes at home and took a cab to the New Orleans International Airport. There were dark circles under her eyes and her face was drawn.

It didn't take her long to spot the woman she was to meet. Gina was dressed the way Sanders had described. Her black dress came down to the middle part of her calf, and she was wearing high heels. She had a welcoming smile, sweetness in her eyes and seemed to be a woman with some class.

After checking their luggage, Gina said, "Our flight won't leave for nearly an hour and a half. Rather than stand around here, let's go to a restaurant and get to know each other." Nathalie agreed, and they walked to the nearest coffee shop. They each ordered a Seven Up, and they split an oyster po' boy sandwich.

Nathalie said, "Tell me about yourself, Gina. I'm interested in knowing you."

"I'm going to be working on an anthropology project in Antigua. It's part of what I have to do to get my Ph.D. from LSU."

The topic of their conversation shifted to Nathalie. She said, "I've lost both of my parents who lived in the highlands of Guatemala, and I'm going there to settle the estate." She didn't feel comfortable telling Gina anymore about herself. They spent the rest of the time before their flight talking about the beauties of Antigua.

Their conversation ended when Gina looked at her watch and said, "We'd better go, Nathalie, our flight will be boarding soon." They got up and went to their departure gate, which was located outside.

Their first stop was Miami, where they made a connection to Guatemala City. After their arrival, they claimed their luggage and went to the front of the terminal to meet their ride to the hotel. Bill Sanders had assured the two women that ground transportation had been arranged. Two men awaited them with a small station wagon equipped with four wheel drive. One was short and fat, and was wearing sunglasses and leather gloves. The other one was even shorter, but was slender. The stout one was the first to step toward the women. He called out, "NATHALIE? GINA?"

They responded to his call and walked to his station wagon. As Nathalie stepped closer, she took one look at the man who seemed to be in charge and thought, "What kind of a chauffeur is this? He's wearing one of those ridiculous straw fedoras, and he looks like he slept in his clothes. He's obese and has a red nose, so he probably drinks too much." Nevertheless, she extended her palm to shake his hand.

A bolt of stark terror struck her when he roughly grabbed her by the arm, put a gloved hand over her mouth and shoved her into the back seat of the vehicle. The next thing Nathalie knew, Gina was sitting next to her. The fat man told the skinny one, "Dump their bags in the back. We don't want to leave any of that behind." The stout one then patted Nathalie down, but didn't make any sexual advances. "Thank God," she thought. She wondered, "Maybe he's searching for weapons, but it's strange that he didn't search Gina too. It's also odd that she didn't put up a struggle and is so calm. She's acting like she has been expecting this to happen. She's not even looking at me."

As they drove through Guatemala City, Nathalie thought, "The skinny man is driving and he seems to be taking orders from the fat one. He didn't give him any directions, so they must have something planned. Is it robbery or, God forbid, rape?" She began to perspire in a cold sweat.

She didn't know that she had fallen into the hands of Solomon Garcia, the bandit Bill Sanders had told her about. His henchman was a Mayan thug named Topec.

In his younger days, Garcia had become known as a great man with a blade. Solomon loved to assault his victims on very hot days. He once tailed his target on foot until the victim reached a place which offered solitude. He then dashed past the unfortunate person and did his dirty deed with quickness and stealth. He kept his knife so sharp that it could penetrate flesh with little pain. The only telltale sign was the victim suddenly feeling wet along their side. At first, they would think it was heavy perspiration caused by the heat of the day. When they reached down to the wet spot and pulled their hand back it was covered in crimson, and then they knew. Solomon had sliced them good, and they would soon be dead.

From a skinny kid who killed so easily, Solomon had grown into a sloppy thirty year old man who carried two hundred pounds on a 5' 7" frame. His capacity for violence and brutality had served him well through his adult years.

Garcia said to Nathalie, "If you keep quiet and don't try anything, I won't tie you up and gag you. Do what you're told, *Gringa*, and we'll get along fine."

She was trembling and sobbing as she asked, "Who are you? Where are we going?"

"Shut up, woman!"

They drove until the paved roads ended, and then continued on until they reached a ramshackle house in a suffocating Guatemalan jungle. It belonged to Tepin, the other Mayan in Garcia's gang. Since Garcia was a mixed breed of Indian and Spanish, he felt an innate superiority to those he led. He sometimes reminded them of his higher status by saying, "Most dirt grows something, but your kind cannot even grow weeds. All you can grow is more dirt."

After they pulled up to Tepin's house, he marched out to meet them. He was a short, taciturn man with a big machete. Solomon chuckled as he said, "I have to take a leak. No indoor plumbing yet?"

"No, *amigo*, just the hole in the back room. Be sure to pour in some water from the bucket next to it and flush everything away." Nathalie thought, "What section of Hell am I in?"

Just then, Gina piped up. The blue eyed blonde asked in a cold tone, "Where's my pay? Who's gonna take me back to the airport? My flight home leaves this evening." Nathalie then realized she had been lured into a trap.

Gina had known all along that they were going to be kidnapped. She was not a Ph.D. candidate, but a high end prostitute at Sal Cardinale's brothel. She was to receive $3,000 for serving as a decoy, payable immediately after the kidnapping. She had done her part and wanted to get back to Gretna as soon as possible.

Garcia walked up to the blue eyed blonde and whispered in her ear, "Follow me and we'll get everything straightened out. I have some money to give you." He pulled a wad of cash from his inside coat pocket and held it in a tantalizing way as he started to walk behind the house. She followed him like an obedient puppy. Within a few steps after they were in the back yard, the rumpled looking thug whipped out a Colt .45 automatic and put a bullet right in the middle of Gina's forehead. Her lifeless body dropped to the ground like a bag of dirty laundry.

When he came back to the front of the house, Nathalie saw blood on his cheap, raggedy suit coat. It was too much for her to handle. She screamed, "MURDERER!"

He responded by grabbing her long blonde hair and slapping her several times on her cheeks. She screamed with pain and begged, "Please don't do this to me." When he let go, she fell to the ground. He growled at her, "*Mujer*, you didn't keep quiet. I am going to have to tie you up and gag you." The trauma was so great for her that she fainted. When she awoke, she was in the back seat of the station wagon again. This time, her hands and ankles were bound and a gag was in her mouth. They were driving somewhere. She hoped they weren't going to kill her or rape her before she could use the code word.

And Love Was Born

And Love Was Born

Chapter Twenty Five

Alfredo was sitting by himself at the desk in his office. His legs were crossed and his right hand was tucked between his thighs. He had a faraway look in his intense eyes as he pondered a business related problem. His deep thoughts were interrupted when the phone rang. It was a call from Guatemala. Marcel was on the line.

His cousin cleared his throat nervously before saying, "Alfredo, it hurts me to have to tell you this, but my contacts just told me something has happened to Nathalie. A police detective saw her get off the plane with another blonde woman, but he lost them in the crowd. He also said she has not checked into her hotel. He thinks they were picked up by someone they knew. I will call as soon as I hear more."

"Thank you, Marcel. I know you will do your best." Alfredo became very worried.

Five hours later, Marcel called again. His voice cracked as he said, "Alfredo, they have found the body of a blonde woman in a remote area outside Guatemala City. She was shot in the forehead, but they have not identified her as yet. They said it appears that whoever did it wanted the body found quickly to show they meant business. We must pray that it is not Nathalie. It could be the woman she was with. I will stay in touch."

There was a deep momentary silence on Alfredo's end, and then all he could manage to say was a weak "Thank you, cousin."

He placed the receiver back in its cradle. Suddenly, he felt a chilling sensation all over his body. His heart skipped a beat and his legs were like wet spaghetti. They gave out when he tried to get up from his chair. He called for his sister, Maria Louisa, but all that came out of his mouth were unrecognizable murmurs. His chest had tightened and he couldn't breathe. In desperation, he picked up a vase and threw it against a wall with as much force as he could muster.

Maria Louisa heard the crashing noise and came rushing into the office. She had been in the back of the house, and it was remarkable how quickly the woman in her fifties came to her brother's aid. She arrived to see a different Alfredo. His face was distorted and he could not respond to any of her questions. She grabbed the phone and told the operator, "Please send an ambulance to 3120 St. Charles Avenue. Alfredo Milla needs help. Also, please contact Dr. Jaime Rodriguez immediately. He is Mr. Milla's cousin."

"The ambulance should be there shortly." Alfredo's sister was relieved as she hung up.

When the ambulance arrived, two attendants got out, accompanied by an intern from Touro Infirmary, which was the closest hospital. The intern took Alfredo's vital signs and performed a preliminary examination. He ruled out a heart attack or a stroke. By the time he had finished, Dr. Rodriguez had shown up.

Alfredo's cousin said, "He's in severe shock. Let's get him to the hospital." The two attendants placed Alfredo on a gurney, fastened belts across his body and lifted him into the ambulance. Dr. Rodriguez said to Maria Louisa, "I'm riding in the ambulance with your brother. I'll be sending someone for my car."

Alfredo was immediately wheeled into the emergency room when the ambulance arrived at Touro. As he was moved from the stretcher to a bed, his cousin ordered the ER nurses to, "Keep him quiet and warm. When you finish wrapping him in blankets, let me alone with him. I must see how he responds to me when I ask him some questions." After covering him up, the nurses left the room.

The doctor said to his patient, "Alfredo, this is your cousin Jaime. Open your eyes. Listen to me. What happened to you?"

All Alfredo responded with was, "Unnnnh."

"Alfredo, work with me. What's wrong with you?"

"My Nathalie…"

"What happened to Nathalie?"

"She… she's gone."

"What do you mean she's gone?"

Alfredo's head began to clear. "She has been kidnapped. She might be dead." After he said it, he was sorry he had. Now the police would be brought in.

Dr. Rodriguez called the nurses back into the room. He said, "Take his B. P. Take a blood sample so I can run some tests."

"B. P. is high, "said one nurse.

"I'm going to sedate him. I want to keep him here overnight until the blood test comes back, and I'll be staying with him." The nurses followed every order. They could see that Alfredo Milla was a very important patient.

One of the nurses came into the room with a nitroglycerin capsule, and Jaime gave his cousin the medicine to lower his blood pressure. Before he sedated him, Dr. Rodriguez tried to find out more about Nathalie's kidnapping. He wanted to make sure it actually happened and wasn't some hallucination. He said, "Alfredo, listen to me. I need to ask you some questions."

"I feel like I'm dying, Jaime."

"You're not dying. I'm running some tests. You'll be here overnight."

"No! I have to go to Guatemala. They took *Munequita*! Let me out of here!" He began to struggle with his cousin, but he was too weak.

The doctor said, "You can't leave, Alfredo." He called for a nurse and said, "Help me sedate him." When they tried to put an IV in his arm, he fought them until Dr. Rodriguez told the nurse, "Bring an orderly and secure the patient to his bed." It was a rough way to treat his cousin, but he had no choice.

After sedating his relative, the physician started to leave the room, then turned and said, "Alfredo, I'll be in touch with Maria Louisa, *tu hermana*. I'm sure she'll call with any news. I'll be here all night with you."

Alfredo was too exhausted to respond. He closed his eyes and drifted into unconsciousness.

And Love Was Born

And Love Was Born

Chapter Twenty Six

Immediately after Gina's murder, Nathalie was driven in Solomon Garcia's four wheel drive vehicle to El Tejar, a village of four thousand that was thirty minutes by car from Antigua. Garcia relaxed in the passenger seat while Topec drove. All along the way, the leader of the gang sipped on *cusha*, a homemade rotgut liquor made from fermented fruit. He was combining business with pleasure while his underling did all the work.

The men who lived in El Tejar produced bricks and tiles for their livelihood. The clay was dug out of nearby hills. Some of them would mix the clay with their feet to break down the chunks, and any chunks not broken down were thrown away. There was only one store in the village. It had an absentee owner, and it was managed by a woman named Piedad.

One of the men in that village was a Mayan Indian named Kark. He worked hard digging clay, but was always in need of money because he gambled and drank. He wasn't too choosy about where his Quetzales came from, and Solomon Garcia took advantage of this character flaw. Garcia gave Kark seventy five dollars to hide Nathalie in his small house, which was painted a bright yellow like the color of the sun.

Kark pocketed the cash and turned over the responsibility for the hostage to his wife, Nicte. He left the small house that they shared, saying, "I'm going to drink with my friends. It is my manly right."

Nicte became curious about the hostage. The Mayan housewife had worked as a maid for an American family when she was young. The family had paid for some of her schooling, and she had become fluent in English. She began talking to Nathalie, who understood every word her captor said.

She said of her husband, "He is a drunk who throws his money away on card games. He loves to play them, but never wins." Her prisoner was limited to communicating with her head and eyes because she was gagged and her hands were tied. Nicte sensed that Nathalie was sympathetic to her, so she decided to untie the hostage and remove the gag after giving a stern warning. "Do not try anything on me. Otherwise, you will again be tied and gagged. I will also tie your ankles." Nicte was much bigger than Nathalie, and it was easy to see that she could carry out her threats.

When the downtrodden wife saw that her captive wasn't going to try to escape or cause any other problems, she served her tea made from allspice leaves. This was a treat for Nicte. She had learned about tea from the American family, but no one else in the village liked it. As they sipped their beverages, they had a long conversation.

It had been quite some time since anyone had listened to what Nicte had to say, and the unappreciated housewife was able to get many things off her chest. After listening to all of Nicte's problems, Nathalie said, "Can't we please go for a walk? Let's get some fresh air. Aren't you tired of being in this little house?"

"Where could we go? I do not have any money."

"Do you have any stores here? I need some toiletries. I have some money in traveler's checks. I'll let you buy some things for yourself."

Nicte's eyes lit up. She thought, "This is a chance to finally get some things I always wanted." She said, "I will take you to the only store we have, but if you say one word of this to my husband, you will be sorry."

As they stepped outside the humble dwelling, Nicte threw a dirt clod at a hornet's nest without any fear of being stung. She then warned Nathalie about the very deadly snake called *barba amarilla*, which is Spanish for yellow beard. She said, "Follow directly behind me. I know where to walk. Take your eyes off the ground for a second and you will trip. Stop and mosquitoes will get you." The Mayan housewife thought, "I don't want her to get bitten by a poisonous snake before I can spend some of her Quetzales." They followed a trail leading to the main part of the village where Piedad's store was located.

They heard a faint buzz, and Nicte ordered, "Stand like a statue!" The two women stood perfectly still as the buzzing increased until thousands of bees whipped around like a golden wind before dissipating over the jungle. Nathalie thought, "No wonder she spends so much time in that little house."

Piedad was behind the counter when they arrived. She and Nicte were good friends. The store manager was also a Mayan with a drunk for a husband, so the two *campesinas* shared a great deal in common. Nicte introduced her hostage by saying, "This is Nathalie. She is from America. She is here on business and wanted me to be a guide for her. She found out about me from the American family I worked for. I have to keep it secret because if Kark finds out, he will take all the money for himself. You know how those men are. Will you take her traveler's checks?"

Piedad replied, "I can take those checks if they are used to buy merchandise. Do not worry. Kark has no way of finding out what you buy, and I am not going to tell him."

Within forty minutes, Nicte had selected shoes, a purse, a dress, two bras, six pairs of panties and a supply of her favorite tea. They were items that were normally difficult for her to buy because her husband gave her very little money. The bill came to over one hundred dollars. Nathalie was glad to pay for it with her checks, and even gave Piedad extra money as a gratuity. After seeing how free spending Nathalie was, Nicte wanted more and thought, "I am going to see how generous this American woman can be. After all, she needs my help."

Everything was working out the way Nathalie hoped it would. The most important thing was to send a distress signal to her bank. It could be done by short wave radio, and the only store in town would surely have one.

Nicte was in such a shopping frenzy that she paid no attention when Nathalie asked Piedad if she could contact her banker in Antigua by radio. "We could ask them to have a messenger bring me more money." The store manager agreed to do it, thinking, "She'll be spending even more and I'll be making a lot of commission."

Nathalie wrote out a message that Piedad read into the microphone word for word. "*Suquita* needs more money." Once the message went through, Nathalie began to worry that Marcel's plan might not work. She had no way of knowing for sure. All that held her together was hope.

Nicte suspected none of this. Nathalie seemed so obedient that there was no question in the Mayan housewife's mind that the rich American woman was under her complete control. After she and her prisoner returned to the humble yellow house at the top of the hill, Nicte was happy to see that Kark was still out with his friends. She was in such a good mood that she decided to fix a feast for just the two of them. She even let Nathalie go outside and clean herself with a hose before dinner. It was the closest thing Kark and Nicte had to a shower. She had to wash herself out in the open, shielded only by a towel hung on a rope.

Nathalie hoped she would be rescued before her captors did anything worse to her. While she was outside and Nicte was busy cooking, the green eyed blonde wrote a letter to Alfredo with a pencil and paper that she had carried in her large purse. When she finished hosing herself and drying off, she concealed it in her bra.

The letter read,

My Love,

When I was kidnapped, I heard echoes of your voice in my head. You gave me the strength to keep on going. If I would have been killed, it would not have mattered because I was surrounded by the repercussion of your voice.

Yours Forever

Nathalie

And Love Was Born

And Love Was Born

Chapter Twenty Seven

Kark stumbled into his house at one in the morning. He was drunk. He woke Nicte up and demanded that she fix him a meal. She dutifully made some tortillas and fried black beans while he slumped over the kitchen table with his weary head resting on his arms. He muttered in his drunken stupor, "*Mujer, te quiero.*" Nicte said under her breath, "Nothing he says is true. He has promised me a bathroom for two years, but drinks up all the money. Everything is for him. And he calls that loving me? What a joke." This time she didn't mind as much because of all the things she had purchased without his knowledge. She thought, "For once, I have the upper hand."

The Mayan husband raised his head from the table and began acting as though he were king. He became angry and shouted, "I DON'T WANT THAT *GRINGA* IN THIS HOUSE! SHE IS BOTHERING MY PEACE. I CANNOT MAKE LOVE TO YOU WHILE SHE IS HERE."

"Where do we put her?"

"Put her where we crap. Put her in *la letrina.*"

Nicte obeyed her husband. When she went to get Nathalie, she startled the hostage out of a sound sleep. The wife said, "Come with me, *Senorita,* and do not make any trouble."

Nathalie had been gagged and tied up after her meal with Nicte, so she couldn't say anything. She sensed something bad was about to happen and she started to resist. When Kark peered through his bloodshot drunkard's eyes and saw this, he became impatient. He said in a rough tone of voice, "Get out of the way, woman. I'll take care of this bitch." He pulled Nathalie to her feet and tried to shove her through the back door of the house, but he stumbled and Nicte had to take over. She wrestled their hostage into a small shed in the back yard that served as the couple's toilet.

It consisted of a big, nasty hole in the middle of the floor. The noxious odor was overwhelming. There was no toilet paper. There was only a pile of banana leaves used for wiping bottoms. Next to the pile was a good sized branch with several leaves that was used to ward off the rats which were constantly around. The most horrific sight was the dozens of fat, winged cockroaches. There were so many clinging to a wall that the wall appeared to move.

When Nathalie was pushed into the disgusting place, she fell to the ground. Nicte threw an Indian blanket on top of her to keep her warm. By then, Kark had sobered up enough to say to his captive, "Hold your legs together." When she obeyed him, he tied her ankles. He then said, "Nicte, tell her to do what I say or I will destroy her face. And also tell her not to make noise." He shook a fist under their prisoner's nose for emphasis. Nicte whispered to Nathalie, "Obey. Obey, *el es malo.*" She had tasted Kark's violence on too many occasions. Meanwhile, her husband experienced a feeling of dominance over a white woman. He had never felt this before. He thought, "I can see myself doing this again." All Natalie could say in response was, "I'll be good."

She was in a state of near shock. She thought, "Oh my Heavenly Lord, I can't take this. Please let me die." She began to sob as she thought, "I can leave this world knowing I am loved by Alfredo." As the door to the outhouse was being shut, Nathalie begged, "God! No! Don't leave me here."

The physical activity had sharpened Kark's appetite, and he went back to the house so he could gorge himself on the tortillas and refried beans Nicte had prepared. When he finished, he took his wife into their bedroom and made her lay down next to him. He wanted to have sex, but he was too drunk to even get his trousers off, and he quickly passed out. Nicte thought, "Thank you, Black Christ, for sparing me."

He had collapsed on the bed diagonally, leaving no room for his wife. This suited her fine. She was more than happy to sleep on the couch.

Nathalie couldn't sleep at all. It was impossible to relax in a place that smelled so bad. She became nauseous and worried about suffocating if she vomited while gagged. She also began to feel furry creatures with claws crawl over her. She thought, "They must be rats!" She began to recite in her mind a prayer from her days at the Ursuline Academy. "Oh my Father, I am heartly sorry for having offended thee and I detest all my sins because I fear the loss of Heaven and the pain of Hell, but most of all because they have offended thee, my Lord, who art all good and deserving of all my love." She was making her last act of contrition because she saw no way of getting out alive.

And Love Was Born

Chapter Twenty Eight

It was three in the morning and everyone in El Tejar was asleep. Three military vehicles rolled into the village through the inky night. The last in line had a red cross on its side signifying that it transported a medic and his equipment. General Hector Rojas rode in the passenger seat of the lead jeep. He wouldn't have missed the trip for the world.

When the code word *suquita* was transmitted from the banker to Guatemala's secret police, Rojas was the man who decided what steps were to be taken. Upon learning the call for help had come from El Tejar, he was compelled to pull rank and lead the assault. His determination bordered on pathological.

Once the general had been told that the woman at risk was a blonde American, he immediately thought of his own blonde daughter, Paquita. She was his only child, and he adored her. She embodied all the hopes and dreams that had driven him to rise from humble beginnings to a top military post.

His daughter had been taken from him two years before. At the time, she was only twenty two, had barely tasted life and was studying to become a physician. She had died horribly at the hands of a wicked band of renegade Guatemalan Indians who had attacked a clinic where she had been volunteering. After raping her, they beheaded her with a machete. None of the perpetrators were caught. Even with all his contacts, the only thing General Rojas was able to determine was that they came from El Tejar.

All the love in his heart turned to hate, and he became impossible to live with. He was never home because he had become obsessed with finding his daughter's killers. He reached the point where he felt justified in killing anyone who lived in El Tejar. He rationalized it by thinking, "None of them are innocent. If they aren't in the gang, they are harboring them. They all must die." His wife could not endure the terrible change in the general, and she left him.

When the convoy of jeeps pulled up in front of the store where the radio message had been sent, General Rojas stepped out of his vehicle and walked to the entrance. He banged on the door loud enough to rouse Piedad from a sound sleep. Her husband hardly noticed because he was sleeping off a night's drinking with his friend Kark.

Piedad turned on a light and saw the general through a front window. She thought, "What is this business? Who is in trouble now? Please don't let it be me."

The general didn't bother to say hello or good morning when she opened the door. All he did was shove a picture of Nathalie in her face and growl, "Woman, where is this blonde American lady? Do you know who took her?"

"*Si, mi general.* She is being kept at Kark and Nicte's house. If you go to the hill that is next to this store and climb close to the top, you will see the house. It is painted in yellow."

General Rojas walked out of the store and looked at the hill. Piedad followed him, and he suddenly heard her say, "*Por favor*, I do not want any trouble with the government. My husband and I work hard for a poor but honest living."

Rojas gave her a glowering look and snapped, "We will go to that house, *mujer*. If we do not find the American woman, you are in trouble." He patted the M1911 Colt .45 automatic he had thrust in a belt around his waist, Mexican style.

"You will find her. They were here. The American woman bought many things." Piedad's complexion grew paler with each word.

The general said to his second in command, "Let's go."

And Love Was Born

Chapter Twenty Nine

The general and his soldiers were cautious when they arrived at Kark and Nicte's home. They wanted to make sure they didn't encounter a vicious dog protecting the property. Once they were sure there was no threat, they approached the entrance. Rojas pounded on the door and shouted, "OPEN UP RIGHT NOW!"

Nicte jumped up from the couch in fright. She said in a loud voice, "I am putting some clothes on. I will open the door. Please do not hurt us."

When she opened the door, Rojas saw a guilty look on her face. He didn't bother to bring out the picture of Nathalie. He simply asked, "Where is the American girl? Show me where she is."

"She is in the outhouse out back. She is tied up and cannot speak because her mouth is gagged."

Suddenly they heard Kark in the background. He shouted, "WHO THE HELL IS HERE?" He tumbled out of bed holding his machete, and came out of the bedroom pointing it at the general.

Rojas gave him an order. "Lay down your weapon or you will be hurt."

"I do not have to do anything I do not want to do. Get out of my home. This is my property."

The general said, "I am telling you again. Put it down now!"

Kark began to move closer to Rojas. The general quickly pulled out his pistol, fired and hit the Mayan in his left hip. Kark screamed in pain, dropped to the floor and passed out. Rojas thought, "I'll finish him off later."

He turned to Nicte and said, "Woman, take us to the hostage." She quickly led them to the outhouse.

One of the soldiers was the first to enter the disgusting place. He moved the beam of his flashlight around until it landed on Nathalie. Rats were jumping all over her, and a tarantula was crawling on her hair. When he saw her condition, he exclaimed, "My god, she is unconscious! I think she is still breathing."

General Rojas turned to the medic and said, "Quick, Juan, bring your jeep here immediately." He then turned his attention to Nicte. He blurted out in anger, "You stupid animal!" He quickly aimed his automatic and put a bullet in the middle of her forehead. He was cool, calm and collected as he pulled the trigger because he felt completely justified in acting as judge, jury and executioner. As the downtrodden but greedy housewife drew her last breath, the general said, "All of your kind should die."

While the soldiers were carefully moving Nathalie from the outhouse and placing her on the back seat of the medic's jeep, tears rolled down her cheeks. She kept saying, "Thank you... thank you for rescuing me. I thought I was going to die."

Kark regained consciousness and made a getaway while Rojas and his men were occupied with Nathalie. It was excruciatingly painful for him to move, but he was fighting for his life. All he could think was, "They want to kill me. I must get to my friends." He continued to lose blood as he crawled. After a couple of hundred yards, he had no more strength and passed out. In his unconscious state, he was unaware that he was surrounded by army ants. The stinging swarms swiftly covered his body.

His skeletal remains were not discovered for two days. They had been picked clean. The only means of identifying him were his clothing and a belt buckle with the initial "K."

And Love Was Born

Chapter Thirty

The next day, Marcel called Alfredo and said, "I now have Nathalie at my home. The soldiers brought her here half an hour ago. She was taken to a hospital where she was disinfected, and they did a thorough checkup. They found nothing wrong. General Rojas assured me that none of what happened was leaked to the press. She needs to rest. My wife is taking care of her. I do not think she is ready to talk to you. She seems to be a bit disoriented. Other than that, she appears okay."

"Oh, Marcel, what have they done to my love? Did they beat her or starve her? Does she have bruises or cuts? Does she look thinner? Is she pale? Is she eating?"

"Calm down, Alfredo. She is all right. She is now in good hands. She is doing okay. I want to give her a couple of days rest before I bring her back up to your arms. I plan to personally travel to New Orleans with her."

"Should I take a plane to Guatemala? I can arrange a Pan American flight immediately."

"There is no need for that. Let her rest. She has gone through a lot. I believe she will need a little counseling when she gets back. I did not want to ask her any questions about her kidnapping. The soldiers briefed me about what happened. They assured me that the plantation and hospital are no longer in danger. I have personally hired a reliable replacement for Rodrigo Ramos, and I will be overseeing all operations. I want Nathalie to talk to me when she wants to. I do not want to force the issue. She will talk when she is ready."

"Marcel, I am not sure I want to stay and wait. I am taking the next flight out of here."

"Listen, Alfredo, you are an intelligent man. You have to understand that coming down here will not help her. She is getting along very well with my wife. We are trying to make her as comfortable as we can."

"I do not know how to repay you," said Alfredo. "You have been my cornerstone. Please call me and give me updates. Maybe by tomorrow she will be feeling better, so I can talk to her and tell her how much she means to me and how much I love her. You have no idea how I prayed for her safe return."

"My wife and I also prayed for her safety," said Marcel, "but now she is safe with us. A soldier is guarding our home. So relax, my cousin, all is taken care of."

"I will call you in a couple of hours for an update."

"That is fine. If she asks to talk to you, I will call you."

"Goodbye, Marcel, and many thanks."

Alfredo put the receiver down. The pain in his stomach was history. He went to the kitchen and told his sister the good news.

And Love Was Born

And Love Was Born

Chapter Thirty One

Nathalie was sitting in the living room of Marcel's home. She could see a guard standing at the front gate. She began to feel more relaxed knowing that no one could come after her again.

Marcel had been calling Alfredo every two hours to give him updates on how she was doing, but Nathalie did not feel ready to talk to her beloved just yet. She wanted to calm her nerves. She thought, "I don't want to start crying in the middle of our conversation. That might upset him." Marcel had told her, "You do not have to talk to him now. Just let me know when you are ready."

The next day after finishing her dinner, she said to Alfredo's cousin, "I think I'm ready to talk to my love Alfredo. I'm beginning to feel better. Thank you so much for providing a guard for this home. I'm beginning to feel more relaxed."

Marcel replied, "I will call him, Nathalie. Come to my office so you can have some privacy."

Marcel dialed the number in New Orleans. Alfredo answered, "*Hola.*"

"It is your cousin. Guess who wants to talk to you?"

"Put her on the phone! I have not been able to eat or sleep. I have to tell her how much I love her."

"Here is Nathalie."

"My love," she said. "I love you so much. It's over, all of it is over. I want to be in your arms. I want to be held close to your heart."

"My *munequita*, I have been with you every moment of the day and with every step you have taken. I love you more each day. Soon we will be together."

"I'm ready to fly back to your arms," she said. "Can you ask Marcel to arrange a flight so I can be there where I belong?"

"Yes, darling. Are you feeling like traveling, or do you want to wait another day or so to recuperate?"

"No, no, I want to be near you as soon as possible. I will heal much better with you holding me."

"Put my cousin on the phone and let me talk to him."

She said with an inner calmness, "Marcel, Alfredo wants to talk."

When Marcel took the receiver from her, Alfredo spoke first. "She is ready to come back. She would like you to make arrangements for her to fly back to New Orleans."

"I will call the manager at Pan American so he can help secure a flight for two o'clock tomorrow."

"Thanks, cousin. Will you call me when you know the itinerary?"

"I will," said Marcel. He looked at Nathalie who was smiling and then said, "I'm giving the phone back to her, and then I will leave you two love birds alone." He handed her the receiver and then left his office.

When Nathalie was back on the line, Alfredo said, "I love you. Soon I will be next to my one and only."

"I will dream of you tonight," she said before placing the receiver back in its cradle. She was ready for bed. Dreaming about Alfredo was all that mattered to her.

Later that evening, Marcel was able to book two seats on a Pan American flight for New Orleans leaving the following day. He told Nathalie, "We will be leaving at two in the afternoon."

She gave Marcel a warm hug and said, "Thank you for all you've done. I'm going to bed early. This will be the first time since my kidnapping that I'll finally be able to sleep." She slept soundly that night.

And Love Was Born

Chapter Thirty Two

Alfredo paced in the terminal of the New Orleans International Airport while awaiting Nathalie and Marcel's arrival. When it was announced that their flight was landing, he hurried to the gate to greet his beloved. He spotted them as they descended the steps from the plane. He could see that his love had lost weight, looked fragile and had circles under her eyes. As they entered the terminal, he took Nathalie into his arms and then greeted his cousin.

"I am returning your treasure," said Marcel. "She is such a lovely lady. We were honored to have her stay with us."

"Thank you, cousin," replied Alfredo. He turned to Nathalie, gave her a kiss and said, "Let us pick up the baggage. We will take a cab to my place. You and Marcel will be staying there."

Nathalie wasn't happy when she heard that. She said, "I can stay at my home."

"No, not tonight," replied Alfredo. "Maybe at a later time. Everything has been arranged."

"I don't want to be a burden to anyone."

"You are not. Do not say that, Nathalie." Alfredo was getting frustrated. He was seeing a different side of his beloved.

She was overly sensitive, and she began to cry and couldn't stop crying. It seemed that being in the airport had triggered a flashback of her kidnapping. When she finally calmed down, they took a cab to Alfredo's home.

They were met by Maria Louisa, who hugged both Nathalie and Marcel. Alfredo's sister led both of the guests to the bedrooms they would be using. She said, "After you refresh yourselves, come down and we will have some snacks."

Marcel went downstairs within a few minutes, but Nathalie didn't come down. Alfredo said to his sister and cousin, "Well, she is being a woman. She will come down shortly." After half an hour went by, he went upstairs to see what had happened to Nathalie. As he approached her room, he heard sounds of her sobs coming through the closed door. He knocked and said, "Nathalie, may I come in?"

He heard her footsteps approaching the bedroom door, and then she opened it. Her eyes were swollen from all the tears she had shed. She exclaimed, "You don't know what they did to me!"

Alfredo took her in his arms and tried to reassure her that everything would be okay. All Nathalie said in response was, "I don't feel well, Alfredo. I'm going back to bed." He decided to leave her alone in hopes that she would be better in the morning.

And Love Was Born

And Love Was Born

Chapter Thirty Three

Alfredo took time from his work to give full attention to Nathalie, but nothing changed after a couple of days. His one and only love was still not the person he had known. She was experiencing repeated flashbacks that caused nightmares which prevented her from getting hardly any sleep. She was also not eating well. The situation grew worse when she started nervously biting her fingernails until she drew blood.

He immediately called his cousin, Dr. Jaime Rodriguez, and the physician admitted her into a hospital for observation. Since her condition was stable, all the doctors could offer were prescription medications to calm her nerves and help her sleep. She was discharged after a week.

Her nail biting had stopped, but her appetite hadn't improved and her nightmares persisted. They became so intense that she would wake up screaming. There were also moments during each day when she would weep uncontrollably. When the doctors were consulted, they prescribed Valium. It calmed her but she hated the side effects. All she seemed to do was sleep. Alfredo thought, "She cannot go on this way. Maybe Matt Logan has some ideas about what to do." While Nathalie was staying with Marcel, Matt had called Alfredo and told him, "I'm willing to do anything I can to help. I know what it's like to have gone through trauma."

Alfredo dialed the lawyer's home number. After Logan answered his phone, Alfredo said, "Matt, I hope that I am not disturbing you."

"Not at all. I heard that Nathalie is back. How's she doing, my friend?"

"She is not doing too well. She seems to be having flashbacks and nightmares. You mentioned that I could call you if I noticed those traits. I am very worried. She left as a very healthy young woman and now she is sickly. You have been through something similar to what she experienced. I think you would be more help to her than even my cousin Jaime, who is a doctor."

"I'd love to have her come over to our home. Janet and I will be able to get a better idea of what we can do to help her."

"Thank you, Matt. When can I bring her to you?"

"How about ten o'clock tomorrow morning."

"Yes, that would be a great time. See you tomorrow."

Alfredo told Nathalie that she would be spending a little time with Matt and Janet Logan. She was agreeable to it because she was aware of the change in her and she didn't want it to continue. Alfredo drove her to the Logan residence the next morning, where she was warmly greeted by the two attorneys. Matt hugged her and said, "You'll be staying here for a while. We want to help you. I've gone through some of the things you have, and I'll do my best to help you get well, Nathalie."

Janet also hugged their guest warmly and said to her, "I'm so glad that you decided to come. I know that you have made the right decision. It will be a treat for us to have you here."

Nathalie replied, "I know that I need help. Since both of you are my friends, I feel comfortable being here with you."

Alfredo said, "Thanks to both of you for being willing to help my beautiful *munequita*. I know that she is in good hands." He turned to Nathalie and said, "I will call you, my darling, and I will come and visit you." He gave her a wink and said, "I want my girl back."

She said to him, "I will get well. I love you." She looked at Matt and Janet and said, "I want to thank both of you for giving your time to me so I can get well." She gave each of them another hug.

Alfredo then took her in his arms and said, "I love you and I always will, my beloved *munequita*. I will leave so you can start getting better."

"I also love you," she said. "I'll soon be better and be back to being the old Nathalie."

"I know you will," he replied, and then he left.

Janet said to Nathalie, "Let me show you your bedroom. I hope you like it. It overlooks the garden, which is filled with flowers. You'll see humming birds."

Nathalie replied, "I love those tiny birds that have their own personalities."

They went upstairs to the guest bedroom. Matt carried Nathalie's suitcase. When they entered the room, their guest said, "It's so airy and pretty, Janet."

"You have your own bathroom and a sitting room next to the bedroom."

"Your home is so comfortable," said Nathalie. "Thank you for having me here."

Matt said, "Nathalie, would you like to go to my office so we could talk?"

"No, I'm not ready for that. I just want to relax, make my mind blank and not think about anything." Matt and Janet could see that their guest was under enormous stress, so they let her be. Nathalie didn't eat a thing during her first night there. She enjoyed a bowl of Janet's homemade chicken soup the following afternoon. She told her hostess, "It's the best I've ever tasted," but declined a second helping. On her third day with them, Nathalie had tea and toast for breakfast and two bowls of chicken soup in the evening. She was pleasant with Matt and Janet, but didn't have much to say to them. She spent most of her time sitting in their garden. Janet was right about there being hummingbirds to watch, and their presence comforted her.

On her fourth day with the Logan's, she approached Matt and said, "I'm ready to talk. The sooner I get to the core of my problems, the sooner I'll be back with the love of my life."

They went into his office. He asked her, "Would you like anything to drink?"

"Some water would be fine, thank you."

Matt brought her a glass of water and started to talk while she sat in a comfortable chair. He said, "I want you to know that I also went through terrible times. It's good to talk about it. I'm your friend, and I'll be able to understand everything that you tell me. Remember, I've been there just like you have."

"Matt, I have to tell you that it was horrible. They tricked me into going to Guatemala. They kidnapped me." She began to cry. He went over to her chair to console her. He said, "Look at me, pretty lady. It's over now. No one else will ever be able to hurt you again. All the bad people are gone. You have your life back. You have a man who adores the ground you walk on. Do you feel like telling me what they did to you? You need to get it all off your chest."

She blurted out, "They hurt me! I was slapped on my face many times!"

He said with a soothing tone to his voice, "It's okay to cry. I shed many tears too."

She looked at him. She finally had someone who would understand. She was beginning to feel better. She then said in a calmer tone, "They tied me up. They tied my hands and ankles and put a gag in my mouth. It was a horrible experience."

He replied, "It's over with. They can't hurt you again."

Nathalie then said, "I don't want to talk about this anymore." It was hurting her too much, and she shut down. After a moment, she added, "Maybe tomorrow we can talk again."

"Nathalie, I can understand. I was the same way. Let's go and see what Janet is up to."

They headed for the kitchen, where they found Matt's wife busy preparing a salad. Janet said, "Matt dear, serve Nathalie some fruit. I stopped at a little stand yesterday. Everyone in the neighborhood goes there because they always have fresh produce."

Nathalie said, "Thank you, Janet. I know I'll enjoy it."

Janet Logan hugged Nathalie and said "We want you to feel at home. We're very fond of you. Don't hesitate to tell us if there's anything we can do for you."

Nathalie said, "Matt and Janet, you both make me feel so welcome."

After Nathalie finished her fruit, Janet said, "I understand that you enjoy reading. We have an extensive library. In addition, a little bird told me how much you like Cajun food. I made gumbo for us to have tonight."

"You've read my mind. I think I'm going to go upstairs and rest for a while. What time will we be eating?"

"How does six sound to you?"

"I'll be down by six. I want to get some rest. I'll be looking forward to your gumbo."

"It's my mother's recipe. She always received compliments whenever she served it."

Nathalie got up from the kitchen table and went to the guest room. As she climbed the stairs, she thought, "I went through a lot, but Heart to Heart Hospital is secure, and so is the plantation. Thank God, thank God. I'll get over my trauma, I know I will. I must be strong. Matt will be a big help to me."

She took her clothes off before she lay on the bed. She could see that she had a few bruises on the upper parts of her legs from being dragged into Nicte and Kark's outhouse. She thought, "I will heal. I'm so grateful that I wasn't bitten by a rat or a tarantula. If my father were alive, he would be proud of me." She was beginning to feel better. She couldn't wait until the next day and another talk with Matt.

Chapter Thirty Four

After a delicious gumbo dinner, Nathalie had trouble getting to sleep. It wasn't the food, and she didn't have any nightmares. It was because she couldn't wait to talk to Matt Logan in the morning. She was ready to give him all the details of what the Guatemalan thugs had done to her. He was probably the only one who could understand what she had gone through and sympathize with her.

When she finally saw the light of a new day, she got out of bed and went downstairs. She could hear Matt and Janet talking in the kitchen. When she joined them, Janet said, "Well, good morning, pretty lady. I hope you were comfortable."

"Yes, I was. Good morning."

"Would you like some coffee? I've made waffles for breakfast."

Nathalie replied, "Can I help you with anything?"

"Everything is ready," said Janet. "Please have a seat at the table near Matt. Enjoy."

When they had finished breakfast, Matt asked Nathalie, "Are you ready to go to the office so we can talk some more?"

"Yes, I want to tell you all about my being captured."

They left the kitchen, went to the office and Nathalie sat in the same chair she had occupied the day before. Matt said, "Let me hear what happened. I'm interested in what you have to say."

"Well, Matt, let me start by telling you how evil those people were. I had been set up. Gina, the woman I was traveling with, was working with them. When we arrived in Guatemala City, they forced me into their car. They screamed at me, and Gina stood there not caring what they did to me. When I asked them why they were treating me that way, they screamed, 'SHUT UP!' They told me that I wasn't allowed to say anything." She began to cry when she said, "One of the men pulled my hair so hard that a chunk of it came out." She bowed her head so that Matt could see the injury. She added, "You can see my crown. The hair is gone."

"Nathalie, it will grow back. The main thing is that all is well now. You're home. You did something special by protecting the coffee plantation and Heart to Heart Hospital. Look at how many people you've helped by what you did. You're a heroine."

"They also hit me. I have bruises on my leg, up close to my thigh. They put me in a filthy outhouse where rats and a tarantula crawled over me."

"I know it was a horrible experience. You have to look at the whole picture, though. They're dead. It's over. It's in the past."

She looked at him with gratitude in her eyes and said, "It's wonderful to talk to someone who understands and has been through something like I have. Thanks for listening to me, Matt. I feel better. I have to be strong. I'm lucky that I was their captive for only two days. I'm getting better. I have to get better so I can be with my only love, Alfredo."

"Yes, Nathalie, he loves you very much. I want you to know that I'll be available anytime you need to talk." She seemed to be on the path to recovery. She looked stronger and determined that nothing was going to hold her back. He thought, "As far as I'm concerned, she can go to her sweetheart tomorrow."

Alfredo took Nathalie to his mansion on St. Charles Avenue where he and his sister Maria Louisa could look after her. Their loving attention and support helped her to recover quickly. It wasn't long until she was back to being her old self. The two lovers offered a prayer of thanks. They realized that it could have been much worse.

And Love Was Born

Chapter Thirty Five

Solomon Garcia dreaded having to tell Bill Sanders that the Ordonez kidnapping had been botched, but he had no choice. He sent a brief short wave transmission which stated, "Your package didn't make it. There was unexpected trouble." Sanders replied, "Will be headed your way to talk to you in person." Garcia became very worried. He remembered something that happened when he was twelve and one of his father's accomplices had stolen some money from him. He saw his father cut off all the fingers from the man's right hand. He wondered, "What is going to happen to me now?"

When the heavyset gang leader met his boss at the Guatemala City airport, he was surprised that Sanders was accompanied by a statuesque redhead named Beatrice. Garcia thought, "She is no *pollita*. She has to be in her thirties. I guess he is a *gringo* who always needs a *puta* to play with." Bill insisted that Solomon drive them to where he lived. Garcia said, "I can do that, but my room is too small for three people to meet in."

"That's all right," replied Sanders. "Is there a *cantina* near there where we can talk and get some good liquor?" Garcia said there was, so he drove to one less than a block from the hotel where he lived.

Solomon was nervous as the three of them sat down at a table. He expected a tongue lashing and maybe worse for the way he and his henchmen had blundered their job. Sanders thought, "He's looking at me like I had just given him a week to live."

Garcia was pleasantly surprised to find Sanders was in a mood to celebrate. The visitor from New Orleans ordered a bottle of Jack Daniels, which was far better than the homemade hooch Garcia usually drank. The Guatemalan thug wondered what the occasion was.

While Beatrice powdered her nose, Sanders said, "All along, I had told the people behind this that it was stupid to kidnap the Ordonez chick and try to scare her into signing papers giving us everything. The best way would be to kill her. They finally wised up. They want her dead, and they're going to pay even more money to have it done. This time, I'm going to pay you four grand instead of two. I'm also giving you an extra two G's so you can hire some good help. I want the best, so don't skimp. Once that Ordonez bitch is dead, I'll give you another two large on top of the four. I'll have the money for you later tonight."

Bill could tell that Solomon was mentally counting what he was going to receive. It would amount to sixty thousand Quetzales. Sanders then said, "Drink up. I'm here to have fun. By the way, did you notice Beatrice? I think she's hot for you. I know she has a thing for *Latino* men. When she gets back, I'll leave you two alone so you can get to know each other better." Just then, Beatrice appeared. Sanders left the two of them and walked from the table to the bar. He handed the bartender some money and said, "Send over another bottle of Jack Daniels to the man and woman at that table." Sanders would have more to do with Garcia, but not until much later that night. In the meantime, he would try his hand at one of the local poker games.

While Beatrice and Solomon were drinking, she sat next to him and talked about how much Hispanic men turned her on. "I don't know why. Maybe it's their accent, their *macho* ways or their hot blood. You are hot blooded, aren't you?" She had a hand on his right thigh, and she was squeezing it to test its firmness. She said, "My, you have strong legs. How are your other muscles?" He became aroused by the way she was flirting with him, and he said in slurred speech, "Lesh go ta my room. We'll have fun next door."

Solomon didn't know that Beatrice was a high end hooker from Sal Cardinale's brothel. She had been promised five thousand dollars to "screw the ugliest, nastiest Guatemalan you could ever imagine." She was also ordered to make sure he would either pass out drunk or fall sound asleep after the sex. She had no pride and would do anything for five grand.

Beatrice tried to get Solomon drunk in the *cantina*, but found that he could hold his liquor better than she first thought. He was beginning to slur his words, but was a long way from unconscious. She bit the bullet, accepted the fact that she was going to have sex with the brute and decided to get it over with as quickly as possible. He took the unopened bottle of Jack Daniels with them, and they made a short walk to his hotel. When they entered the sparsely furnished lobby, the clerk was sound asleep in his chair behind the front desk. As they walked up the dark and dreary worn down stairway to the top floor of the two story structure, Garcia said with pride in his voice, "I've got the besht room in the place... even has a shower."

After he unlocked the door, a terrible odor nearly made Beatrice nauseous. She thought, "Jesus Christ, what have I gotten myself into? They should pay me ten times what I'm gonna get." She couldn't back out because she knew she'd get no sympathy from her employers. They were the sort who wouldn't hesitate to kill anyone who reneged. Once she had agreed to do something for them, it was either do it or die.

The room had only a bed and a shabby dresser with a drawer missing. There was no mirror, and the walls were filthy. Another room was behind a curtain. She pulled it aside to find a shower head coming out of a wall, a hole in the floor and two buckets. One was filled with water, the other was empty. Her host explained in slurred speech, "The hole ishh the toilet. If ya gotta use it, flush it with the full one."

It was obvious that the bed linens hadn't been changed for some time because the white sheets looked gray. Things became hopeful for Beatrice when Solomon had problems removing his shoes. She thought, "Maybe he's so drunk he'll pass out quick." She tried to put him to bed, figuring he'd go out like a light once his head hit the oil stained pillow. She managed to remove the shoes, but he pushed her away when she tried to help him take off his suit coat. He pulled out a pistol from his shoulder holster and growled, "Get naked, bitch."

"Okay, okay," she replied. She kicked her heels off, unzipped her dress, slipped it off, and then removed her bra and panties. He stood up, undid his belt with one hand while holding the pistol with the other and let his trousers drop to the floor. He wore no underwear and after he stepped out of his pants, he fell onto the bed. He said, "Get on. You do the work."

She replied, "Mind if I have a drink while we're doing it."

"Go ahead."

She grabbed the Jack Daniels. She wanted to be nearly unconscious while she was doing the nasty deed, so she raised the bottle to her lips and took the biggest swallow she could.

She had sex with him for what seemed like hours, but was only three minutes. She was amazed at how he could become aroused and stay that way after drinking so much. Finally, he went limp and she heard him snore. Mission accomplished.

She got up to take a shower before Bill Sanders arrived. As the water ran over her, she was glad to feel somewhat clean again. She didn't even mind that the water was cold, there was no soap or towels and she had to stand still while the water dripped off her. While she waited to get dry, she kept drinking the liquor. Her eyes became bloodshot and heavy, and she passed out at the foot of Solomon's raggedy bed.

When Sanders showed up, he thought, "Perfect. They're both passed out." He injected the two of them with lethal doses of morphine. He thought, "It's the perfect method of murder. Even if an autopsy is performed, which is doubtful, the cause of death for both will be 'acute alcoholism.'" Bill had eliminated two problems with one cold blooded move. Garcia was killed for blundering the kidnapping and Beatrice was a high line hooker well past her prime earning years. Sal Cardinale wanted her eliminated and had given Sanders the task of disposing of her. Once again, the cleanup man had earned his keep.

And Love Was Born

And Love Was Born

Chapter Thirty Six

After she felt much better, Nathalie and Alfredo took a trip to Guatemala and went to his villa in Antigua. They spent a few pleasant days seeing the sights. Nathalie was inspired to write a poem.

At The Other Side Of The Mountain

When I first saw you, I could see,

A gentle and passive heart.

I told myself this could not be,

But somehow you and I,

Became a part.

A heart so full of kindness,

A man of somewhat shyness,

Our eyes, how they were hypnotized,

And we were both in paradise,

Close to your romantic fountain,

At the other side of the mountain.

How we trembled as we touched.

No, no, it could not be too much.

How we vowed our purest love,

And Love Was Born

With the shining stars above.

We vowed our purest love,

Like the whiteness of a dove.

Please don't ever let me go,

Hold me close and hold me so.

For you are my other part,

And you are totally in my heart,

Close to your romantic fountain,

At the other side of the mountain.

And Love Was Born

Chapter Thirty Seven

Alfredo had an important business meeting in Guatemala City. This meant Nathalie would be left alone for the day in the Antigua villa. The only other person in the residence was a maid named Maria.

It was a quiet morning, and the weather was gorgeous. After breakfast, Nathalie thought it would be very relaxing to be outside and sit by the beautiful fountain in the back yard. She would have a majestic view of the surrounding mountains. The garden was filled with bougainvilleas, roses and other attractive foliage in blossom. It was like being in the middle of a rainbow.

She had obtained a book with many pictures on the history of Guatemala. She wanted to learn more about the beautiful country which had intrigued her ever since she had been making trips to visit her parents. The beautiful sights, the sound of the water in the fountain and the interesting book promised a most pleasant afternoon.

Suddenly, she noticed a satiny blue butterfly that had been attracted to the flowers. The beautiful winged creature inspired her to write a poem.

Butterfly

I gaze at my flower bed.

My eye catches a Zinnia Red.

In a sudden moment,

I see a swift movement,

A bantering butterfly.

How gently she plays,

Like music she sways.

Is she telling me something?

Or is it nothing?

While she gracefully, playfully pauses,

What are you saying,

As you are swaying,

And playfully playing,

You dizzying butterfly?

Are you in love,

As you flit to and fro?

Where is your partner,

Or does it not matter?

When you fly toward the sunset,

Like a dancing marionette,

Are you looking for lost love?

You have gone.

You have left me.

Now you're free.

After writing the poem, she heard the phone in the villa ring. Nathalie ran to pick it up before the maid could answer it, thinking it was her beloved calling her. She was excited by the thought of reading her poem to him. When she placed the receiver to her ear, she found that another woman was on the line. The woman said, "Hello. Is this Nathalie?"

"Yes. Who is calling?"

"This is Isabel Martinez."

Nathalie thought it was a business call, so she said, "Alfredo is not here."

"I do not want to talk to him. I want to talk to you."

"I have no idea what I could help you with. I don't know you."

"I want to let you know that Alfredo and I have a child together."

Nathalie froze. She suddenly had problems catching her breath, but she managed to get out the words, "Am I hearing correctly? You have a child that is yours and Alfredo's?"

"That is right. He is the father. The child is named after him. He is one year old and looks just like him."

"That can't be possible. He has never told me that he fathered a child."

"Well he has. I am sorry I had to be the one to break the news to you, but I thought you should know."

"What is your name again?"

"Isabel Martinez. He will know who I am. I have to go now. Bye, Nathalie."

Nathalie felt a chill come over her entire body as she put the receiver down. She asked herself, "How could Alfredo do this to me? I came into our relationship pure. How could he hurt me this way?" She went into the living room, sat on a couch and cried. She felt her soul leave her body. It was as though she were floating into some unknown horrible place. She thought, "God, if there is a Hell, I am in it. Why is this happening to me?"

She needed to go to the bathroom and get some Kleenex to wipe her eyes and blow her nose. After that was done, she took two aspirins and went into her bedroom to lie down. She lay on the bed and sobbed. The shock was too much for her.

Maria heard her crying and came to see what was wrong. When the maid entered the bedroom, she saw a Nathalie she had never known. She asked in a concerned voice, "Miss Nathalie, are you sick?"

All Nathalie said was, "I just want to be left alone."

"I'll bring some juice to calm you down."

Nathalie hadn't heard a word Maria said. She was still in shock from the phone call.

The maid returned with a glass of orange juice and set it on the night stand. She said, "Please drink the juice, Miss Nathalie. Should I call Mr. Milla?"

"No. Please don't call him. He's too busy. I'll talk to him when he gets home." Nathalie couldn't hold back her tears as she said that. Maria thought, "Maybe I should call Mr. Milla anyway. Miss Nathalie is not herself. On second thought, he'll be back later today. He's probably busy. I won't bother him right now."

Maria quickly exited the bedroom. She wondered what it could have been that made Miss Nathalie so upset. It must have had something to do with the phone call she had received.

After the maid left her, Nathalie sat up in the bed and began talking out loud. She was not afraid to do that because she knew Maria had gone to her own quarters. She said, "Why didn't he tell me? Why did he keep his fatherhood a secret? Why did he ruin our pure love in such a horrible way?" There were no answers, only silence.

She thought, "How could he break up our togetherness this way? The thread of our love has been broken. He has hurt me badly. I'll never heal from this. And to think that I loved him so much that I would have given my life for him. I feel like I've been stung by five thousand bumble bees. Every muscle in my body hurts. Maybe I went into this relationship and gave him all I had because I was naive, and that made me blind to who he really is."

When it was time for lunch, Maria began to set the table. Once everything was ready, she went to the bedroom and said, "Miss Nathalie, please come and eat."

Nathalie saw the worried look on the maid's face and replied, "Okay, Maria. I will try to eat."

The food smelled good, but she found it almost impossible to digest it. Each bite was like trying to take down a glass of bitter medicine. Her taste buds were shot, and her heart was aching.

She finished eating, but all that was on her mind was her questions about Alfredo. If someone had asked her what she had just eaten, she wouldn't have been able to tell them. She was beginning to have a horrible headache, so she went back to her bedroom and closed the door.

She would stay in bed until Alfredo arrived home. She had to figure out the best way to confront him.

Chapter Thirty Eight

The disturbing phone call Nathalie received was the final link in a chain of events that had begun with a festive scene in El Sibonay, the most popular club in Antigua. It was owned by Pedro Carrillo, who was a good friend of Alfredo's, and it was frequented by Pablo, the multimillionaire's stalwart chauffeur. The two of them inadvertently exposed Milla to the danger of being exploited by two women. One of the women was avaricious and the other insanely jealous.

Pablo was so happy at the thought of a wonderful woman like Nathalie becoming part of his employer's family that he couldn't contain his joy. He just had to celebrate with a glass or two of his favorite libation in the company of his friends at El Sibonay.

Pedro happened to be there when Alfredo's driver walked in. Pablo rushed up to the club owner and excitedly said, "Alfredo has found a classy lady to marry. She is *muy bonita*!"

Carrillo replied, "This calls for a toast to our good friend. Let us share a bottle of Chivas Regal, and it is all on me." He had his bartender set a bottle of the costly whiskey and two glasses with ice on the bar. After Pedro poured a double shot in each glass, Pablo loudly offered a toast. "To Alfredo Milla, the greatest man in the world who has found true love!" He and the club owner clicked glasses.

The chauffeur's loud toast was heard by Aurora Gomez, a nurse who was a regular customer of the bar. Like all nurses in that country, her days were spent at the beck and call of patients with lots of money. She was under constant tension to satisfy their demands because even the slightest criticism would result in her termination. She had been doing it for too long and was looking for a way out. She was part Indian, and her heritage resulted in her having reddish skin, black hair and black eyes. She was 5' 3" and weighed 155 pounds. Her weight problem wasn't helped by her hearty appetite for beer. Her low status and unappealing looks left her with no hope of marrying well.

Aurora had a plan, though. She had been plotting for a year and a half in hopes of riches. She had planted her crops and when she heard Pablo's toast, she knew harvest time had arrived. The nurse became so excited that she uncharacteristically got up from her bar stool and left a glass of ice cold beer that she had only taken two sips from. She went to the home of her best friend and co-conspirator, Isabel Martinez.

Nurse Gomez rang the doorbell and Isabel greeted her with, "*Hola, amiga.* What brings you here?"

"I have some good news hot off the press."

"Come to the living room. Tell me, tell me."

"Alfredo Milla has found a wife."

Isabel's face turned red with anger. She exclaimed, "I will fix him!"

"We will fix him together, just like we planned," interjected Aurora.

"*Si*," agreed Isabel.

"We have been waiting for this to happen. Now is the time to attack his bank account and make him jump."

Their wicked plans had started to take shape a year and a half before when Isabel confided to Aurora that she was pregnant by Jacobo Sanchez. She had said, "He loves me, but he has very little except his hopes and dreams. He is very bright and is going to school. He has plans to become an architect."

Aurora was not at all impressed. She said to her friend, "How bright can he be? He has fathered a child out of wedlock and has no job. Hopes and dreams do not put food on the table." The nurse thought for a moment and then asked, "Do you love this dreamer?"

"Not completely. Maybe after he graduates and shows me that he can produce, I may feel different." It was only natural that Isabel should be concerned about her unborn child's future.

The nurse had a steely-eyed look on her face when she said, "You are a fool. You have a gold mine, and I can help you make a lot of money for both of us."

"What are you talking about?"

"Well, is it not true that you dated Alfredo Milla?"

"*Si*, and I loved every bit of it."

"Did you go to bed with him?"

"*Si*, and it was wonderful."

"How many times?"

"Only twice, and I wish it had been more. He was deliciously good at it."

"Well, now it is time for him to pay for his fun."

"What do you mean?"

"Well, he went to bed with you, he had a great time and now he must pay."

"What are you planning?"

"I will help you have the child in my home. If it is a boy, we will name him Alfredo."

"What if it is a girl?"

"We will name her Maria Louisa after his sister."

"What about the birth certificate?"

"I have a relative who happens to be a doctor. He will fill out the document the way we want if there is a little something in it for him. He probably would not put down that Alfredo is the father, but I am sure he will agree to leave that space blank. We can work with that."

Isabel thought for a moment and then said, "I am in with you. God, I hope it is a boy and he looks something like Alfredo."

And Love Was Born

And Love Was Born

Chapter Thirty Nine

Nathalie felt apprehensive when she heard Alfredo's Mercedes pull into the driveway of the villa. She watched him get out of the car and walk to the door once again carrying a dozen yellow roses. He was smiling. She thought, "How could he be happy when he's carrying such a dark secret inside?"

Alfredo had a smile on his face because he was thinking of Nathalie's beauty. He couldn't wait to take her in his arms and tell her that she had made him the happiest man alive. He opened the front door, stepped into his villa and said with excitement in his voice, "Where's *Munequita Linda*?" There was no answer.

At first, he thought, "Nathalie must be in her bedroom." He was about to head in that direction, but she came into the living room. Her eyes were red and swollen from crying and she had a tissue in her hand. She cleared her throat and said coldly, "I'm here."

Alfredo handed her the bouquet of yellow roses. He also yearned to put his arms around her, but his sixth sense warned him not to. He was seeing a different Nathalie.

Without saying a word, she took the roses and dropped them on the dining room table. He was unaware that Nathalie didn't like to speak when she was extremely upset. He was totally shocked at her demeanor. He asked, "What is bothering you, my love? Your expression does not fit you. Are you feeling well? Are you ill? Should I take you to a doctor?" She had nothing to say to him. All the solicitous questions only made her angrier.

She handed him a white envelope and said, "I want you to read this. Let's sit at the dining room table."

After Alfredo had taken a seat, he opened the envelope and read her note. It stated,

Alfredo,

I received a phone call today from Isabel Martinez. She told me that you have fathered a child with her; a son. I thought you were a decent man. You did not let me know anything about your fatherhood. I came into this relationship clean and pure, but it seems that you did not. You have not mentioned child support, which I hope you are paying. It is not the fault of the child to come into this world as he did. It is your fault and Isabel's I need time to digest what you have done and decide whether I want to continue moving forward in this relationship. I am writing this note with a broken heart, and I know that my heart will cry as I hand this message to you. I wish this were a love note but because of your actions, it isn't. I also know that we have to always be honest with each other. I love you more than life. You are my everything.

Nathalie

After reading the note, Alfredo cleared his throat. He was in shock, his hands trembled and he had a desperate look on his face. A mistake he had made in the past had come back to haunt him. His eyes met Nathalie's, and he began to speak. He said, "I can explain everything to you. Please do not be distant with me. I love only you, Nathalie. I must confess that I did have an affair with Isabel, but that was before I laid eyes on you. It was a foolish thing that lasted only a little over a week. The child that she claims is ours was not fathered by me. That woman has been with other men. She has a reputation for being easy. Think about it, Nathalie. If the child were mine, is it not true she would have told me the moment she learned that she was pregnant? Of course she would have. She would have wanted to collect child support from me. I have no idea why she is causing trouble between us. I promise that I will get to the bottom of all these lies. The child is not mine. You have to believe what I tell you, Nathalie. Please do not throw what we have away. Without you, I would have nothing to live for."

Nathalie didn't say a word. She stared at him and then excused herself from the table. She went to her bedroom and closed the door. She wanted to be by herself in her sorrow.

Alfredo was angry. He thought, "How could that dirty Indian Isabel have the nerve to call the woman I love and plant all those lies?"

He and Isabel had met a year and a half before Nathalie came into his life. Isabel worked as a bank teller in Antigua. She was flirtatious with every man who appeared capable of giving her a better life, and he was no exception. She was a *chola*, a mixture of Indian and Hispanic. To some, a *chola* was close to a prostitute. He also knew she was called "The Antigua Telegram" because she couldn't keep any secrets.

That made no difference to him at the time. He thought, "She looks clean. I will take her to a so so restaurant and then we can have some fun." They went on three dates and had two sexual encounters. He would have never tried any of that with a woman of the same upper class he belonged to. He had forgotten that it only takes one encounter to get a woman pregnant. He had also forgotten that a man inevitably becomes the choices he makes.

Chapter Forty

After Isabel's phone call brought turmoil into his home, Alfredo knew what he had to do. He was being assaulted by riffraff, so this required fighting fire with fire. He composed himself, picked up the phone and called his good friend Pedro Carrillo. In addition to being the most popular club in Antigua, El Sibonay offered high stakes poker games in a back room. This enabled Pedro to keep his finger on the pulse of anything seedy in that city.

The line was busy when he dialed his friend's number. He hung up, waited a few minutes and then tried again. This time, Pedro answered.

"*Hola.*"

"Pedro, it is Alfredo."

"*Como estas, amigo*?"

"I need a big favor. A woman I dated a couple of times has brought chaos into my house. You know her. She goes to your club. Her name is Isabel Martinez."

"*Si, si.* Isabel is often in my place. I see her with different men all the time."

"She claims I have fathered a child with her."

"Fathered a child!" exclaimed Pedro. "No way! She was on the rebound when you broke it off. It seemed like I saw her with a different man every time she came in. Who knows who the child belongs to. She has mentioned to the guys who play poker in my back room that she was sorry you broke up with her. She often talked about what a good catch you were. I always had a feeling she was nothing but trouble."

Alfredo said, "What I did with Isabel was just an encounter and nothing more. Can you help me find out who the real father is? I know you have many connections. I need to get to the bottom of this lie. Nathalie is beside herself. She has been crying all day long. The sooner this is over, the better it will be. I feel as though someone has punched me in the gut. Nathalie might break up with me because of this, and I could never live without her."

"Take it easy, *amigo.* Isabel is just one of those mean women you hear about. I will do everything to help you."

"Thanks, Pedro. You are a good friend."

"*De nada, amigo.*"

After he put down the receiver, Alfredo went to Nathalie's bedroom and knocked on the door. "Nathalie, please open the door," he said. "We need to talk."

"Talk about what. You have hurt me."

"Please, please, Nathalie. Open the door."

The door opened. Nathalie stood there looking pale and drawn. Alfredo took her in his arms and held her. He tried to reassure her that he loved her by saying, "Love of my life, you are the only one I love. Don't you remember our many kisses, our warm hugs, our talks, our numerous words and our feelings? Nothing can come between us. We are solid as a rock. I have given myself to you completely and unconditionally. My mind, my emotions and the inner part of my heart is yours forever. You have become my eternal love. When I am with you, I live. We have become a force that nothing can penetrate. What we have is so special and possesses such energy that it only happens once in a lifetime. My true love for you has no end."

Nathalie replied, "Alfredo, I love you, but I have to make sure that the child is not your son. Let us delay our engagement until you have an answer. I'm sure you can understand my feelings. I have been hurt, and a hurt takes its own time to heal."

"I understand. Why don't I take you out of the house tonight? Maybe that will refresh your mind. I do not want you thinking anymore about something that is not true."

"No. I'm not going out tonight. If you want to, you go. I'm going to stay home. I don't want to be bothered. What you have done has given me great pain."

"Nathalie, what Isabel told you is a complete lie."

"You will have to prove that to me beyond a shadow of a doubt. Just leave me alone, Alfredo. Just leave me alone. I want to think things over." She gently closed the bedroom door.

He tried to talk to her through the closed door. "Nathalie, you have to believe me." There was no response from her. After a couple of minutes, he walked away. He thought, "How am I going to prove beyond the shadow of a doubt that I am not the father of that woman's child?"

Nathalie spent some of her time alone writing a poem which she sent to Alfredo's office in Guatemala City.

And Love Was Born

Lover Who Is Far Away

I take my pen and a small piece of paper.

I go to my refuge and write to you.

I write how much I love you,

And how much I think of you, my love.

I am your love who is far away,

And this cursed distance that separates us.

There is not a day that passes,

That I don't feel your kisses,

Even though you are far, so far away.

I maintain loving you.

I think of you day and night.

How I wish my brains would turn into bones,

So I could never love you again.

You tell me that you love me with an eternal love,

But you have placed an arrow like a killer.

My heart is bleeding slowly.

My condition is fragile.

When my writing was finished,

A solitary tear fell on this paper.

I filled it with a thousand kisses,

With my trembling lips,

And sent it to you.

Alfredo was so taken by her poem that he translated it into Spanish.

And Love Was Born

And Love Was Born
Amada De Lejos

TOMANDO ESTA PEQUENA PLUMA,

Y ESTE PEDACITO DE PAPEL,

VOY A MI REFUGIO TE ESCRIBO,

TE ESCRIBO CUANTO TE QUIERO,

Y CUANTO TE PIENSO AMOR.

SOY TU AMAD DE LEJOS,

Y CON ESTA MALDITA DISTANCIA,

QUE A LOS DOS NOS SEPARA,

NO HAY DIA QUE PASA,

QUE NO SIENTO TUS BESOS,

AUNQUE ESTAS LEJOS TAN LEJOS.

AMANDOTE ME MANTENGO,

DIA Y NOCHE TE PIENSO,

COMO QUISIERA QUE TODOS MIS SESOS,

SE VOLVIERAN SOLO HUESOS,

PARA AMARTE NUNCA MAS.

DICES AMARME CON ETERNO CARINO,

PUCISTE ESTA FLECHA COMO UN ACECINO,

MI CORAZON SANGRA LENTAMENTE,

MI CONDICION FRAGILMENTE.

TERMINANDO MI ESCRITURA,

CAYO UNA SOLITARIA LAGRIMA,

And Love Was Born

EN ESTE PAQUENO PAPEL,

LO LLENE CON MIL BESOS,

CON MIS TEMBLOROSOS LAVIOS, PARA MANDARTE A TI.

He responded by sending Nathalie a poem he had written.

The anguish that I feel,

Without you,

Is like,

An asthma attack.

It leaves me breathless;

Sick, then weak.

I'm so sorry that woman put those lies in your head.

He also sent her a note which read, "In my solitude, I think of you constantly. Love, Alfredo."

A few days later, he sent her another poem he had written.

As a beautiful rainbow,

You appeared,

And you became encrusted in me forever.

Nathalie had inspired Alfredo to express himself in ways he had never done before. He continued sending her his poems.

And Love Was Born

Impossible To Forget You

How can I forget you if my mind,

Draws your silhouette constantly.

How can I forget you if my eyes are like mirrors,

That reflect your face even though you are far away.

How can I forget you if my ears hear your voice,

Like when we were together.

How can I forget you if the air that I breathe,

Has your fragrance even though you are far away.

How can I forget you if your hands feel that they are in mine,

Though so many days have passed.

To forget you is impossible,

The only way it will be

Is if death comes to me.

She reciprocated by sending him her own poems. One of them read,

And Love Was Born

And Love Was Born

Without You

To Alfredo Milla, a Man Full of Kindness, a Man of Somewhat Shy-

ness,

Awakening without you today,

I felt intoxicated as if I

Had consumed a bottle of cheap wine.

Losing my balance,

Feeling in a semi-daze,

I took the phone and called you

To hear your precious voice.

Oh! The feeling that invaded my body

When the call ended

Completely confirmed

My immense love for you.

And Love Was Born

The muse visited Alfredo once again while he was sitting at his desk. He wrote a short poem to Nathalie and sent it to her.

Sitting in my office,

I get thoughts

In my head,

Visions of you,

Constantly.

She responded with,

This feeling of bliss

I can't dismiss

When you placed a kiss

Upon my lips.

And Love Was Born

Chapter Forty One

In addition to the call she made to Nathalie, the vicious Isabel had also sent Alfredo a note that read, "I will go to a dark place, darker than the darkest night, where I will find silence and where I can forget you." After reading that, he thought, "Her name should be Jezebel Martinez."

Aurora and Isabel wasted no time in pressing their claim. The swarthy complex-ioned nurse called Alfredo at his office. She told the receptionist, "I want to speak to Mr. Milla, *por favor*. Tell him that a representative of Isabel is calling."

Alfredo took the call. He asked, "Who am I speaking to?"

"My name is Aurora Gomez, *Senor*. I am the nurse who assisted Isabel when she had your son." She touched a nerve with that statement.

"My son? What are you talking about? I do not have a son. You are talking to the wrong man."

"Oh no, Senor, I am talking to the right man. Who would know better than the woman who brought the child from Isabel's womb."

"What are you looking for?"

"Only the birthright of your son."

"I will not discuss this further until I meet with my attorney."

"You can meet with whoever you want. He is still your son." She gave him the phone number where she could be reached, and then she hung up.

He immediately contacted his attorney, Ricardo Duran. Ricardo strongly suggested that a meeting with the two women be arranged as quickly as possible. The encounter took place in Duran's office. There were four people in the room; Alfredo, his lawyer, the nurse and the scorned woman.

Aurora placed the birth certificate on the attorney's desk. Duran looked it over and then said, "The space for the name of the father was left blank." His eyes quickly shifted to Isabel, and she looked him straight in the eye. She wasn't about to back down after coming this far. He asked her in a stern voice, "Who is the father of your son? Think carefully before you answer. If you lie, it could mean very harsh punishment."

Isabel had been as calm as if ice water was in her veins, but her emotions suddenly erupted. She blurted, "He was with me twice, and it only takes once to be a father! It was the right time of the month." She riveted her gaze on Alfredo and added, "Even though you treated me so badly, *mi amor*, I still have love for you and I cherish the son you blessed me with. I appeal to your sense of honor. You have broken my heart, but I can go on. I plead with you to do the right thing for your namesake." She punctuated her statement with sobs. Alfredo thought, "She is shedding crocodile tears."

The lawyer was amazed to see how unshakeable Isabel was. He thought, "She is the most motivated liar I have ever seen, and this makes her dangerous for my client." He ended the meeting by saying, "I will look further into the matter. I have your numbers, *Senoras*, and I will be getting back to both of you."

When the two female con artists had left, Ricardo turned to Alfredo and said, "Do not make the mistake of taking this personally. All of this is about money. It would be far more expensive to fight this than to give them one hundred thousand Quetzales. That is only ten thousand dollars American money. They will think it is all the money in the world, and I will make sure that they sign an iron clad agreement not to bother you anymore."

Alfredo looked his lawyer in the eye, took a deep breath and said, "I hope you know me well enough to understand why I will not give them a single Quetzal. Paying them anything would be admitting their claim has some merit. I fear that Nathalie, the love of my life, would not accept that of me. I will fight them and I will win because I have right on my side."

Duran replied, "How are you going to prove beyond a doubt that you are not the father? She can put on quite a performance."

"I noticed the date of birth. I was in New Orleans for nearly a year before her son was born. I will supply you with business records and statements from witnesses which will prove that."

"Well, that gives me something to work with, but it does not completely solve your problem. You are a wealthy man who had the money to take quick trips back and forth for secret rendezvous with her. She is very persuasive, especially when the tears start to fall."

"I do not care," said Alfredo. "I must fight for what is right, even though it may cost me millions." He made an emphatic gesture by forming a circle with his right thumb and index finger and then slowly gesturing downward.

Chapter Forty Two

Alfredo was busy organizing the records he would be taking to Ricardo Duran when he received a call from Pedro Carrillo. The club owner said, "*Amigo*, come down here right away. I have someone you want to meet. He is going to help you with your problem."

When Aurora and Isabel's intended prey arrived at El Sibonay, the bartender pointed to the back room and said, "The boss is waiting for you in there." Alfredo entered that room and found Pedro sitting at a table with a strange man. The club owner said, "I want you to meet Jacobo. You will find him very interesting."

"Why is that?"

"Because Mr. Sanchez is the father of Isabel's son."

Alfredo looked at Jacobo and said, "How can you prove he is yours?"

The architectural student replied, "My son has a dimple on each cheek, just like me. He also has slender legs and long, slim fingers like I do."

Pedro handed Alfredo an envelope containing enlarged photographs of both the father and the son. He said, "I had them made up for you from snapshots Jacobo let me use. They are additional proof that he is the father."

Jacobo added, "I am willing to state in writing exactly how many times I was with Isabela and when each time happened."

"Why are you doing this?" asked Alfredo.

"Mr. Milla, you do not deserve what those two women are trying to do to you. I try to be a man of honor, and I want my son to be the same way. I come from a poor but honest family, and I am studying to be an architect. I will have a good job someday, and I will see that my son is taken care of. I will not give one Quetzal to his mother, though, because she is a blackmailer."

"Will you testify under oath?"

"Of course I will. It is the right thing to do."

They shook hands. Alfredo's problem had been solved by an honest man who stepped up when needed. As he turned to leave the room, the multimillionaire said, "Your actions will not go unnoticed. I will pay for your schooling and when you graduate, I will hire you."

The next day, Alfredo took the photographs and all the information about Jacobo Sanchez to Ricardo Duran. The lawyer said, "I will obtain a statement from Sanchez right away. That, together with the pictures, will end any trouble those two women might try to cause."

Alfredo said, "I want to keep the photos until I show them to Nathalie. I will get them back to you in the next day or so."

He went straight to the villa from Duran's office. She was there to greet him when he opened the front door. She was a stunning vision in a green outfit that matched her eyes. He put his arms around her and said, "This has been a wonderful day, *mi amor*. I have something to show you."

He walked her over to a table, kissed her and then handed her the photos. They both sat down, and she began to study the pictures. After a few minutes, she said, "Alfredo, this boy does not look at all like you."

"Nathalie, my love, have you looked at his father?"

She looked closely at the pictures of Jacobo and said, "This child looks exactly like his father; the dimples, the legs, the hands. Oh, Alfredo, I'm so sorry that I doubted you. You have always been truthful with me. I promise that I will never let something like this to happen to us again."

"*Munequita Linda*, it was not your fault. Let us forget what happened and continue living our love for each other to the fullest. We will be picking up our engagement rings in a few days, and then we will consummate our love in each other's arms. I can't wait until you are mine completely. Tonight, we will go to the Hotel Antigua, your favorite place." Alfredo gently caressed her face with his hands and tenderly kissed her.

"I'll get ready, Alfredo. I think a change of scene will do me good."

"Yes, my love. It won't be long before we have each other fully and completely. Then, the rose and the carnation will shed their last petals and we will be able to drink from each other's nectars forever."

And Love Was Born

Chapter Forty Three

Alfredo's chauffeur Pedro drove the couple to the Hotel Antigua in the Mercedes Benz. The hotel's restaurant offered outdoor seating covered by a roof overlooking a pool. Alfredo asked the maitre d for a table as far away as possible from the other patrons. They were taken to seating for two that was in a courtyard with a four tiered fountain. The water made a very pleasant sound as it cascaded from a lion's mouth. They were surrounded by lush foliage and flowers in bloom. Their waiter asked, "Would you care for something from the bar?" Alfredo said to Nathalie, "I think a glass of wine would be good. Do you agree?"

"Yes, I would like some wine. Today has been stressful for me."

"How about a red wine, my love?"

"That would be fine, darling."

He ordered a vintage cabernet sauvignon from the wine list. He gazed intently at Nathalie and said, "You look beautiful tonight."

"I'm glad you find me beautiful."

He took her hand, kissed it and said, "You have to understand that there are mean *envidiosas* in this world who want to destroy the happiness of others. Isabel is one of those people but like all those who do wrong, she will pay for it."

Alfredo was interrupted when the waiter returned with a bottle of cabernet sauvignon. He poured a small amount into a glass, handed it to Alfredo and awaited his approval. After sniffing the aroma of the wine, Alfredo took a small sip and rolled it around his mouth so that his taste buds would encounter the full flavor of the best to be found in the hotel's cellar. He announced his decision by simply saying, "Very good."

The waiter then filled Nathalie's glass before he filled that of the man who loved her so much. Alfredo lifted his glass and made a toast. He said, "To the woman in my life whom I adore more than life itself. Before I knew you, life was colorless. The love between us has brought a rainbow into my world. You are everything a man could ever desire in a woman."

Nathalie lifted her glass and toasted the man whom she had grown to love with such intensity. She said, "To the great love for you that lives within me."

After drinking to each other, Alfredo moved his chair closer to hers and kissed her on the lips. She returned his kiss gently. He said, "Thank you for believing in me despite all that has happened. Your standing by me makes me love you all the more."

She replied, "Alfredo, I had time to think during the drive here. It was foolish of me to believe gossip without concrete evidence. I will not let anyone manipulate me like that ever again."

He said, "You have shown wisdom beyond your years, my love."

"Thanks. I think I'm ready for dinner. I wasn't able to eat much today. I now have an appetite for the Guatemalan food that I've become so fond of." Their relationship was once more on course.

And Love Was Born

Chapter Forty Four

Alfredo was up early when the day they had so anxiously awaited finally arrived. He hadn't slept well and was tense because he had been anticipating the day their love would be consummated. The rules of the Castilian Spanish culture dictated that there was to be no love making until after the woman accepted the man's proposal and a ring was placed on her finger. Alfredo had proven to Nathalie that he was manly enough to wait for her. This had not been easy for him. In the months they had known each other, there had been many times when he wanted to take her in his arms, savor her, love her passionately and make her totally his. Now that the day was here, he thought, "Taking things slow was good for us. We started with a special kind of affection and it has blossomed into a relationship that is immense and solid. Our love for each other is so deep that it is hard for me to imagine anyone else experiencing what we share."

Their busy week had started with a visit to the local authorities in order to sign all the documents which officially made them man and wife. Once that was taken care of, they went to Javier Cordova, Guatemala's most renowned jeweler, to order their rings. After they arrived at the shop, Alfredo told the jeweler, "We are so much in love. I would like something very special. I want a diamond in the shape of a heart." He turned to Nathalie and said, "I want your ring to be in the shape of a heart because my heart belongs to you."

She began to cry tears of joy when she replied, "You always think of such unique things." Alfredo's choice of design was very rare in 1969, when everyone wore round diamonds.

They were to pick up their rings a week later at eleven in the morning. This meant another trip to Guatemala City, and they would have to leave no later than ten to get there on time. Alfredo was ready to go at eight o'clock, and he patiently waited for Nathalie to finish doing all the things a woman of style, grace and bearing must do before appearing in public. When he heard her moving around in her bedroom, a sudden desire came upon him to open her door, take her in his arms, caress her body, kiss her sensuous lips and have her, but he knew that was impossible. That would have to wait until after they were engaged.

He tried as hard as he could to push thoughts of sensual pleasure from his mind, but he couldn't control his emotions. They were reaching an intensity that could not be reined in and his entire body pulsed with desire for her. He went out to the courtyard hoping to cool off his ardent feelings. He stood there thinking of all the exciting things he expected to happen that day. These pleasant thoughts were interrupted when Nathalie appeared at the entrance to the courtyard and said, "Where are you, Alfredo?"

"I am here, *Munequita*, next to the romantic fountain you like so much."

He was surprised to see her wearing a pink negligee. He said, "You look stunning. Pink is definitely your color." He put his arms around her and became aroused. She could feel how excited he was.

Alfredo said, "I came out here to cool down, and now I am again aroused by your beauty. You have no idea what you do to me. All that keeps me from going crazy is my knowing that today is our day. In another few hours, we will be in each other's arms and will taste each other's nectar. I love you and only you. I will love you for the rest of my life."

He began kissing her neck and stroking her shoulders and arms with a feather light touch. He was on the verge of exploding and he could tell that he had given her goose bumps. Each touch and kiss sent electrical shocks through Nathalie's entire body. She was able to keep from giving in only because she had been taught to respect herself above all else. She said, "It hasn't been easy for me either. I have wanted you so many times. I'm so happy that this day is finally here. I want to give myself to you. I want you to have the precious gift of my virginity." She began kissing Alfredo passionately.

He became breathless, but quickly recovered to say, "Darling, we must stop!"

"Yes, we must. It won't be long until we have each other completely." Nathalie went to her bedroom to get ready. Alfredo took a shower to cool off.

Pablo, the chauffeur, arrived at nine thirty. Alfredo had ordered a bouquet of various colored flowers and asked his driver to pick them up on the way to the villa. When the black Mercedes Benz pulled into the driveway, Alfredo immediately went to the car to retrieve the colorful bouquet. With the flowers in hand, he stepped back into the villa and called out, "NATHALIE, ARE YOU ALMOST READY?"

"I only have to put on my lipstick. I've already packed my overnight bag."

She emerged from her bedroom wearing a pink suit with white trim on the collar. The glow about her was enhanced by the lighting in the airy dining room. Alfredo handed her the bouquet and said, "I greet you with these flowers. You are the flower of my life."

Nathalie was surprised at his gesture of courtship. She had not expected Alfredo to give her flowers. "Thank you so much," she said. "You have a way that makes me feel like a total woman."

"You will always be the total woman in my life." He reached for her and kissed her lips.

"I'll put water in a vase for them," she said.

"Let me do that for you, Nathalie."

He placed the flowers in a vase, poured some water into the container and then put it on a table in her bedroom. "We have to go now," he said.

Alfredo handed their two small pieces of luggage to the chauffeur, who placed them in the trunk of the car. The happy couple got into the Mercedes. As they pulled away from the villa, Pablo offered them his congratulations.

Chapter Forty Five

Upon arriving at Javier's jewelry store, the chauffeur parked the car right in front of the shop and then opened the door for them. Alfredo got out first and then offered his hand to Nathalie. She was smiling when she exited the vehicle. Javier was waiting for them at the entrance and remarked, "There's a glow in both of your faces."

"We are happy," said a smiling Alfredo. "Today is our special day."

"I am very happy to be helping to make it so special," said the jeweler. "Both of you must try on your rings one last time to make sure they fit perfectly."

"I am sure they will be fine," replied Alfredo. "My friends and relatives have vouched for the excellent work that you do."

"Follow me to the back room," said Javier. "I will bring the rings to you. Please have a seat. I will be back shortly."

They were seated in a small room with a table. Two chairs were on one side of the table and a stool was on the other. A lamp with bright lighting had been placed on the table. Nathalie spoke first.

"Alfredo, I can hardly wait to see Javier's new design, which he said incorporated a heart shaped diamond. You have done such a special thing by ordering that ring for me. I will be the only woman with such an unusual ring. All I can say is thank you, darling." She reached over and gave him a kiss.

It wasn't long before Javier entered carrying two small boxes. He sat on the stool, removed their rings from the boxes and then displayed them on a black velvet pillow. Nathalie quickly picked up her ring off the velvet. She was stunned by its beauty. It had a heart shaped diamond that weighed three carats and was mounted in a plain platinum setting. The diamond was colorless. It had been designed so that nothing distracted from its heart shape, and it was the best money could buy. Her eyes were filled with tears of joy. She cleared her throat and said, "I'm so touched by your generosity. The ring is beautiful. It is more than I ever imagined it would be. I don't know what words to use to thank you enough." She let her actions do her talking when she reached over and kissed him again.

He said, "I could not just pledge my love to you. I had to show you how much you mean to me."

"Well, you've certainly done that," she replied.

Javier said, "Let me place the ring on your finger. I have to make sure it fits." After he slid it on, he announced his decision by simply saying, "Perfect fit." She beamed with pride as she gazed at both the three carat dazzler and her beloved Alfredo.

Alfredo gave an approving look and said, "It is exquisite, Javier. You have exceeded your reputation for quality work."

Nathalie's eyes were full of love for her one and only. Javier broke her spell by saying, "Now it is time try your ring on, Alfredo."

After slipping the ring on Alfredo's finger, the master jeweler smiled and said, "Perfect fit. I'll be expecting an invitation to the wedding. I would never miss it. Both of you look so happy."

"We are," said Alfredo. "It is the best thing that has ever happened to me. I will be giving my *munequita* the ring at the Hotel Antigua while mariachis play *Munequita Linda*."

"The perfect song!" exclaimed Javier. The song they were talking about was a lovely ballad about blonde women. Its lyrics included "Tell me that you love me like I love you, pretty doll with hair of gold, teeth of pearl and ruby lips."

"Let me put the rings back in their boxes," said the jeweler. "I see that you have a purse, Nathalie. Why not put the two boxes in it for safety?"

"That's a good idea. I'll see that nothing happens to them. Thank you for the lovely work you have done for us."

"Please wait here for me, my darling," said Alfredo. "I have to settle the bill."

He was gone briefly. When he returned, he said, "I love you, Nathalie. Let us celebrate our engagement with a bottle of Dom Perignon."

"Yes, I want to celebrate our most important day. I am ready to give myself completely to you. I am yours forever, my darling. I love you with all my being."

He took her in his arms and kissed her several times. They held hands as they walked to his Mercedes. Pablo helped them enter the vehicle, and then drove them to the Hotel Antigua for their celebration.

And Love Was Born

Chapter Forty Six

Before sitting down to dinner in the Hotel Antigua's restaurant, Alfredo asked Nathalie for the box containing her ring. She handed it to him, having no idea of what he was about to do. He took her hand and knelt in front of her on the tile floor. He looked into her green eyes with intensity and said, "Will you marry me? I will make you the happiest woman in the world. I will treat you like a princess. I love you more than life itself."

Nathalie blushed as she heard the people around her clap with joy. She replied, "Yes, I accept your proposal. I love you as much as you love me." They kissed as the crowd in the restaurant watched teary eyed.

They enjoyed their meal, but were very excited about what lay ahead that evening. The Dom Perignon helped to relax them. Before they knew it, their waiter had removed their plates from the table. Alfredo took Nathalie's hand and then held her close. He kissed her tenderly, then said, "We have waited so long for what we are about to share. I will do all I can to make it wonderful. *Te amo, Munequita Linda*." They left the restaurant and headed for their room.

The time had finally arrived when Nathalie would give Alfredo every inch of herself. She prepared in the bathroom by putting on her pink lingerie and looking in the mirror. It would be the last time she did that as a virgin. Nathalie possessed absolutely no sexual experience. She had saved herself for the right man and was happy that she had. Her face was filled with joy, but she was also a little nervous. She had taken a mild sedative prescribed by a physician.

She opened the bathroom door and found that numerous candles had been lit. She turned off the light so that she and Alfredo could bask in the romantic glow. He was wearing a light blue robe. He took her hands gently, pulled her close to him and said, "You look absolutely gorgeous, my princess. You do not know how I have waited for this day to come. *Te amo y te adoro*, Nathalie."

His lips sought hers. His kisses were passionate, but also tender. He led her by the hand to the bed. She was pleasantly surprised to find that he had spread petals from a yellow rose and a red carnation all over the sheets.

Alfredo spoke softly and said, "Our being together has made me the happiest man in the world."

"Darling," she replied, "I only know that my feelings for you are bigger than this world. You are the man I have waited for." She kissed him with a tenderness that only a woman could offer.

"You are making me feel like a true man," he said, "and you have awakened a powerful desire for you." They sat on the bed amidst the petals. Alfredo again told her how beautiful she looked. As she softly stretched out, she could smell the fragrance of the flowers. He lay next to her, gently took her in his arms and said, "I want to look at you, Nathalie. Let me feast my eyes on you."

He slowly removed her negligee. Nathalie was a bit nervous because she knew that she would soon be giving herself to the man she loved. Alfredo had a calming effect on her, but she was still tense because of her virginity.

Alfredo gazed upon the loveliness of her body with love in his heart and in his eyes. He reassured her that he would be gentle. He began stroking her with a softness and tenderness reserved for new born babies. Soon, he began to kiss her delectable form. He kissed her all over her body which now glowed in the candlelight. She was excited at his every touch, and she began to moan despite still being nervous. He whispered softly in her ear, "Darling, you are so beautiful. You look like a Venus."

"Thank you, my love," she replied. "I'm almost ready to give all of myself to you. I love you." Nathalie wanted to savor more of his tender touches. With each touch, her body yearned for him. Alfredo slightly lifted her from the bed as he took her in his arms. He kissed her forehead, cheeks and lips. Between his kisses, he whispered to her, "I adore you. I want you." His words made Nathalie even more excited.

He put her back on the bed and lay next to her. She began caressing his body. She thought, "Alfredo feels so manly to me." He became more excited as she explored his body with her fingers. She said, "I love you. I am so in love with you that I am ready to give myself to you."

He kissed her, and then he made love to her. When Nathalie let out a cry, Alfredo said, "Oh, darling! I love you," and he climaxed.

He covered her mouth with tender kisses and reassured her of his immense love for her. He held her against his body and could feel her trembling, so he covered her with his physique as if he were her blanket. She felt him all over her, and it was a delicious moment. After a few minutes, he lay on his back to rest. He spoke to her as he rested, saying, "Thank you for giving me the best gift of all, which is you. My love is yours forever, Nathalie."

He noticed that she had experienced some discomfort. He held her tenderly and whispered, "How can I help you to feel better, my darling?"

"Just hold me and tell me how much you love me. Tell me you will be mine forever."

They lay together listening to themselves breathe before falling asleep in each other's arms. He had been inside her heart and inside her soul. There were times during the night when he reached over and held her close to him. Nathalie enjoyed those tender touches.

Alfredo knew that his beloved had experienced a big change, so he approached her with tender words in the morning. He had been told that a woman goes through a few days of pain after losing her virginity. He wanted his true love to know that he would always be there for her.

The next day, Nathalie wrote a poem and placed it under Alfredo's pillow to surprise him.

And Love Was Born

Under the sky,

Beneath mysterious clouds,

Colorful clouds of crimson and gold,

Like a bouquet of marigolds,

We lay in bed and talked,

And loved passionately.

Soon we closed we our eyes,

And sank into our tomorrows.

I awakened the next day,

Entwined in your arms,

Feeling an intoxication for you.

The day after that, she wrote another poem and left it for her beloved on his bathroom dresser.

You put magic in me;

Sounds of rhapsodies.

It feels as if I'm in a galaxy

When you are close to me.

Our lovemaking was absolutely delicious.

In reply, Alfredo left a note for Nathalie on her bed which read, "Oh! This love has a charming ring. Musical bells you bring. Love, Alfredo."

While he was away on one of his trips, he sent a note to her which included a poem he had written.

Why do I sit in a stupor

Gazing at the sky,

Wishing I had wings

So I could fly to you.

He added a brief comment at the end. "Your love has more brightness than the light of June."

Nathalie wrote another poem to Alfredo which she put in an envelope. When she handed him the envelope, she gave him a kiss. The poem read,

As we held each other

In a fierce embrace

Consumed with purest love

That we waited for and longed for,

As our plasma intertwined

Inside our bodies

In a dance of love,

We kissed passionately.

As we whispered to each other

From now on, it is our right.

This pleasure will be ours forever.

We kissed savagely.

We both said I love you as we fell asleep.

After reading it, Alfredo said, "What have I done to deserve so much love in my life? Not many women are like you, and I am blessed to have you. I not only love you, Nathalie, I adore you."

Chapter Forty Seven

The soreness Nathalie experienced when she gave her virginity to Alfredo lasted two weeks. During the time she was healing, they found intimate pleasure in ways other than intercourse. One evening while they were in bed, Alfredo took her in his arms and removed her nightgown. As he took the garment off, he re-assured her of the great love he felt. He started to caress her naked body, saying, "You are so beautiful, Nathalie. I want to please you." He kissed her breasts, and suddenly her nipples became hard. She became so excited that she eagerly uncovered his body and began feasting on his strong shoulders and hairy chest. She said, "The hair on your chest excites me. It's a sign of manliness to me."

Alfredo replied, "It is for you only, *mi amor*." He then pulled her close to him and said, "I want my body to feel yours."

She answered, "You arouse me. You feel so good!"

He tenderly held her face in his hands and kissed her lips. She hungrily returned his kisses. He reached down to her private parts and gently caressed them until she came. She exclaimed, "Oh, oh my love, I feel like I'm in heaven!" As they French kissed, she took his manhood in her hand and tenderly massaged it until he climaxed. Under his breath, he gasped, "I love you so much, my Nathalie." He kissed her again and said, "I am the luckiest man in the world to have you." After she replied, "I'm the luckiest woman in the world," they slowly drifted into slumber with her head on his chest.

When the soreness had left her, Nathalie and Alfredo happened to attend a tenth wedding anniversary party for his friends Amalia and Leonardo. After returning to his villa from the country club where the event had been held, Nathalie said to the love of her life, "They reminded me of us, darling. Their joy just poured out of their skin."

"That is true," he replied, "but I believe we are happier." He punctuated his remark by putting his arms around her waist and moving his body close to hers. He could tell that they both wanted to feel themselves close against each other once again. He lightly ran his fingers through her silky hair, and then he placed his hands on her breasts in a tender way. Even though she was clothed, he awakened a need within her to have him. She said flirtatiously, "You feel so exciting to me, *amor*."

He looked into the depths of her green eyes and replied, "I want you and need you. I am full of love for you, my princess."

"Your words and tenderness have awakened beautiful desires within me. I want to have you, to feel your body and receive your nectar by making passionate love. I will get ready. When you hear our song playing, I will be in bed waiting for you."

He kissed her in response. It felt so delicious to her that she relaxed and closed her eyes. Anything her Alfredo did produced ecstasy. She thought, "I guess that's what happens when two people truly love each other." He tenderly kissed her eyelids and gave her a loving pat on her behind.

He undressed her with his eyes while she gracefully walked to her bedroom. She looked so lovely, sexy and classy. He remembered the first time he had made love to her. She was so innocent and so delectable. They would be making love for the second time, and he was ready to savor her even more. This time, he would make sure that it would be a pleasant encounter for her as well. He knew how she had suffered for a few days after giving her virginity to him. He went over in his head his plan for making it a wonderful night. After two weeks of healing, he was going to slowly and tenderly teach her variations in love making.

He went to his bathroom and prepared himself by taking a shower, then putting on his robe. Suddenly, he heard their song, A Woman in Love by Issa El Saieh, playing on the stereo. It was time, and he quickly made his way to the bedroom.

The only illumination was provided by candles that Nathalie had placed all over the room. The atmosphere was most inviting. She looked beautiful in her green baby doll lingerie. He was about to say, "*Munequita*, you look so…" when his words failed him. Her loveliness had made him speechless because all five of his senses were riveted on his love for her. Somehow, he was able to finish his sentence by saying, "You are my everything. I love you so much." He was literally panting with desire. After a moment, he was able to say, "I can't express how I feel about you. It's just too big. All I can say is that you became part of my life." As he started to disrobe, he said, "I'm crazy with love for you. I want you."

He got on the bed next to her and gently removed her negligee. After they were both naked, he began kissing every part of her body. He was learning every part of her loveliness with his lips, and she enjoyed everything he was doing. When he reached her mouth, they French kissed and then she left his embrace to begin kissing him on his hairy chest that turned her on so much. She went from there to kiss his neck, and then both of his cheeks. She said, "I will be enjoying you tonight. Kiss me all over my body again. It makes me feel good. Take me to paradise!"

Alfredo continued to caress and kiss her body with love and affection. He wanted to make sure she would be ready for him. It wasn't long before she blurted out, "Oh Alfredo, I want you so much! I want to feel every part of your body!"

He slowly got on top of her. She was ready, and she gradually opened her legs to receive him. He entered her with tenderness, saying, "You feel so perfect. I love you."

She replied, "I'm intoxicated with love for you."

After a few minutes of mutual enjoyment, he exclaimed, "Oh Nathalie, I am coming! You are my one and only! I adore you!"

Seconds later, she moaned as she climaxed. "Ummmh! Owwh! Owwh! Ummmh!" When she finally recovered and was able to get her breath back, she tenderly said, "You have taught me what love is, Alfredo. I love you."

They had consummated their love once again. They fell into slumber entwined in each other's arms. In the middle of the night, Alfredo slipped his strong arms around Nathalie's waist and pulled her close to his body. He could tell he had awakened her because she murmured softly. He whispered, "You are the fire that burns inside of me. I have a mystical attraction to you. I give you a piece of my soul because the soul is eternal. I love you."

At the dawn of the next day, their bodies were touching as if they had become one, and love was born again between them.

And Love Was Born

And Love Was Born

Chapter Forty Eight

They returned to New Orleans so that Alfredo could attend to some business matters. Since they had not yet been married in the church, they lived in their separate homes while in that city.

During this time, Nathalie's cousin Juan Eduardo Ordonez made a trip from his home in Ecuador to New York. Along the way, he stopped off in New Orleans to see her. It had been thirteen years since they had last seen each other. He wanted to surprise her and also share the good news of his engagement. His fiancée was a beautiful woman from a fine family. He checked into the Ponce De Leon Hotel in the French Quarter, and then called from the hotel to see if Nathalie was home. She was ecstatic when she heard his voice. She said, "I'll be there to pick you up in a half hour."

"I'll be waiting in the lobby, cousin."

They went to the Court of Two Sisters for lunch, which was in the same part of the Crescent City as the hotel. She was excited because she hadn't seen him in such a long time. When they entered the restaurant, they were spotted by Alfredo's friend Rodolfo Munez. He saw Juan Eduardo hold Nathalie close to his body and put his arm around her waist. He watched her respond to that gesture by placing her left arm around her cousin's left shoulder and glancing at him in a warm way. It shocked Rodolfo to see the man kiss Nathalie on her cheeks, and she returned his kisses.

Rodolfo also saw him talking to her. He was too far away to hear the conversation, but the man she was with may have been saying some intimate things to her because it was clear that he was showing her a great deal of affection. He even tenderly patted her on the cheeks.

Alfredo's friend thought, "This is unacceptable! How could she let down a man who adores her? I never expected her to be like that. She looked like a classy human being. I just have to tell Alfredo what I saw. He cannot make the mistake of marrying a woman like her. My gosh, can you trust any woman anymore?"

Rodolfo had been drinking a martini before ordering his meal. The sight of Nathalie and the strange man had unnerved him, and he needed another drink right away. The waiter brought it to him just the way he ordered it; stirred, not shaken. He paid the waiter so that he wouldn't be approached again. He wanted solitude while he watched every move Nathalie made with the other man because now he was protecting his friend.

He saw her point toward a cozy nook some distance from his vantage point and nod her head yes. Rodolfo was a regular customer at the Court of Two Sisters, and he knew that nook was usually occupied by lovers seeking privacy. Between sips of his drink, he analyzed what he was observing. As they walked to the nook, they were joyful and holding each other very close. When they sat down, the man moved his chair closer to hers and began talking to Nathalie in a very enthusiastic manner. They kept on holding hands and acting very affectionately toward each other.

Nathalie and her cousin Juan Eduardo were not aware that they were being watched. The last time he had seen her was when he was fifteen and she was thirteen. He thought, "I cannot believe how Nathalie has grown into such a beautiful woman! A man could easily become lost in her green eyes. Alfredo Milla is a lucky man to have such a beautiful, intelligent woman of integrity for his own." The more he talked to his cousin, the more he gestured excitedly with his hands.

Meanwhile, the alcohol had calmed Rodolfo Munez and he began to put together in his head what he would tell Alfredo. He had to break this horrible news to his best friend, a man who had invited him to his wedding. He thought, "Alfredo will be so devastated that he might kill himself, but I will tell him so he can call off the wedding. He can't go through with it. He just can't. Not after what I have seen." He still couldn't get over it. He kept thinking, "The nerve of that woman! Can you trust any of them anymore?"

Rodolfo knew that his friend was in Slidell, Louisiana on business. He thought, "Maybe when he gets back I'll invite him to lunch. It won't be here at the Court of Two Sisters. It would have to be somewhere else. It might be best to have him come to my house. This would allow me to spend enough time going over each point of what happened between Nathalie and the other man." He took a pad and pen from the inside pocket of his suit coat and began writing a detailed report of everything he witnessed, including the time of day. A private investigator couldn't have done better.

After he finished writing and consumed the last drops of his martini, he was disgusted. His stomach was twirling, and he felt like vomiting. He was so upset about everything that he got up from the table and left.

When Rodolfo arrived home that Thursday night, he called the Milla house. Maria Louisa, the sister, answered the phone. She recognized who he was and said, "My brother isn't home from his trip yet. He isn't expected back until Saturday."

"Could you ask him to call me as soon as he gets back? Please tell him it's urgent."

"I will."

"Thank you very much, Maria Louisa. Goodbye."

And Love Was Born

Chapter Forty Nine

The drive from Slidell had been safe and uneventful for Alfredo. His midnight blue Cadillac had performed beautifully. Before heading for his mansion, he stopped by Nathalie's place with a bouquet of yellow roses. She greeted him passionately. She said, "Oh my darling, I'm so happy to see you! You have no idea how much I've missed you. I was lonely without you. For us to be separated is horrible for me. I love you." He wanted to stay longer, but he had to go to home to check his mail and see how his sister was. He said, "I will call you later this evening, my love. Maybe we will go out for a late dinner."

When he arrived home, Maria Louisa said to Alfredo, "You had a telephone call from your friend Rodolfo Munez. He said it was urgent that you call him as soon as you got in."

Alfredo immediately called his best friend. Rodolfo said, "I'd like to invite you to dinner at my house. I have something very important to talk over with you. My wife will be making something special for you. What time can you be here?"

Alfredo replied, "I cannot make it until Monday evening. I have things to do after being on the road for a few days."

"*Mi amigo*, you must be at my place tonight. I have something urgent to tell you."

"Can I bring Nathalie?"

"No, no! We need to talk to you alone."

"Is it something about business?"

"It is something bigger than business. When you get here, you will find out what it is."

Rodolfo was sounding very mysterious. Alfredo wondered what was going on. Maybe one of his friend's relatives had died. He reluctantly said, "Okay, I will be there at six. I cannot stay more than an hour because I want to see my love Nathalie."

"All right. It won't take that long, but you need to come."

Alfredo arrived at his friend's home. After he was greeted by Rodolfo's wife, Angelina, his friend immediately escorted him to the library. Rodolfo closed the door and said to him, "First of all, I don't like to interfere in any relationships, but I have to tell you what I saw at the Court of Two Sisters this past Thursday afternoon. I am only telling you this because I am your friend. I saw Nathalie walk in with another man. They were hugging each other, and he and she were kissing on the cheek... not on the mouth. I guess they were not kissing on the mouth because they were in a restaurant, but they could have."

Alfredo had a look of total disbelief. He said, "Is this your idea of a joke? You must be kidding! Nathalie wouldn't do that! I called her during my trip, and she didn't mention going to lunch at the Court of Two Sisters with anybody."

Rodolfo adamantly replied, "She was with a man. They were kissing and looking at each other passionately! He had his arm around her waist! She put her arm around his shoulder and was patting him! They were sitting in the corner far away from everybody, the place where lovers sit. He even moved his chair to be closer to her. They were both together, laughing and having fun! Can you understand! I am a man, and I know affection when I see it. I am upset, Alfredo. I am so upset it is difficult for me to talk about it. I hate to have to pass this news to you. You do not deserve this. You are a good man. You do not know what effect this has had on me, but I had to tell you before you made a mistake."

Alfredo was speechless. He turned white. He said, "I am going home. Please tell your wife that I am sorry, but I cannot eat. My stomach hurts. I am beside myself."

"I understand," said his friend. "I will explain it to Angelina. Get some rest, and please take care of yourself. It has been very hard for me to tell you this. I talked to Angelina about it, and she agreed that I had to tell you and not just let it go."

"Thanks for being a friend," said Alfredo. "I am going home. I have a lot to sort through. I will call you later. I need to think about all this. I am absolutely, absolutely heartbroken." He left and drove straight home. He was in a daze when he pulled up in his driveway. He had no recollection of how he had gotten there. It was a miracle he didn't have an accident on the way.

He walked into his home with his head and shoulders down as if he had been totally defeated. Maria Louisa saw there was something wrong with her brother and asked, "What has happened to you? Are you sick?"

All he said was, "No. Something has happened." He didn't want to talk about any of it. He said, "I have to get away from everyone. I am going into my bedroom. I need to get away from everything, Maria Louisa, so I can think clearly."

After he left her, she thought, "What is going on? He has never been like this. I hope it is nothing serious."

Once he was along in his bedroom, Alfredo sat down, put his hands to his face and sobbed. The tears were falling like rain. He had never cried so much in his life. He said aloud, "I cannot believe this. It cannot be possible after I showed her all my love and gave her my heart, myself, my entire being. God, what have I done to deserve this?"

He left the bedroom and went downstairs to his bar. He poured himself a double shot of whiskey, the strongest drink he had on hand. He went back upstairs to his bedroom so he could sit in his favorite chair and digest what his friend had told him without interruptions. He was a broken man at that point. He thought, "All I want to do is get drunk. My pain is too hard; too hard to bear." After he finished his drink, he went back downstairs and poured himself another double. He returned to the bedroom and drained his glass for a second time. He said aloud, "I cannot believe it. How could she do that to me after we had just made love?" He fell asleep in a drunken stupor.

Nathalie called that night. Maria Louisa told her, "Alfredo was tired from the trip and had a headache. He went to bed early."

"That's unusual. He always calls me when he says he's going to call. He said he was going to call me, and that we were going out to dinner. Maybe he has the flu or a virus of some kind."

"All I know is that his face was white. There is something wrong with him. I hope it is nothing serious."

Nathalie answered, "I'll call him early tomorrow morning."

She put the receiver down and thought, "Omigosh, I'm sorry he wasn't in. I wanted so much to tell him how much I love him. I needed to hear his voice. I needed to be touched tenderly by him. I wanted to make love with him. I wanted to hear him call me *Munequita Linda* again. I wanted to have him. I needed our togetherness, but he's not available."

She decided to get ready for bed. She took a bath, put her negligee on, made a cup of tea, went to her library and started reading one of her favorite collections of New Orleans ghost stories. The phone rang. It was Tisha.

Nathalie answered by saying, "Hi, Tisha. Alfredo came by today and gave me a dozen yellow roses. I put them in a vase in my library. I'm looking at them and thinking about him while I'm reading some ghost stories. I couldn't talk to him tonight because he wasn't feeling well. His sister told me he went to bed early. I hope it's nothing serious. Other than that, everything is fine. Hopefully, we can get together tomorrow and do some fun things. We haven't seen each other for almost a week. I love him so much, Tisha."

Her friend replied, "Did you have a good time with your cousin?"

"We went to the Court of Two Sisters, and we had a great time. We laughed and joked like we used to do thirteen years ago, when we last saw each other. We talked a lot about my relatives back in Ecuador, and he brought me up to date. He has grown to be a very nice looking man. He's tall and handsome. He's engaged to a beautiful woman. Anyway, that's all that's going on. How's John?"

"Just fine. We talked about marriage. We'll be getting married in six months. We'll be shopping for engagement rings next week. I'm so happy to be his Jewish princess. We're going out tomorrow night. I wish you guys would come with us."

"I don't know what we'll be doing, but I think I'll pass on that. I'd like to be alone with Alfredo since I haven't seen him for so many days."

"Okay, Nathalie. Take care. I'll talk to you tomorrow. Have a good night."

"We'll talk. Good night."

And Love Was Born

Chapter Fifty

Alfredo called Rodolfo on Sunday morning. He still couldn't believe what he had been told. He asked his friend, "Are you sure you saw Nathalie with another man? Maybe you were mistaken. You might have seen a woman who looks like her." He was hoping his friend was at least a little doubtful about what he had seen.

Rodolfo replied, "I am absolutely positive. She was wearing the heart shaped diamond ring you gave her. Nothing is more positive than that. I also heard her voice and her laughter. It was her, Alfredo. It was her."

Alfredo said, "Well, *amigo*, I have to go." His voice was cracking and he had to get off the phone before bursting into tears.

He started dialing Nathalie's number, but stopped. He had a splitting headache, and he just couldn't bring himself to do it. He thought, "I will take a couple of aspirins to ease my pain and lay down for a while before I call her. I need to recuperate from the shock."

He found it impossible to sleep. After twenty minutes, he got up and went to his phone. He dialed Nathalie's number. She answered, "Hello" in her special way.

"Nathalie, I need to talk to you." She sensed something was wrong because he referred to her as "Nathalie," not *"Munequita"* or "my love."

"Alfredo, love, I'm so happy that you called. I called you last night and left a message. Did Maria Louisa give it to you?"

"Yes, I got the message this morning."

"Alfredo, I want to see you. I want to be with you. We haven't seen each other for almost a week. It seems like a year."

He said coldly, "I need to talk to you, Nathalie."

"What's wrong with you? You have never talked to me in that tone of voice before."

"There is nothing at all wrong with me. I need to talk to you. Let me come to your house. What time will you be ready?"

"I'm ready right now."

"Are you dressed?"

"Well, I have my negligee on. That should be enough."

"Please get dressed. I am in no mood to play around. I will be there in forty five minutes."

"Alfredo, what's wrong with you? I don't like the tone of your voice."

"I need to talk to you, and we will leave it at that. I will be there in forty five minutes. Goodbye."

He drank two cups of strong coffee so that he would be alert and able to quickly grasp the nuances of every possible way she might respond. He wanted to make sure there would be no misunderstandings.

He drove his Cadillac over to her place. After he rang the doorbell, she opened the front door and greeted him with a bright smile. She said, "Hello," and approached him to give him a hug. He shocked her by pushing her away.

She looked at him in disbelief and said, "Alfredo, what in the world is wrong with you?"

He replied in a cold, distant tone, "I need to talk to you. Let us sit in your living room."

"Okay, but why are you this way with me? I haven't done anything."

"Oh, Nathalie, I am not sure of that."

They walked to the living room apart. They sat at opposite ends of the sofa. He spoke first.

"I know you were in the Court of Two Sisters on Thursday afternoon while I was in Slidell on business."

"Of course I was there."

"Nathalie, I know you were with a man, the man was holding you, you had your arm around his shoulders, you were kissing each other's cheeks and then the two of you went to a little hiding place used by lovers. You sat there with that man making goo goo eyes. What has gotten into you? What made you do that?"

Nathalie tried to defend herself, but Alfredo was in charge of the conversation. She found it impossible to break in. He continued his rant by saying, "What possessed you? You did something horrible to me. I thought you were a woman of standards, but you turned around and betrayed me. I cannot marry you! I have to break our engagement."

Nathalie sat there frozen. For a long minute, she found it impossible to say anything. When she gathered her thoughts, she said, "Alfredo, you don't understand."

"What is there to understand? What you have done is as plain as day. I have a witness who saw all of it; my best friend Rodolfo." Alfredo then got up and headed for the front door.

She ran after him saying, "Stop, stop, Alfredo! Hear my side of the story."

"What side are you talking about? You were with another man."

"Alfredo, come to your senses. We have to talk. You need to hear what I'm about to say. Let's go back to the living room."

"No, I am going to listen, but I am standing next to the door. Whatever it is you say might not be the truth. If I begin to think you are lying to me, I am leaving."

"Alfredo, how can you accuse me of having another man in my life?"

"My friend saw you, that is how."

"No, no, I did nothing wrong. The man he saw me with was my cousin Juan

Eduardo from Ecuador, whom I had not seen in thirteen years. He's two years older than me. We were so happy to see each other that we hugged and kissed each other on the cheek. We were excited to share so many childhood memories and to celebrate that both of us had become engaged."

"Oh, Nathalie, you are telling me a lie to cover up your sin." He opened her front door, walked out and slammed the door behind him. He was the most angry he had ever been in his life.

Nathalie stood frozen like a piece of ice. She had never seen Alfredo behave in such a vicious way. She thought, "He was so jealous that he didn't want to give me a chance to say anything." She took a moment to calm down and then thought, "I'm going to check into a hotel and get away from the house so that he can't contact me. When he calls or comes by, he'll be upset, but it will serve him right. I have to think about whether I want to continue our relationship. Maybe I should call our wedding off."

She went to her bedroom and packed a small suitcase. She decided to stay at the Pontchartrain Hotel for a few days.

And Love Was Born

Chapter Fifty One

Alfredo went straight to his office when he arrived home. His sister, Maria Louisa, noticed his troubled demeanor, but said nothing to him. After a while, he came out of the office, walked towards the bar and poured himself a double whiskey sour. He drank it quickly, but it didn't relax him at all. He needed to talk to someone, so he walked into the kitchen where Maria Louisa was washing some dishes. He said in a trembling voice, "You will not believe what happened. Nathalie was seen with another man! My friend Roberto saw her at the Court of Two Sisters. He was kissing her and holding her close to his body. They sat in a corner where lovers sit, and they were holding hands. He moved his chair closer to hers as they dined. Oh sister, I am so heartbroken. I thought…" He began to sob.

"Calm down, brother."

"How can I calm down? She has torn my heart into shreds. I went to her house and confronted her, and then I left." Alfredo went back to the bar and poured himself another double. Maria Louisa followed him and said, "Alfredo, there must be a good reason why she was with that man. She loves you. I have seen it in her face. You must give her a chance to explain things to you. You sometimes jump to conclusions too fast. Why not give her a call after you settle down?"

"I have a splitting headache right now," he answered. "I will give her a call in a couple of hours."

"It might not be anything, Alfredo. You might be making something out of nothing."

"I love you, sister. You always give me such good advice." He finished his drink and went upstairs to lie down.

When Nathalie arrived at the hotel, she gave the doorman the keys to her Mercedes, walked into the lobby and checked in. A bell hop carried her small piece of luggage to her room. She was happy that the Pontchartrain Hotel was not far from her home. She entered the room, and the young man placed her suitcase on a stand. Nathalie tipped him and then locked the door.

She said aloud, "Well, I'm here. I have to take time to think things out. Can I live with Alfredo's recent behavior, or should I forget about marrying him?"

While Nathalie was getting settled in her hotel room, Alfredo was getting up from his bed. He no longer had a headache. He decided to call Nathalie. He thought, "Maybe I have been behaving like a child." He went to his office and dialed her number. There was no answer. He decided to wait an hour and try again.

He began to do some paper work, but found that he couldn't stay focused. He couldn't keep from staring at the clock on the wall, and the hands didn't seem to move at all. His emotional state was such that he began to think they were moving backwards. He couldn't stand it any longer, so he decided to drive to Nathalie's place. He backed his Cadillac out of the garage and left.

And Love Was Born

When he arrived at her house, he sensed that something was not right. He got out of his car, went to the front door and rang the bell. No one answered. It was very unusual for her not to be at home at six in the evening. He got back into the blue Cadillac and drove home.

Meanwhile, Nathalie called Tisha to let her know where she was staying and what had happened between her and Alfredo. Tisha was shocked and said, "Nathalie, you should sort things out carefully. Alfredo is a good man."

"How can you say that after he accused me without knowing what really happened? Tisha, you don't do that to a woman you say you love."

"I'm glad you're taking a little time to be by yourself. It'll help you make the right decision. This is a problem that only the two of you can solve, but I'm here for you in case you need me."

"Thanks, Tisha. I think I'll go to bed early. I want to be fresh tomorrow so I can try to solve this problem. I can't stand his accusing me the way he did without having all the facts."

"Take it easy, girlfriend. I'm here if you need me. Try to get some sleep."

"I will. Once again, thanks, Tisha."

Alfredo was beside himself when he walked into his home. He went straight to his office and called Tisha. He wanted to know if she had heard from *Munequita*. She picked up after two rings. "Hello, this is Tisha."

"Tisha, I am coming apart. Do you know what has happened to Nathalie? I have been calling her home and she is not there. I have driven there and no one was around. Do you know her whereabouts?"

"Yes, Alfredo. She is at the Pontchartrain Hotel. She needed to be by herself."

"Thanks for the information. I will call her."

"I wouldn't call her tonight. I think tomorrow would be better."

"I cannot wait to do that. I have to talk to her, Tisha. Thanks for the information."

Immediately after he hung up, he went to the phone book and found the number for the hotel. The front desk connected him with her room. Nathalie answered, "Hello."

"It is I. I miss you and love you."

"Oh Alfredo, I don't feel like talking."

"Can I call you later?"

"Tomorrow would be better. I have things to sort out. We'll talk tomorrow."

"I love you."

"Goodnight, Alfredo."

It was a cold response, but he had it coming. He was beginning to be sorry for what he had said to her.

And Love Was Born

Alfredo spent a horrible night. His only thought was, "Somehow, I have to make it through to tomorrow."

He waited until ten o'clock in the morning to call Nathalie. When he heard her voice on the other end of the line, he said, "Nathalie, I want to see you."

"No, Alfredo. I thought about everything that happened the other day. I decided that I want to postpone our wedding. For a while, I was thinking of calling it off completely. I just don't know if I can live with someone who can accuse me the way you did without knowing the truth."

"I did not mean to. I love you so much. Please do not throw our love away. Please forgive me for hurting you the way I did."

"I don't want to see you, Alfredo. I need to be by myself. Bye."

Alfredo sat for nearly a minute still holding the receiver in his hand. He began to sob. He thought, "How can our love be finished? It cannot be. She has to understand that I love her with all my being."

He went to his bedroom and stayed there the rest of the day. He didn't come down to have lunch or dinner. His sister became very worried about him.

It was midnight when he got out of bed and went into his office. He sat at his desk and wrote a poem for Nathalie.

Listen my friends.

Let me tell you

How I loved her.

I loved her

With every inch of my heart.

Now, she has left me forever.

Show me how to live without her love.

I will go into the darkness of the night,

The darkness that is darker than the night,

Where in my solitude

I can convince myself

Not to love her anymore.

Friends, come and console me

Of this pain that I feel

And Love Was Born

That is breaking my heart

Into small pieces that no one can pick up.

I will be with the darkness,

The darkness of the night,

So that maybe somehow

I can forget her forever.

After he finished writing the poem, he addressed an envelope to Nathalie in care of the Pontchartain Hotel, folded the paper he had written his work on, placed it in the envelope and drove to the closest mailbox.

She received the poem a day later. She thought, "Perhaps I've been a little too hard on Alfredo." She began to soften her feelings. Finally, she called him. When he answered, she said, "I hope that now you'll let me explain what happened that afternoon at the Court of Two Sisters."

Alfredo replied, "Nathalie, you do not have to explain. I trust you. It was foolish on my part to act as I did. I am sorry. I acted like a child. I love you. You are my whole life."

"I'm going home tomorrow," she said. "I'd like to explain everything to you. Won't you come for coffee and cake?"

"I would love to."

"I'll call you to let you know when I'm home."

"I will be there. See you tomorrow."

When they met at her house, she told him all about her cousin Juan Eduardo. She said, "As a matter of fact, Juan Eduardo is still here in New Orleans. I want you to meet him."

Alfredo took her in his arms and said, "*Munequita*, I am so glad that it was your cousin. We will take him to Commander's Palace tonight."

The three of them had a great evening. Alfredo verified that all was well. Nathalie entertained them with a story from her days at the Ursuline Academy. She said, "We took all our meals in a dining hall, and breakfast, lunch and dinner were never any fun. We had to say Grace before lifting any utensils. We had to sit up straight with both feet on the floor while eating. Only one of our hands could be on the table. Our other hands were kept in our laps along with cloth napkins we were expected to use. We had to keep our napkins in our laps throughout the meal, and we were taught how use the corners of the napkins to wipe the corners of our mouths. We were also taught the correct way to hold our forks, and we were allowed to pick up only small portions with them. We couldn't overfill our mouths or talk with food in our mouths. If we wanted to talk to each other, we had to use what the nuns called our 'inside voices' and speak in low volume. The

174

nuns would hover over us to make sure none of the rules were broken. If anyone violated a rule, a nun would bang a yardstick on the end of the table and call out the name of the person who did it. When we finished eating, we had to fold our napkins in a certain way and place them next to our plates. Then we got up from the table, walked behind our chairs and pushed the chairs back into their original positions."

After listening to her story, Juan Eduardo said, "Well, you know everyone from our family went to strict private schools. You were no different than all of our cousins. We all marched the same way to the same tune."

Alfredo looked lovingly at Nathalie and said with pride, "I have a polished girl."

He couldn't wait to make love to her that night. The next morning, they woke up with the same love they had before the misunderstanding.

Later that day, she wrote a poem. Nathalie waited until Alfredo hung up his suit coat and then she slipped it into the inside pocket. He discovered it after he arrived at a meeting the next day.

The Day That You Love Me

The day that you love me,

The birds will sing like a quartet,

In perfect harmony,

As they wink at us.

The ocean waves,

Will caress us,

With a tender touch,

As if they were angels.

The day that you love me,

The sun will warm our skins,

Like our first kiss,

And Love Was Born

That we gave each other.

The flowers will suddenly open,

Showing us their petals,

In many dimensional colors,

For us to feast on.

The day that you love me,

The parks will open their gates,

To show us their flowers,

With their perfumed aromas.

The day that you love me,

I will appear like a beautiful rose,

All dressed in pink,

For your eyes to see.

The day that you love me,

Your voice will sound,

Like musical bells,

Bringing me your love songs.

Chapter Fifty Two

Matt Logan was in his office reading the wedding invitation he had received from Alfredo and Nathalie when a call came through for him. His secretary Louise said, "A Bill Sanders is on the line. He says he knows Nathalie Ordonez." Matt took the call and said, "What can I do for you?"

Sanders replied in his husky voice, "We have to talk. I know who's behind everything that happened to your friend. I also have hard evidence that she is in even greater danger. I'll meet you in the lobby of the Ponce de Leon Hotel at seven o'clock. I'll be wearing a white sport coat over a blue turtle neck."

The thought of Nathalie being in danger again turned his blood into ice. His heart stopped for an instant, and he thought, "She won't survive another trauma. I can't let that happen."

He knew he couldn't tell Alfredo because the love of Nathalie's life would panic just as he had before. He would probably do something stupid that would play right into the hands of the bad guys. His shoulders slumped as he resigned himself to what had to be done. He thought, "I'm the only one who can stop them."

Matt showed up at precisely the appointed time. The mysterious person who had called him turned out to be a strange looking man. He had a burr head haircut, broad shoulders and his hands were larger than normal, but his high cheekbones and soft features could have been those of a woman. Logan dismissed that notion after he happened to notice the man's size eleven feet. He thought, "No woman has hands and feet that big."

The lawyer asked the stranger, "Who are you and why should I be talking to you?"

"I told you that my name is Bill Sanders. I'm Sal Cardinale's second in command at his brothel in Gretna, which is actually a Mob operation."

Hearing Sal's name made Matt cringe. He said, "I didn't know Cardinale had a second in command."

"Well, he does, and I'm it."

"I've never had any respect for him. I'm not even sure he's human."

"He doesn't think much of you either. Once in a while, he talks about what a poor excuse of a man you are and how you're not fit to live."

"So what does all this have to do with me?"

"Sal is the one behind everything that's happened to Nathalie Ordonez. I can supply you with hard evidence that can get Sal the death penalty." This statement got Matt's attention. He wondered if it were true.

"Why are you willing to do this?"

"Sal is a greedy bastard. He gives me peanuts. He supplies my food, housing,

And Love Was Born

cars, the works, but he pays me peanuts. I do all the work, but he gets practically all the gravy. With him out of the picture, I can take over. I'll give you the evidence, but you have to promise that you'll keep me out of it when you go to the authorities."

Matt was definitely interested. He said, "Where is this evidence?"

"I'll meet you tomorrow night at nine at this address." He handed Logan a slip of paper containing an address in Gretna. Immediately after Matt agreed to be there, Sanders got up and left without another word. The lawyer began to have second thoughts about what he had gotten himself into. He thought, "Having Cardinale reenter my life is worse than the bubonic plague. He's ruthless and relentless. He'll stop at nothing to get what he wants."

What Matt Logan knew of Sal Cardinale barely scratched the surface. He was an embodiment of evil who kept his life shrouded in mystery. No one knew the true story of where he came from because he kept the chilling tale a closely guarded secret.

BOOK TWO
SAL AND LUCRETIA'S STORY:
YEARS SPENT RACING
TOWARD DEATH

DEATH FOLLOWED

CHAPTER ONE

Nathalie and Alfredo were in serious danger because of a man who never really knew his true name. All he was able to piece together was that he was born sometime in 1924 and was an infant when his mother booked passage on an ocean liner. For some reason which he never found out, the ship sank. It was a debacle and in all the confusion, the mother and infant were unable to secure a seat in any of the lifeboats. Out of desperation, she placed her baby on the door to a medical cabinet which had a red cross painted on it and happened to float by them. There wasn't enough room for her on the small makeshift raft, so she must have paddled alongside for as long as she could. Hypothermia probably overwhelmed her. The likelihood was that she drifted off into an endless sleep as she was swept into the abyss.

Fortune smiled upon the infant when he was spotted by the lookout of a freighter under the command of Captain Frank Carter. By this time, the baby had miraculously survived being adrift for several days, but had been reduced to just a shriveled up little thing. He was nursed back to health by Dang, who was the Asian sea wife of Hunk Welles. Hunk was a massive Cherokee Indian who served as the ship's second mate.

The Cherokee second mate went to the captain and asked, "What do you plan to do with the baby?"

"Our next port of call is Venezuela, Hunk. He looks white, so we'll keep him onboard until we get back to the States and he can put in a seaman's orphanage."

"Captain, I want to adopt him."

"Why do you want to do that?"

"Any child who survived what this one went through will live a very long life, and our ship will be blessed by having him aboard."

Like all seafarers, Frank Carter was a bit superstitious, and he went along with what the 6' 6" 300 pound Cherokee proposed. According to traditional maritime law, the captain was the sole authority aboard any ship. He was entitled to act as judge, jury and executioner. The captain exercised his privilege and decreed that the baby boy was Hunk Welles' adopted son. The big Indian named the child Young Welles. This did not please the other Indians onboard. They hated the infant because they were still angry about what the white man had done to their ancestors and because they believed that strangers found adrift in the ocean brought bad medicine with them when taken onboard.

Hunk and Dang acted as the baby's parents, even though they were not married. Their relationship of seaman and sea wife was a type that has long been forgotten, but sea wives were once part of traditional maritime life. It has been said that sea wives existed through the course of history, and that even Christopher Columbus had one.

DEATH FOLLOWED

The ship's captain was the decision maker when it came to a vessel's policy on sea wives. Most ships allowed them. If the captain allowed sea wives onboard, he would usually make sure he had the best looking one on his ship. Practically all of the officers had wives at home they were legally married to, and the sea wives were never taken seriously. They were just women who took care of these men while they were out to sea. It is doubtful if any seaman ever told his "land wife" about his sea wife.

Sea wives came onboard of their own free will as young girls and were assigned to cabins occupied by ranking ship's officers. Most were Filipino, Indonesian, Chinese or from Southeast Asia, but some came from South America. They were all from very poor families, and they were doing it strictly for money. They were paid from a pool of cash that accumulated from what the crew would ante up for each hand of their frequent poker games. Once the pool reached a certain amount, it was distributed to the sea wives so they could send it to their families. Sometimes they were given "bonuses" of a bag of beans or a bag of rice to send home. When a new captain, officer or engineer came onboard, he would be assigned both a cabin and the sea wife that came with it, whether she liked it or not. Although it was permitted for a sea wife to be taken to another ship, most officers and engineers chose not to do so when they transferred vessels. The majority of sea wives were aboard the same ships for many years.

Each of them was assigned a job on the ship. When working, they wore baggy one piece coveralls, just like the ones a mechanic would be expected to wear. A large locker in the engine room contained hundreds of the coveralls in various sizes and colors.

DEATH FOLLOWED

CHAPTER TWO

Five years after Young Welles had come onboard the ship, Herman Richter took over as captain. Hunk was pleased at first because the change of command resulted in his being promoted to first mate. This meant he was second in rank only to the captain. The big Indian was to find out that there would be a bad side to the transition. It started when he introduced his five year old boy to the new skipper. He said, "This is my son, Young Welles."

Richter was a big, balding and powerful man. He was 6' 2" and weighed 260 pounds. He wore a white captain's cap and a black double breasted coat with epaulets, gold buttons and gold braid on the cuffs. His outfit also included a white shirt, black tie, black trousers and black boots. Everyone onboard would soon learn that Captain Richter's way of dressing would never vary, no matter how hot or cold the weather was.

The captain looked at the boy in a strange way, as if he were trying to place a connection with him in his mind. Richter started asking Hunk many questions about the child's background, since it was obvious that he was not an Indian. Hunk answered as many as he could before finally saying, "You can check the ship's log for more information, skipper."

Several days later, the boy was confronted by both Captain Richter and Hunk. The captain grasped the youngster around his ribs with big, strong hands and lifted him into the air. He exclaimed, "You are my lost son... and now I've found you!" He hugged him in an emotional way, but Young Welles showed no emotion at all because he was very confused.

Captain Richter took the boy into his cabin. He crouched down in front of him, placed his hands on the boy's shoulders and said, "You are a very courageous lad. You are my long lost son, and now you are here with me! Bring your head close to mine and look into this mirror with me. Don't you see the resemblance?" The boy had to admit there was somewhat of a resemblance. They both had dark hair and dark eyes and some of their features were similar.

Hunk took this development in stride. He seemed happy that the boy was reunited with, as he put it, "A father more closely related to him." Captain Richter respected Hunk for all he had done for the boy. Hunk, however, didn't tell the new captain about everything he had done for the kid. He never mentioned the way the other Cherokees had tortured and abused the child. He wanted to do all he could to prevent any retaliation against members of his own tribe.

The captain renamed the boy Ernst Richter. In the beginning of their relationship, Captain Richter was the happiest man on the seas, and the boy was just as happy. He was hungry for affection and attention from someone he could relate to; somebody who was just like him. He respected Hunk and Dang for all they had done for him, but he didn't quite love them. After all, Hunk was a Cherokee Indian and Dang was an Asian. There was always a separation between them and the boy. He believed that the big burly Caucasian sea captain would give him what he had been seeking.

DEATH FOLLOWED

Herman Richter possessed a strong and very complicated personality. There seemed to be a fathomless depth to the man's persona. He was born in 1889. He followed in the footsteps of his father, who had also been a sea captain. He was a German and very proud of it, even though his fatherland had lost the Great War and had to endure humiliating reparations because of the Treaty of Versailles. Even though he had immigrated to America, Richter's heart was always with his homeland.

Captain Richter was also an Aryan. He firmly believed that the most advanced cultures came from Northern Europe and that white people were destined to dominate the world. His two gods were Neptune and Charles Darwin. Neptune was the god of water and the sea in Roman mythology. The planet Neptune was named after the god because its deep blue gas clouds gave early astronomers the impression of great oceans. One of the first lessons the captain taught the boy was, "The sea has always existed from the very beginning. When you are at sea, you are with Neptune. You are also with all those who have been at sea and will be at sea. All of these people are with you, right at your side. They are like ghostly legions ahead of you and behind you. The sea is our destiny and our future. Neptune will always protect you as long as you honor him as the god of the sea."

Darwin was an English naturalist and geologist who contributed to the theory of evolution and wrote a book titled On the Origin of Species. Herman Richter cited Darwin's writings as proof of the superiority of Caucasians over the other races, even though very little of it was about humans. He told the boy, "From the beginning of mankind, infanticide and complete destruction of the enemy were encouraged to keep our race pure and strong. We must do all we can to prevent intermarriage of Caucasians with those of impure races, otherwise it would cause a polluting process."

The captain added, "Land lovers ruined things, especially with their 'Ten Commandments.' Those commandments are ridiculous, especially the fifth one; 'Thou shalt not kill.' Killing is part of the natural order. Nature is all about killing and being killed. Life is for the strong, to be lived by the strong and, if need be, taken by the strong. There should be a return to the natural order where the strong dominate the weak. The destruction of the weak and the sick is more humane than protecting them. Neptune and Darwin have proved this is so. Human beings are not equal. Just take a look at the Indians and Asians on this ship. They have dull brains to begin with, and they do excessively stupid things."

Needless to say, Herman Richter wanted his adopted son to have little to do with Dang because she was an Asian, and he considered that an impure race. He wanted to end any bonds of affection between the woman and the boy. He told Ernst, "I am both your mother and your father." He also detested the Cherokees. He was good to Hunk, but he treated the other members of the tribe harshly. If they broke his rules, he administered their punishments himself with an enormous whip known as a knout. There were two occasions when his lashings resulted in death.

DEATH FOLLOWED

CHAPTER THREE

The tall, muscular sea captain took charge of the boy's schooling and drilled him intensively each and every day of the week. The captain knew seven languages, and he taught all of them to his adopted son. He also taught the child mathematics and navigation. The kid was made to read every word of Darwin's On the Origin of Species and Mein Kampf, a book written by a German political prisoner named Adolf Hitler. Every night without fail, the captain quizzed the lad on those two books. Herman Richter was not only strict, but very demanding. He wanted more and more from the boy. He never seemed to be satisfied.

In addition to all the academic work, the child was given self-defense training from the age of eight on. He was instructed in hand to hand combat and the use of knives, pistols and rifles. Despite being barely five feet tall, he was an able bodied seaman at the age of ten and a child capable of violence.

For the most part, Herman Richter was cold, distant and stone faced. He seldom grinned and didn't smile excessively. Ernst hungered for any sign of affection from his father and would do anything to gain his approval.

Captain Richter wanted the boy to become comfortable with killing and to experience a living thing die at his hand as early as possible. When Ernst was eight years old, he ordered the youngster to slit a pig's throat. The captain held the creature down while the boy killed it. While it was happening, Herman Richter said, "Feel the knife as it cuts through its flesh. Watch the animal as it becomes silenced. Savor it."

Ernst was very worried that he might not please his father, and the tension helped him to focus on what he had to do. A strange thing occurred while the pig was dying. His father ordered him to hold the creature close enough to feel its life depart and as he did this, Ernst became aroused. The boy felt a release of sexual tension as he saw the look of approval from his father that he had always craved.

Captain Richter was not only satisfied, but elated at what his adopted son had done. He hugged the boy lovingly for the first time and exclaimed, "I'm proud of you, my son! You have done the creature a favor by taking it out of its miserable existence. Animals have only legs and instinct. Instinct is no match for reason, and creatures without reason have no real life at all."

Four years later, Ernst killed his first man. It happened when head hunters from a remote island stormed the ship while it was anchored. The crew fought them off, and Ernst threw a knife at one of the spear wielding attackers. The blade hit the savage in the neck, and he fell to the deck face first. The lad's knife had penetrated a main artery, causing almost immediate death.

DEATH FOLLOWED

After the fighting was over, the proud father brought his son's knife back to him. Once more, he was elated and gave Ernst an affectionate hug. Captain Richter had a broad smile on his face as he said, "Be proud that nature has made you a killer. You have earned the right to kill, for you are one of the superior humans truly fit to live. Never forget that." He had no idea of how sexually satisfying it had been for the boy.

DEATH FOLLOWED

CHAPTER FOUR

Ernst Richter's fourteenth birthday proved to be the most memorable of his entire life. His father insisted that he put in a full day of work, and the celebration really began when the sun went down. Fortunately, the sea was calm that night, which enhanced the festivities.

The party was for officers only. None of the sailors and sea wives took part. It was not just a boy's birthday party. It was going to be a rite of passage.

Captain Richter poured the boy a tall glass of rum and toasted him by saying, "Today, my son, you are a man. You have earned a place among the officers of this vessel. This means you are entitled to your own cabin. Here's the key. Go and inspect your new quarters. Do it right now."

Ernst was lightheaded from the rum while walking toward his new housing, but he also felt grown up. It would be the first time he had a cabin of his own. For years, he had slept in a hammock attached to walls in his father's cabin. Three people occupied the captain's quarters during that time; Herman Richter, his sea wife and Ernst.

Before he had left his party, his father also mentioned that it was time for him to begin learning the responsibilities of an officer. He wasn't told exactly what they were, and he wondered, "When will the lessons start. Will they begin tomorrow?"

Ernst's new quarters were just below the bridge. As he unlocked the door, he expected it to be emptied out. When he turned on the light, he was surprised to find a woman in the bed. She didn't have a stitch of clothing on.

He had seen enough Filipinos to recognize her race and knew she was one of them. She was older than him; possibly in her twenties. Her eyes were dark and lovely, but her full breasts immediately got his attention. He had seen women who were completely naked before, but he was captivated by her well-proportioned figure

She got up from the bed, took him by the hand and began undressing him. When he was naked, they lay next to each other. She knew very little English; just enough to say, "My name Babae." (She pronounced her name "Baby"). He had no idea that "Babae" in her native tongue meant "woman."

She began kissing him all over his body. When he became aroused, she showed him what to do and they began having intercourse. She was very experienced, but Ernst picked up the hang of it and kept up with her, thrust for thrust. After he climaxed, she asked, "You like?"

He vigorously nodded his head, and then made a gesture indicating he would like to do it again. She nodded her head, and they kept going.

DEATH FOLLOWED

He climaxed a second time, and then they fell asleep in each other's arms. Babae awakened when he did, showered with him and scrubbed his back. She would have shaved him too, but all he had was peach fuzz. He then went to breakfast, but she did not join him in the officer's galley because sea wives were not allowed to eat there.

Captain Richter had his son sit with him during breakfast. He asked the boy, "What did you think of her?"

"She's very pretty and very nice."

"She is part of your training to be a sea captain. You will have to observe how I trained my sea wife to fulfill my needs. Use my methods as examples of how to treat your woman. Always remember that she will do anything you ask because money is being sent to her family. The family is everything to such a person. If she doesn't do what you tell her, let me know about it and we'll get you another beautiful young girl from a family who would be grateful for big bags of rice or beans and some candy bars."

Ernst soon found out that Babae was nearly twice his age. She was assigned to the galley and worked as a cook. She had no interest in learning English, but was a nonstop talker. He asked his father if he should learn her native language, but the captain told him not to do it. Captain Richter saw no need for having long conversations with any of the sea wives, including his. Babae insisted on sex every night, and they enjoyed their physical intimacy.

After a week went by, Captain Richter took the boy aside and lectured him. He said, "A seaman should not be able to impregnate women from ports all over the world because that will bring more degenerates. Your sea wife was ordered to use the Queen Anne's Lace tea to avoid getting pregnant, but I don't want to take any chances of my son being trapped into a marriage with a member of an impure race. You will have to be castrated."

The captain had not used the correct word to describe what he wanted done. It would actually be a crudely performed vasectomy.

Herman Richter was so dominating that the boy was too frightened to protest. He was old enough to know that his father was the captain of the ship and the ultimate law on that vessel. He felt he had no choice, so he went along.

The operation was performed on a wooden table in the galley. There was no physician aboard, so it was done by an officer who had some previous experience as a medic. Ernst was given no anesthetic, not even rum to drink. All that was done to lessen his agony was the officer shoving a chunk of ice up against the lad's crotch and holding it there until it felt numb. The mate sliced open his testicles, cut two tubes and tied them off. Captain Richter held his son down. The boy screamed throughout the procedure. He was covered in his own blood when he passed out from the pain.

DEATH FOLLOWED

CHAPTER FIVE

Ernst suffered intense pain in his left side for a week after the crudely performed medical procedure. As time went on, he noticed that one of his testicles was shrinking and he could no longer achieve a hard erection. There was nothing he could do about it but keep quiet and bear the pain alone. He knew that if he went to his father, he would probably be told that he was a weakling who dishonored his superior race. He might even kill him.

Even though his sea wife was very attractive, he no longer had any desire for sexual intercourse. It was possible that he associated intercourse with intense pain. The man who performed the vasectomy may have botched the procedure in some way, or the less than hygienic sanitary conditions may have contributed to the problem. The instruments used may have been unclean and pools of blood had been allowed to form on the galley table. It would eventually dawn on the boy that the only way he could achieve sexual release was through killing.

Since he no longer liked having sex, he refused Babae's overtures with absolutely no embarrassment on his part. The sea wife became angry, which was a big mistake. After he told his father that he no longer wanted her, she was put off the ship at the next port. He was allowed to choose her replacement, and he selected an older woman who became content with a sexless relationship. When Ernst made his strange choice, Captain Richter thought, "Beauty is in the eye of the beholder. Maybe he wants a woman who will mother him."

The captain was unaware that forcing the boy to have the vasectomy had not only ended their relationship but fueled enormous hate in him. Ernst subconsciously felt that he was trapped, and he shut down emotionally. There was no more love within him. He continued to obey Captain Richter, but it had nothing to do with the captain being his father. It was strictly because of the power of fear and the fear of his father's power. Ernst vowed to either escape or kill the captain, and he made sure Herman Richter had no inkling of what he thought. If the captain ever found out, it would mean certain death. The boy bided his time until he could make his move. That finally took place in 1941, when Ernst was seventeen.

By then, Captain Richter's consumption of alcohol had gotten out of hand. His behavior had become erratic, and the man who had once taken such pride in his appearance became sloppy and careless. He was starting to make more mistakes and overlook things. He was also having problems with his sea wife. She was attractive, but she wouldn't mind him as much as he would have liked. The captain regarded Ernst's sea wife as far more trustworthy than his. He told his adopted son, "The only reason I wouldn't have her for my own is her looks. I don't know how you can handle sleeping with such an ugly woman." He had no idea that Ernst had become celibate.

The teenager's opportunity for escape began to take form on a night when Captain Richter became very drunk on rum. He had a habit of locking his door, and then sometimes taking stock of his valuable possessions before turning into

DEATH FOLLOWED

bed. On this night, he left the door open after stumbling back into his cabin. Ernst happened to see the light from the open door and went to look in on the man he hated so much. When he arrived at the doorway, he saw the captain dozing with one of the ship's old log books in his arms. The captain's sea wife was sound asleep, and Ernst was careful not to awaken either of them. His curiosity was aroused, so he stealthily moved close enough to examine what the captain was holding. He was startled when he discovered that the book had been hollowed out and was a hiding place for a lot of gold coins. He was able to determine that the book was the ship's log for 1914, and then he suddenly remembered that 1914 was the year before Captain Frank Carter had taken command of the vessel.

Money was something Ernst had little experience with. Captain Richter kept a tight rein on the young man by never giving him any. After seeing the gold coins, the lad suddenly became obsessed with it. He dreamed about having money, and he patiently waited for his chance. His opportunity arrived six weeks later when the ship made port in Seattle, Washington.

Herman Richter decided to go on shore leave, and he ordered Ernst to see that his sea wife cleaned their cabin. He said, "Make sure that lazy sea wife of mine finishes that job. I locked her in to make sure she did it. Bring her some food in a couple of hours, and make sure it is done properly. Here's the key to the cabin." This was the opportunity the teenager had been waiting for.

Ernst brought the sea wife her food. She was so hungry that she paid no attention to him while she was eating. He was able to take the 1914 ship's log without her noticing. He gave the key to the captain's cabin to his sea wife and said, "Tell my father that I fed his sea wife and locked her in. Tell him I went on shore leave and give him back his key." This surprised her because he had never gone on shore leave before, but she didn't say anything. She thought, "He's always acted strange, but he treats me well."

He left the ship carrying his plunder in a duffel bag. The young seaman got away from the waterfront as quickly as he could. He didn't want to attract attention, so he checked into a sleazy unheated two dollar a week room. He locked the door to the room and then pulled the log book out of his duffle bag. When Ernst opened it, he found two hundred twenty dollar gold pieces; two thousand dollars in cash. He was rich.

DEATH FOLLOWED

CHAPTER SIX

There was no need to stick around Seattle. Ernst immediately went to a barbershop for a shave and a haircut, and then he purchased a low priced but serviceable suit, a white shirt, a tie, new shoes and a decent piece of luggage. He ditched his seaman's clothes and left town on the first outbound train. The ex-sailor was pleasantly surprised when no one bothered him at the terminal. Apparently Captain Richter had not reported him to the police. Ernst thought, "He probably wants the pleasure of hunting me down and killing me himself. Maybe he thinks I couldn't make it on shore with all the land lovers, but he's wrong." He didn't want to take any chance that the captain he had betrayed might catch up with him. He had seen enough of Herman Richter's violence and brutality to know that his adoptive father could lay claim to the title of "the most dangerous man in the world."

America was still in the Great Depression when Ernst went on the run. Homeless men with criminal records were a dime a dozen. No one paid attention to drifters as long as they kept moving. Wages were pitifully low; some men were laboring for a dollar a day. Ernst had plenty of money, but he wanted to make it last. He was also very secretive about his finances because he felt it would be dangerous not to be that way.

Captain Richter had repeatedly told him about how difficult it would be to live on land. Ernst found the pace of life was much faster than being aboard a ship, but he enjoyed the increased tempo. As he traveled southward, he considered various means of transportation available. Those with little or no money hitched rides on freight cars, but that could be very dangerous. Buying a car was not always a good idea back then. Engines had to be warmed up, and tires were not as durable. Automobiles had to follow the primitive roads which existed prior to the interstate highway system. Many were unpaved, and not necessarily the shortest distance between two points. Horses were still being used, but they had to be corralled or stabled. Many horses did not like to travel at night, especially when taking short cuts over rough terrain. There was also the option of walking. A man on foot could start out whenever he wanted and could travel all night without stopping, but Ernst regarded walking as a last resort.

He got off the train in Los Angeles, and then caught a bus which took him into Arizona. He met a trucker who appreciated his company while driving non-stop to Dallas. After the trucker let him off in Big D, the wanderer began to make the rounds.

He encountered a dark haired, dark eyed young man like himself named Sal Cardinale. Sal was a couple of years older. He said he had been born in Italy and that he had fled his homeland to avoid being forced to join Mussolini's army. Sal had an interest in prize fighting, and he hoped to pick up some money as a pro-

DEATH FOLLOWED

fessional boxer. His plan was to go to New Orleans. He had heard about a famous trainer named Whitey Esnault, who ran the St. Mary's Italian Gym along the waterfront. Ernst asked him, "Can you make any money at that?" For a young man who had only recently had any bucks, he had become obsessed with it.

"The purses aren't much; twenty dollars for four rounds, forty for six rounds and sixty for an eight round main event. The real money is made from side bets."

"It doesn't sound like much for getting your head beat in."

"If you know how to box, you can keep from getting beat up. The best fighters don't look like fighters. I know how to move, jab, slip punches and avoid a beating."

The Italian encouraged his new friend to join him at the gym where he was working out while waiting for a fight to come along. After Ernst showed that he had a fast pair of dukes, his new buddy started giving the former seaman some training tips. Sal was very encouraging. Ernst became intrigued when the young Italian told him, "Use your right hand to protect your chin, and your left hand as your sword." That was something the young man who was so talented with a knife could relate to.

After working with his new pal, Sal said, "If you improved your skills, you could become a great boxer. Right now, you're just a brawler." Ernst could see that the Italian might be useful. He paid attention to what the young boxer was teaching him and sharpened up his technique by mastering the subtleties of the jab and the left hook.

Ernst became curious about Cardinale's financial situation, especially after he began paying regular visits to the aspiring prizefighter's living quarters. Sal rented a cottage in a sparsely populated section of town. It consisted of a twelve by eighteen foot room, plus a bathroom. At one end of the room was an oil heater. Eighteen inches away from the heater was a kitchen and dining area. The opposite end contained a closet and the bathroom, which included a shower stall and a hot water heater. It was a cozy residence finished in pine trim and wall board. The floor was covered in linoleum, and the place was spotless.

Ernst said to his friend, "If you don't mind my asking, how much do you pay for this?"

"Forty dollars a month, plus utilities."

"Not bad."

Sal added, "I had to pay two months in advance. It's owned by a cabinet maker who has a shop nearby. He was a funny guy to deal with. The lease was written on a blank sheet of paper in pencil. He kept the only copy. He told me, 'Since you don't have a filing cabinet, I'll keep this in my files over at the shop. Any time you want to see it, stop by, go to my filing cabinet and look for it. It'll be under 'L' for lease, or maybe 'C' for cottage.'"

On his way back to his own place, Ernst wondered, "What does Sal do for money? He's at the gym practically every day, and he doesn't seem to have a job."

DEATH FOLLOWED

Early one morning, Ernst went by Sal's cottage as usual. When he knocked on the door this time, he found it was unlocked. He stepped inside and saw Sal's corpse. Someone had used a shotgun on him and blown away his face, making him nearly impossible to identify. A piece of paper with a black hand drawn on it was pinned to the boxer's chest. Ernst had heard enough about the Mafia and the Camorra from Captain Richter to realize that the problem Sal had been running away from was not Mussolini, but a vendetta. He made an on the spot decision to adopt Sal's identity. He took the drawing, Sal's identification, his watch, his jewelry and all his cash, which amounted to thirty dollars. He thought, "He has to have more than this. Maybe he's hidden some loot in his other belongings." He was just about to begin searching the clothes in the closet or looking for hollowed out books like the one Captain Richter had, when he felt something in the leather belt that was in Sal's slacks. Upon closer examination, he discovered a zipper on the inside of the belt. When he opened it, he found eleven diamonds. Ernst thought, "He was probably shot by a hired killer who had been in too big a hurry to search for valuables." The stones were later appraised at fifteen thousand dollars. With his new identity and nest egg, it was time to move on.

DEATH FOLLOWED

DEATH FOLLOWED

CHAPTER SEVEN

The former seaman made his way to Louisiana as Sal Cardinale. He began working along the docks in New Orleans where shipbuilding was in high gear. Nearly two years after he had left the ship, Sal happened to run into an old sailor in a waterfront bar who was too old to be part of a ship's crew. He felt comfortable enough to mention to the old man that he also been to sea. He said, "I realized it was not for me when I saw giant rocks with razor sharp edges that seemed to crouch like sea monsters with their jaws wide open."

The older man agreed. "They could crush a ship like a boot heel grinding down a walnut on a hardwood floor."

"By the way," said Sal, "did you ever hear of a Captain Herman Richter?"

The old salt surprised him. He not only knew Captain Richter, but revealed two amazing things. The first was that Richter had been relieved of command, forcibly removed from his ship and placed in an institution for the insane. The old seaman said, "I visited him once, and that was enough. I could only look at him through a small glass window in a door. He had been thrown in with other madmen. He was constantly walking in a circle and drooling. His face was twisted, his eyes were vacant and there was human waste around him on the floor." When Sal asked him if he had ever met the captain's wife, the old seaman confided, "He never had a wife. What decent woman would marry a brute like him?" After hearing that, Sal realized that all the talk by the captain about being his long lost son was a delusion. It all fell into place.

Sal thought, "Herman Richter wanted to take control of me, mold me and shape me in his image as if I were a mound of clay, keep me around forever and make me his slave. This proves it wasn't luck or the will of any god that I escaped. I'm part of a superior species fit to survive. In fact, what that captain did to my manhood was a blessing. I am no longer vulnerable to women. Thanks to him, I learned about the ultimate excitement: Taking a human life. I now know I am above any laws made by man."

Since he could make up his own rules, he had no problem with engaging in criminal behavior for profit. He gathered bits and pieces about the national crime syndicate that had a major presence in the New Orleans area. He learned that the local big boss was Carlos Marcello, and that Jefferson Parish, on the other side of the Mississippi, had one of the biggest concentrations of gambling houses in America. There was a door to opportunity. He just had to find the key.

Things fell into place when he encountered an unusual woman in a waterfront bar. She had a beautiful face, but nature had mistreated her. She was 5' 11" and had broad shoulders, huge hands and big feet. He thought, "She has to wear at least a size eleven shoe." She came across as a big boned showgirl.

The first time he saw her, she was in a poker game with four men. There was a woman sitting next her, and they acted very affectionately; almost like boyfriend and girlfriend. A hefty pot amounting to two hundred dollars was on the table. It all came down to her and a man who weighed a good two hundred pounds. He held a pair of aces, but she had three of a kind. She won the pot, but the big guy accused her of cheating. Despite a thirty five pound weight disadvantage, she pounded the daylights out of him and thought that settled the issue. Unfortunately, she was wrong. He turned out to be a relative of somebody important. She was arrested and charged with assault and battery.

Sal thought, "Any woman as tough as her has to be useful." He learned that her name was Lucretia Stevens, but she preferred being called Luke. He was also told that the woman sitting next to her at the poker game was her lover.

Sal settled her legal problems by bailing her out, paying her fine and handing money for medical expenses to the man she had knocked out. He took her to an oyster bar because he wanted to discuss a business partnership with her. Her first question was, "Why are you doing this?" She told him, "I won't put out for you. I don't like men. I'm a lesbian."

He replied, "So what else is new. I could tell that a mile away." He assured her he was not interested in anything sexual. He needed a woman to pose as his wife because he wanted to become part of organized crime. He said, "The Mob is huge here in New Orleans. The top man is Carlos Marcello. He's connected with Frank Costello, the head of the syndicate in New York. I heard that they gave Huey Long a million dollars to see that slot machines were legalized in Louisiana, and that they took in two million the first year. I'm from Italy, but in order for me to be accepted, I have to be married and have children." She asked, "What about the kids? How are we going to have any if we don't have sex?"

"We can buy some. Orphanages around the world are trying to sell them, just like potatoes."

Since he seemed to be putting his cards on the table, she told him her story. He had told her he was twenty one, and she said she was four years older than that. He had lied to her, though. The papers he carried for his assumed identity showed he was twenty one, but he was actually six years younger than her.

Luke had come from a farm in the Midwest, near where the states of Nebraska, South Dakota, Iowa and Minnesota converge. It was a place where hard working farmers prospered, but her family didn't. The hard scrabble existence she grew up in would today be regarded as abject poverty. Her mother ran around with other men. Her father suffered from ill health that made him unable to work steadily. He used his medical issues as an excuse to get drunk as often as he could afford to. He was of such weak character that he did nothing about his wife's cheating ways except call his only daughter the same dirty names that he called his wife. Her brothers left the farm as soon as they were old enough.

She was fight-crazy from the time she was a little girl. She loved mixing it up with boys, and she always threw the first punch. All of them were afraid of the unusually strong, big boned girl. The girls used to call her "our bodyguard," and she became an enforcer willing to beat up anyone for any perceived disrespect toward her friends. She had to keep her lesbian desires a secret because if any of her girlfriends knew about them, she would have been ostracized. Her sexual frustration eventually fueled so much rage within her that by the time she left home at the age of sixteen, Luke showed the eye of the beast to all she looked at. By then, her parents couldn't control her, and they believed she was a bad seed. When she finally ran away, no one seemed to care.

She looked older than her age, and was able to hang out in bars where she met her first lesbian lovers. She also began turning tricks, but quickly decided that it was more lucrative to get her customers drunk or knock them out and then roll them for whatever money they had. She was tough enough and vicious enough to handle any who fought back. She loved attending prize fights, and she learned a great deal about how to deliver a punch. The rough girl from the farm country became talented not only with her fists, but with a straight razor.

As time went on, Luke developed into a skillful poker player. It was no longer a game but an industry for her. She also fell into the lesbian lifestyle. She ended the story of her background by saying, "I think I was born too late. Back in the days of the Old West, whores, gamblers and coyotes were accepted. Now, they've all been made outlaws."

He replied, "It's the so called respectable people who are the biggest thieves. Don't worry about that. We're declaring war against society. We'll make ourselves acceptable, but we'll live according to our own rules."

She didn't ask him about his life and he didn't offer any information. As the years went by, his true identity would remain a secret. Since she had no problems with his being so mysterious, the unlikely duo quickly formed an alliance. They would lead an unconventional lifestyle. With Sal, she felt free to do many of the things she wanted. As far he was concerned, she was strictly property that would serve his needs. They were not lovers in any sense of the word. They were lethal allies; partners in crime who found joy in committing violent acts.

DEATH FOLLOWED

DEATH FOLLOWED

CHAPTER EIGHT

Sal and Lucretia were married in a civil ceremony before a probate judge with no witnesses. It was strictly a marriage of convenience. He made contact with the Mob and was accepted by Carmen Zontini, an old timer who took him on as an apprentice. The newcomer's first assignment was to eliminate a member of the underworld who had withheld money from the Mob. Sal efficiently performed the assassination by sneaking up behind his victim, putting him in a choke hold and slitting his throat with his trusty Bowie knife. He went to the additional effort of cutting off both of the man's hands. He brought the severed extremities, complete with the rings which adorned them, to Carmen and said, "I decided to send a strong message to any scumbag who might think of stealing money from *La Familia*."

With his undeniable propensity to kill, Sal quickly moved up in the organization. He also won the mobsters over with his sense of humor. A practical joke that he had learned while aboard Captain Richter's ship was the thing that put him over during the first Mob get together he attended.

One of the older members of the syndicate had become bored during the proceedings and dozed off. Sal very quietly went to the sleeping mobster and stuck a book of matches along the side of one of his shoes. He had folded back the cover to expose all the matches. When he ignited them, they burst into flame with a whoosh. To the amusement of all present, the gangster jumped up from his nap and feverishly tried to keep his trousers from catching fire. The one conducting the meeting said, "Kid, you're all right. You're one of us." Even the victim of the joke laughed at what Sal had done.

After being brought into the Mob, he started out doing muscle work; collecting for loan sharks and contract killings. He was put on a retainer of one hundred fifty dollars per week and was paid a negotiated fee for each contract hit. They were impressed with his ability to pull off assassinations using knives. They always offered him firearms, but he would say, "Thanks, but no thanks. I prefer a 'blade' to a "piece.' Knives don't jam like pistols, you don't have to worry about bullets and there's no need to use a silencer. Besides, killings should be done up close and personal." Sal was so vicious that he was given the nickname *Pazzo*, which meant deranged.

As talented as he was as a professional assassin, he realized that he would have to prove that he could be a "good earner" in order to advance in the organization. Several of the bosses told him, "Gangsters don't spend their time killing people. Making money is what should be on their minds."

He won their trust, and they had big plans for him. In 1944, the Mob bosses were becoming concerned about their members being targeted by ambitious politicians seeking to gain favorable publicity. Sal had told them that he was from Italy, and this put him at risk of being deported. If he enlisted in the service, he would be granted citizenship. Giuseppe Bertolani, a jeweler in the French Quarter, was chosen to talk to Cardinale about going in the Army.

Giuseppe was hesitant to do it. He thought, "It would mean not only putting his life at risk, but also leaving his wife at home. Sal and Luke seem to be a very close couple. Her being alone would be very hard because they have no children, even though I'm sure they've been trying very hard to have some."

The jeweler was surprised when Sal said, "I would be proud to serve the country that has welcomed me with open arms. Luke knows how much I love America, and she's willing to make such a great sacrifice. The only thing that's held me back is my shady past. I don't what can be done about that."

Giuseppe replied, "Don't worry. We have connections."

Sal thought, "This means I will have government records, photographs and fingerprints verifying that I'm Sal Cardinale. My reinvention will be complete."

He enlisted in the Army without any problems. By sheer coincidence, he was assigned to a unit being sent to the Pacific that included Matt Logan.

Matt had come from wealth. In addition to being a successful attorney, his father was an excellent role model who did all he could to encourage his son becoming a man among men. This included getting him into boxing. He sent his son to the St. Mary's Italian Gym in the French Quarter by the waterfront. It occupied a twenty four foot by sixty foot space sandwiched between a saloon and a funeral parlor. It was run by Whitey Esnault, a Navy veteran of World War I. Matt's father encouraged him to go there because he wanted him to become exposed to all levels of society and not turn out to be a "butlered adult with an anchor for a heart"

From the moment Matt and Sal first met, they hated each other. Sal considered Matt a member of a pure race, but a weakling. In Cardinale's view, the son of the prominent New Orleans attorney wasn't emotionally strong enough. He was a "bleeding heart." Matt regarded Cardinale as a brute and sensed there was nothing but evil within him.

The Italian boxer whose identity Cardinale stole had wanted to be trained by Esnault. When Sal heard about Logan's boxing experiences, he said to him, "Whitey once offered to train me, but I got sidetracked when I married, and then the war came along. We'll have to spar some time." He relished the thought of getting the rich boy in the ring, busting his nose and then knocking him out. Matt Logan had met some rough characters in the fight game, but he was to find that none were as vicious as Sal Cardinale.

Their unit was sent to New Guinea. The voyage took nearly a month, and water was in short supply. Sal "appropriated" a fire bucket filled with sand. He dumped the sand out and used it to catch rainwater, which was plentiful because brief showers fell practically every day. He padlocked the bucket to one of the chains supporting his hammock so that it wouldn't "walk off." Cardinale was one of the few GI's who were able to bath and shave regularly and he didn't share his bucket with anyone else.

There were nineteen highly insubordinate characters in Matt and Sal's unit. The officers referred to them as "misfits" or "hard cases." They had either been in trouble with the law or had been small time criminals. After their ship finally landed, they were constantly looking for ways to get out of assigned duties and always scrounging for liquor. They weren't very successful because they had been sent to a place with dense forests and jungles and no local merchants. One of the men was Jewish, and he would often say, "I was paid for my brain and not my brawn when I was a civilian. I'm not going to do anymore backbreaking work when the war is over. I'm too smart for that."

Sal quickly earned a reputation as a man with invincible nerve who could be counted on to carry out the most grisly and hazardous assignments without any mistakes. He had no qualms about crawling on his belly or back through mud or wet ground to infiltrate behind enemy lines. He successfully completed numerous nighttime missions and killed several enemy soldiers in the process. The enlisted man from New Orleans had an uncanny ability to remain silent and stationary for extended periods of time, which enhanced his chances of sneaking up on the enemy at night. None of the men he served with understood the joy Sal experienced on these missions. He thought, "I could never explain how exciting it is to kill at night. It's much better than daylight hours but to me, there's no such thing as a bad kill." Taking lives gave him the ultimate high, and no one could imagine how it sexually aroused him. He also had "command presence;" another term for charisma. The lieutenant in charge relied on Cardinale to keep the misfits in line, and he had no problem doing it because they were scared to death of him.

DEATH FOLLOWED

DEATH FOLLOWED

CHAPTER NINE

Fighting in New Guinea was an ordeal. The military brass failed to send the number of soldiers needed, and the situation was made worse by the ones there having been rushed into combat with insufficient training. They had to contend with insects that bit them savagely, dense vegetation and soft ground. In addition, water and mud dominated their lives. There were times when it rained every day for an entire month. It got to the point where they no longer noticed they were wet. They lived with mud every day and bedded down with it at night. After the war, the ones who made it back home thought of New Guinea whenever they saw mud.

The lieutenant in command of Matt and Sal's platoon was fair complexioned, small and wiry. Matt thought, "He's so fair skinned that he probably didn't have to shave until he was twenty five." With so many draftees from coal mines, cotton mills and small farms among Logan's fellow infantrymen, many of them became frightened when they faced the enemy. Even the hard cases froze when things got nasty. Lieutenants and sergeants were supposed to tell the ones showing fear, "Just stay close to me and give me an extra set of eyes. You let me know where the enemy is, and I'll shoot them." Sal and Matt's lieutenant couldn't bring himself to fill that role. Sal thought, "He doesn't have any balls. Guess I'll have to take over." Many officers would have been concerned that Cardinale was much too comfortable with killing and that he had a mental disorder, but Sal and his lieutenant came to an unspoken understanding. The lieutenant relied on him to perform the nastiest assignments and in return, the Crescent City G.I. was allowed to do practically anything he wanted.

Even though he couldn't bring himself to actually take a human life, the lieutenant intensely hated the Japanese and wanted them exterminated so badly that he was willing to use his own money to give his men additional motivation. He started the "Dime a Dozen Club." The lieutenant was making a little less than eighty dollars a month, but he was willing to pay ten cents for every twelve Japanese soldiers his men killed. Each kill had to be witnessed. Sal never failed to collect enough to keep him in beer money.

Sal was the best armed man in his unit. He obtained any weapon he wanted by whatever means it took; whether begging, borrowing or stealing. In addition to his knives and M 1 carbine, he had a Thompson submachine gun that used the same bullets as his M1911 Colt .45 pistol, plus he had a shotgun. He used hand grenades, when available, and would sometimes make Molotov cocktails by filling empty plasma bottles with gasoline. He also had his fists, which he mainly used during his leisure time activities.

The days in the Pacific were not entirely about combat and bloodshed. Entertainment was provided. The soldiers were shown Hollywood films on big screens that had been set up outside. It could be miserable to watch outdoor movies in the tropics because of all the rain. Sal won even more support from the guys in his platoon when he managed to barter for some alcohol. The men would mix it with fruit juice and fill their canteens with the concoction on movie nights. It made the night fun even though they were soaking wet.

A young soldier named Irv Abramson from Brooklyn provided a needed diversion during the times when the enemy wasn't being engaged. Abramson was serving in the Army Air Corps. He was a gunner for a unit known as "Kelly's Darlings," and ended up flying sixty four missions. He also staged boxing shows for the troops in the Pacific. The shows attracted crowds as large as fourteen thousand, and there was a lot of wagering on the fights.

One of the biggest matches Abramson staged was a light heavyweight bout between Matt Logan and Sal Cardinale. Since both fighters claimed New Orleans as home, Abramson dubbed it "The Crescent City Showdown." There was heavy betting action, and Sal was a seven to five favorite.

Their bout went the full eight rounds, and Matt won a split decision. Each of the two judges voted for a different fighter, so the deciding vote was cast by the referee. The referee was a medic, who was also a closet homosexual. The decision infuriated Sal, and he vowed to pay the ref back. Cardinale baited the medic by going on a nude walk in the jungle. Once he had maneuvered the medic into a secluded place, he strangled him.

Sal reported finding the medic's corpse to fair skinned lieutenant. He said, "The Japs must have done him in. It's a shame because everybody liked him so much." Even though he suspected Sal was lying, the lieutenant protected him as he always did, and the murder ended up being swept under the rug. Matt couldn't get over it. It suddenly dawned on him how evil Sal was. He thought, "We had the best medic of all, and Sal put us in jeopardy by killing him. And all because of a boxing match." The medic's death was another bad memory which contributed to Logan's post war nightmares.

Matt was traumatized by the bloody Pacific campaign, but Cardinale reveled in it. Their personalities were complete opposites, but they were thrust together by fate and hated each other's guts from their very first meeting. When the war ended and they went their separate ways, Matt tried to forget about Sal. Cardinale, on the other hand, carried within him a strong desire to kill Logan simply because Matt had dishonored his race and wasn't fit to live.

DEATH FOLLOWED

CHAPTER TEN

Sal came back a decorated war hero with the rank of first sergeant. He was even awarded a good conduct medal. Matt Logan thought, "If they only knew the truth." Cardinale flaunted his heroism, played the role to the hilt and milked it for all it was worth. He became very prominent within the American Legion because of his war record, his martial prowess and his chivalric grandeur. They loved his *macho* comments. "The worst day of my life was putting on civilian clothes. Only the civilians want to forget the war. It's all tattooed in my head." A country western singer who belonged to the Legion serenaded him with a song written in his honor.

> Cardinale, you fought hard,
>
> Cardinale, you tried.
>
> You were a good soldier,
>
> So hold your head high.
>
> Some great ones faltered,
>
> But you'd never fall.
>
> Cardinale the brave,
>
> You gave your all.

The first order of business after the war for Sal and his wife Luke was a trip to Mexico. He had learned of an orphanage in San Pedro that was making appeals to Americans for donations to solve their financial difficulties. He kept the purpose of their trip a secret and told his Mob associates, "Luke and I are going to Mexico for a homecoming celebration. We've got to make up for lost time. I've been away from her for too long." The truth was that their only relationship during the war was her cashing his allotment checks.

Luke loved playing the role of Mrs. Cardinale. Her sham marriage was the perfect cover for her lesbian activities which spiked during the war. Her height, large hands and large feet made it possible for her to pass as a man and pick up women. She added to the deception by removing the hairpiece that hid her buzz cut and wearing turtle neck sweaters to conceal her not having an Adam's apple. Luke would also stuff a rolled up sock into the front of her underwear so she could masquerade as a well-endowed male. She trolled social clubs and charitable organizations for willing sex partners. There was a man shortage due to so many being in the service, and more women seemed willing to experiment. Luke had as much fun during the war as Sal did.

DEATH FOLLOWED

The orphanage Sal and Luke visited was surrounded by an adobe wall with an elaborately carved large wooden gate. They were met there by a nun who escorted them to Father Alexis Mendoza, the priest who was in charge. The priest said, "It is my understanding from our mutual friend that you wish to make a generous donation to our institution."

"Correct, Father." Sal pulled a thick envelope from an inside pocket of his white linen suit coat and handed it to the *padre*. "You don't have to count it. That's fifty thousand pesos."

"May the blessings of the Lord be with both you and your lovely wife."

"I ask one indulgence, Father. My wife and I are childless. We would like to provide a good home to a male baby."

The priest wasn't the sort to look a gift horse in the mouth. He said, "That is possible, but there are certain expenses involved."

"Would twenty thousand pesos cover those additional expenses?"

"That would be most generous."

Sal reached into a briefcase he had carried with him and produced another envelope. He said, "No need to count it. It's all there."

Father Mendoza dispatched a nun to bring a charcoal haired male infant to the Cardinales'. He also said to the good sister, "Make sure the appropriate documents are prepared for them."

Having concluded their transaction, Father Al said, "Would you care for some wine? The Lord has blessed me with a barrel of an excellent vintage."

Sal and Luke nodded in agreement, whereupon the priest opened a cabinet and brought out a tray with a crystal carafe filled with red wine and three glasses. The padre offered up a toast. He said, "To devout believers, to generous donations, to compassionate parents and to excellent wine."

Sal chose to name the baby boy Stefano, and he would call him Steve. In order to maintain secrecy, Sal sent Luke and Steve to a remote but surprisingly pleasant island off the northern coast of French Guiana he had discovered during his days as a seaman. It was a penal colony for women known as Whore Island. The warden was corrupt, and he allowed his prisoners to sell their bodies to the crews of passing ships. For five thousand francs, Sal gained his full cooperation. Luke enjoyed her stay there immensely. Many of the inmates had babies of their own, the food was great, she was able to sunbath in the nude, achieve a magnificent tan and have her choice of several willing female sex partners.

DEATH FOLLOWED

Sal told all his friends and acquaintances that Luke had gone back up to her home in the Midwest to have their child. When the mother and baby son arrived back in New Orleans, he hosted a party celebrating the reunion and made a public presentation to her of a magnificent piece of jewelry. It was an eighteen carat gold medallion which was two inches in diameter, surrounded by diamonds and accompanied by a heavy gold chain. The front of the medallion bore the initials "S. C." and "L. C." and the back was inscribed "My lover forever." It set Sal back $300, the price of a good used car back then, but it was all a show for the benefit of his Mafia associates. Everyone there mentioned that, "Luke looks fantastic and the *bambino* looks just like the *papa*." Sal thought, "It doesn't take much to fool people who want to believe something is true."

DEATH FOLLOWED

DEATH FOLLOWED

CHAPTER ELEVEN

The Mob placed Cardinale in charge of the most lucrative high end brothel in the South. It was located at 1410 Monroe Street in Gretna, Louisiana. Gretna once had a large German population and was in Jefferson Parish, known for all its gambling houses. When Matt Logan heard tales of what his old sergeant was up to, he immediately put them out of his mind. He thought, "He's a mad dog capable of anything. Nothing he does would surprise me."

Sal's bordello was a very low key operation that didn't need signage, neon lights or advertising. Its clientele knew how to get there, and they were assured that whatever went on remained a secret. Each customer received five star accommodations. All twenty suites in the brothel were beautifully decorated and featured first class linens, goose down pillows, larger than normal towels, the better soaps and shampoos, luxurious carpeting, quality glassware and twenty four hour room service. The Mob preferred that their involvement be kept quiet. Some of the customers suspected an underworld connection, but none of them knew for sure.

The girls who worked there did not know they were working for the Mob. They were not allowed to collect for their services. Each of their customers opened an account, and a bill was sent to their home for any hospitality they enjoyed at the Gretna bordello. The invoice was printed "Southland Service and Supply." A number of Sal's regulars confided that they used the invoices as tax deductions for business expenses. The underworld appreciated Sal's efforts to avoid publicity at all cost. He assured them, "If the politicians ever come after me, I won't challenge them. That would be a losing game. The secret is to do things in ways that don't attract attention."

The Mob's desire to keep what went on at Sal's brothel so secretive worked against them in one sense. In most U.S. cities back then, the Mob ran the gay and lesbian social clubs. Luke's sexual preference would have become known where it not for the money the brothel generated and the underworld's confidence in Sal Cardinale. He and Luke were remarkable in their ability to deceive the crime syndicate.

Sal's elite whore house became renowned among wealthy and powerful men from all over the nation wishing to act out their sexual fantasies. It was always busy, but especially so during Sugar Bowl season, Mardi Gras and Spring Fiesta time. He built it into a real moneymaker for the underworld, but Sal realized that, like all other hoodlums, he was only a cog in a big wheel. He often thought, "When you work with the Mob, sooner or later you lose your independence."

DEATH FOLLOWED

He was very sociable and outgoing at public appearances, but behind the doors of his brothel, Sal's severe gaze glinted out of an impassive face. He had Luke to deal with the whores, so he seldom left his suite on the top floor. His meals were brought to him by a mulatto woman who was the only person of color employed at the bordello. She was the only one allowed to clean his quarters, and he often tested her honesty by leaving twenty dollar bills on the floor. She always passed the test. Her fear of her employer kept her in line.

The main room of his large suite served as his office. His desk was on a round platform which was raised four inches above the floor, and steps on both sides made it easier to get up and down from it. Anyone who took a seat in front of his desk had to look up to him. One wall was a hideaway door which tilted and opened into his bedroom. The bedroom was huge and luxurious. The bed was covered with a black bedspread. Framed photographs of Sal with celebrities hung on the walls. Some of the celebrities were customers of the brothel. A portrait of a pig was displayed between two Bowie knives. It reminded him of his first kill. A large glass cabinet contained "trophies," objects he had taken from his victims.

He wore fine silk or tweed jackets and Countess Mara ties in bold colors. A fresh red carnation was in his lapel each and every day. His mulatto maid saw to it that there were always three carnations in a vase on the night table in his bedroom. Each morning, he would take a pair of scissors, snip the stem of a carnation and place the flower in his lapel. His footwear was either Cuban heels or cowboy boots. His favorite pair of boots was made of pure white ostrich and brown kangaroo. They had an intricate western design, were nicely pointed and perfectly modeled. The tops were soft and pliable, and there was firmness over the instep. They fit so well that when he flexed his toes, the ripple of his tendons could be seen under the leather. Even though he was six feet tall, he often wore three inch lifts in his footwear to make him appear even more menacing.

The proprietor of the house of debauchery was always armed with his specially designed Bowie knife that he carried in a sheath attached to a shoulder harness. Its handle was made of ebony, the same material used for castanets and clarinets, and its deadly blade was ten and a quarter inches long. The weapon had been crafted for Sal by a maker of surgical instruments. It had been blued and bore gold decorations, and was kept sharp enough to take a man's arm off with one swipe. He thought if it as "my Excalibur."

Sal wore dark glasses as often as possible to prevent people from noticing the cold, distant look in his eyes. His trademark became a taupe broad brimmed hat he always wore. Its sides were folded up, and it was decorated with three miniature daggers. Two of the daggers were used to pin the sides of the hat, while the third was an emblem placed on the front of the crown. No one knew how much the daggers meant to Sal.

The tip of each dagger came from knives which were very significant in his life. He used one to kill the pig when he was eight years old, under orders from the insane Captain Richter. He used another to kill his first man. The third was used to kill his first woman. His hat was his symbol; his *rubrica*.

DEATH FOLLOWED

He often hobnobbed with other mobsters to maintain his reputation. He once made a huge impression by challenging them to a hot sauce eating contest. He produced a large container of a condiment made from extremely hot Mexican chili peppers. When his opposition placed tablespoons of the concoction in their mouths, their eyes popped out and their throats closed up as tight as drums. He gave them no sympathy and said, "It's a throat burner, eye glazer and stomach murderer, but I can handle it."

Sal boldly excavated a heaping spoonful of the stuff from the jar he had brought to the gathering, opened his mouth and placed it on his tongue. He held it in his mouth and savored the fiery substance. His color changed, his face turned red, his eyes began to tear up and he rose up from the table. While standing, he placed another heaping spoonful between his teeth and his left cheek, as if it were a chaw of tobacco. He then put a third spoonful between his teeth and right cheek so that his mouth was thoroughly saturated with hot sauce. Sal's face perspired and his skin turned the color of a ripe tomato. He startled all the others by standing on his chair and screaming. It was hard to tell whether it was a scream of agony or a roar of triumph, possibly a combination of both. They couldn't take their eyes off him as he stepped down from the chair. Everyone was amazed that he didn't spit out any of the volcanic substance.

Cardinale looked at all the expressions of amazement and exclaimed, "Ah, there's nothing better than experiencing food and hot sensation at the same time!" Word spread throughout the Mob that Sal was one tough SOB capable of anything.

He was doing well enough financially to purchase a second baby from Father Mendoza's orphanage in San Pedro, Mexico. He gave the child Michele, a common Italian name for boys. He told his underworld buddies, "Call the kid Mike." Having a second boy made him the envy of his fellow mobsters. They never thought of Luke as being attractive, but one remarked, "She's certainly fertile enough to produce two masculine children. I wish mine were as fertile. All six of my kids are girls."

DEATH FOLLOWED

DEATH FOLLOWED

CHAPTER TWELVE

The leaders of the national crime syndicate never interfered with Sal Cardinale's highly lucrative operation, but they once made a discrete visit to the brothel in hopes of learning the secret of its success. Sal's place was bringing in more money than any other whore house in America. They told him, "Your house runs like a finely made Swiss watch." His fellow mobsters said that he ran the place like a stable of race horses, but that wasn't true. Owners of horses often have an emotional connection to their steeds. Sal showed no more feelings toward his prostitutes than if he were running a meat processing plant.

He provided his sex workers with housing, meals, wardrobes, cosmetics and anything else they might require. He also had a physician, Dr. Bert Schultz, who tended to any of the courtesans' medical needs. Sal never let on to Bert that they had both spent many years at sea. Dr. Schultz had previously served as a ship's doctor for an ocean liner, back when such vessels were the preferred means of traveling abroad. He lost his position after he was caught in bed with the wife of a very wealthy passenger. The doctor had a weakness for the sensation of masculine power he experienced whenever he sampled the brothel's merchandise. This was fine with Sal because it was a way to reduce the medical expenses by allowing Dr. Schultz to take some of his fees out in trade.

Cardinale kept fifty percent of what each whore brought in. He kept track of all their expenses, no matter how big or small, and made sure he got every penny back. Since none of them knew they were working for a Mob operation, they thought Sal was in complete charge. As far as the government was concerned, the whores were employed by "Southland Service and Supply" as sales representatives working on straight commission. He believed in the motivational value of keeping his prostitutes on edge, so he had them sign written contracts that allowed their services to be terminated on only three days' notice.

He told them, "Don't worry if your reported earnings are very low. This way you'll pay very little, if any, taxes. Besides we have a great retirement plan." He assured them that when they became thirty and were starting to no longer command top dollar, they would be able to retire. He promised them all a "nice little home someplace where it's never too hot or too cold." In reality, he "retired" them by killing them, then dumping the bodies in nearby swamps to be devoured by alligators. He would boast to the new hires, "I've been trying to hold a reunion of the girls who used to work here for years, but I can't pull it off. They're all so caught up in their new lives that they can never make it back here. If you follow orders, the same thing will happen to you."

To Sal, killing was better than sex. The act of slitting a whore's throat was the buildup; the foreplay. His victim's moment of death produced a climax which released him from his sexual tension. He never forgot the time he killed two whores in the same session. One watched while he slit the other's throat, and he really got off on the looks of fear he saw in their eyes. The Mob knew nothing about these murders. They were not only impressed with all the money he brought in, but also the fact that none of Sal's girls ever had anything bad to say about him. As far as they were concerned, he could do no wrong and they let him run things his way. After all, he was lining their pockets.

The brothel was a four story structure with an elevator. Each of the eighteen courtesans was assigned a suite to live in and service their customers. It was hard to become one of Sal's whores; only one out of four applicants made it. Most were eighteen to twenty four years old. Sal looked for sex workers who were soft young girls with limited perspective and limited understanding who saw things in black and white and who didn't like to think... and they had to be pretty. He preferred those from abject poverty willing to do anything to survive. He referred to the selection process as "separating squirrels from lambs." Lambs were easy to control, while squirrels were too unpredictable to suit him.

Most of the new hires were inclined to be sexually passive, which was contrary to the way prostitutes had to be. Luke had to show them what to do, and she performed that job with relish. She loved having sex with them by using her hands and mouth. She was definitely a "butch." She had never enjoyed caring for her hair the way most women did and much preferred buzz cuts. She always wore long blonde wigs when she appeared in public as Mrs. Cardinale. The task of keeping up Luke's appearances was handled by a beautician who lived on the premises. She also served the function of changing the whores' hair color, makeup and hair style to suit the johns.

Luke graded the whores in thirty four categories, including how well they listened, how warmly they greeted their customers, their punctuality and how well they made sure they looked their best. Any whose grades fell below a certain standard were fined fifteen dollars. The girls were also fined fifteen dollars if they wore slacks, since most of the clientele were of a generation who regarded slacks as being too masculine. It would cost them fifteen dollars if they failed to be carefully made up, got drunk or used a piece of furniture as a footrest. If they needed some cash, Luke would loan them small sums and charge them weekly interest. She kept the records in a little leather covered black book, and no one ever stiffed her. They knew she would have taken it out of their hides. The lesbian with the broad shoulders, large hands and big feet loved to play poker with the whores. She was far better at it than any of them. It was just another means of taking away their earnings.

Sal allowed Luke to keep all the money she made from poker, fines and small loans. That was the extent of the cash she had coming in. Practically all of her creature comforts were Sal's property, including the clothes on her back. He maintained his control by often reminding her of that fact, and he hoped that one day she would become completely dependent upon him.

Luke's bedroom was furnished with a circular bed and a mirror on the ceiling. The bedspread was brown with a large bronze stripe in the middle. There were plain chairs upholstered in the same color scheme as the bedspread. The walls were painted beige. There were no flowers or candles.

DEATH FOLLOWED

She was constantly looking for new experiences through a variety of lesbian encounters. She collected bras and panties worn by her most memorable lovers. She knew that there would always be an end to their times together. When they were past the age of thirty, they would inevitably come up missing. If anyone asked their whereabouts, she would reply, "She went to see Sal and put in for her retirement. I guess she had enough of the business. I'll miss her."

A whore named Mercedes was one of those who had been disposed of. She had fallen hard for Luke, and she even wrote a poem that she placed with a rose on the madam's pillow.

Thanks for being there for me.

You've made life a revelry.

To hug and frolic between the sheets

Makes it all so complete.

Who needs boys for our joys.

I thank you so much.

Thanks for being there for me.

You're the most appealing person I've ever seen.

Imagine when we're done

With all our games and fun

And all the pleasures we will taste,

My one and only luscious cake.

I thank you so much.

I love you, Luke.

Mercedes

Luke had the poem framed, and it occupied a place of honor on her wall. No one else had ever written a poem to her, certainly not her husband in name only.

The women who worked as courtesans were afraid of Luke, but were even more fearful of Sal. They considered him the most demanding and uncomfortable person they had ever been around. His only reactions to them were icy glares and rebukes. He would occasionally assemble them for a lecture on their roles in his operation. He would begin his comments by saying, "Cling to every word I say." He also told them, "I assure you that your wardrobe and living conditions will be first class, so I expect performance. Each customer is a test. If they're satisfied and pay, you pass the test. Otherwise, you'll be gone. Just remember; I can buy and sell any of you any time I want."

He enjoyed keeping them on edge by unexpectedly walking into their rooms and seeing if they immediately stood up to acknowledge his presence and give him a cherry, "How are you, Mr. Cardinale." If they failed to do so, he would conduct a punishment drill. He would enter and reenter the room fifty times, and have them stand and greet him each time. When the drill was over, he'd say, "I'll bet you'll never forget to do that again."

Whenever any of the boys in the Mob asked him, "Do you ever sample any of your merchandise," Sal would reply, "I don't sleep with morons. Besides, Luke gives me all I can handle, and more."

DEATH FOLLOWED

CHAPTER THIRTEEN

Raising children is always difficult and even though his two boys were actually props purchased to keep up appearances, Sal Cardinale had his share of problems. When they were very young, he tried to make things as simple as possible by sending his sons to a Franciscan monastery in Mexico, where they would remain until they were in their late teens. The priests in charge were happy to cooperate with the whore master because of large sums of money he gave them to restore their old and crumbling structures. When his Mob associates asked about his sons, Sal would reply, "I sent them to private schools in Switzerland. It costs a load, but Luke and I have to take care of the most precious things in our lives. We have been blessed with two wonderful sons, and we must do our best for them." When they returned from Mexico, both he and Luke called them Stevie and Mikey. Neither son knew anything about where they had come from or about Sal's Mob ties.

Stevie and Mikey Cardinale didn't come back to New Orleans to stay until they were old enough to perform menial tasks around the brothel. Sal remained distant from them because they were the spawn of degenerates and there was a good chance that they would be trouble. He was willing to tolerate them as long as they were useful.

Stevie was good looking, but not in a ruggedly handsome way. He had dark eyes, black hair and delicate features. He was consumed by his appearance and always had to be perfectly groomed. Every hair had to be in place. Sal thought, "He's a young Rock Hudson." Stevie turned out to be a homosexual. It would have been pretty embarrassing for Sal if word of that got out, since his underworld associates were not just racist but homophobes as well.

His dad heard about it when Stevie made a pass at one of the johns. The client owned television stations in a number of states. He needed FCC approval to acquire new stations, and was greasing the path toward gaining approval by paying for frequent visits to the bordello made by high level bureaucrats. Stevie approached the television CEO, flirted with him in a soft, low voice and gave him a certain look. This made the important client very uncomfortable. He went to Sal and said, "I hate to tell you, but I think your son Steve is queer. He touched my shoulder, but did it in a way men don't. He squeezed it, and he looked at me weird." That was all Sal had to hear. He nipped the problem in the bud by slitting Stevie's throat and dumping his body in the swamp.

For the first few years after his return from Mexico, Mikey appeared to be a useful addition to Sal's operation. He was put in charge of the supply room, a position that came with a degree of responsibility. He had to keep track of the toiletries, towels, sheets, pillowcases, toilet paper and other things each whore required as part of their living conditions. This was important because they were charged for each item they received. He was detail oriented, and performed this job well. Sal never complimented him, however. He was always cold and harsh with Mikey. All he ever had to say to him was, "Take care of your mother."

His mother wasn't much better. Luke treated him like a servant, not a son. She repeatedly asked, "Mikey, sweetheart, can you do a hard favor for me." He was afraid to say no.

Still a virgin at the age of twenty, he became infatuated with one of the whores. Her name was Lynn and she had just turned thirty. He was very kind to her, giving her supplies without marking them down so that she wasn't charged. He was the first man who ever treated her as a gentleman, and she saw that as a sign of vulnerability. She decided to spend time with the youngest Cardinale and see how much she could exploit his father.

They arranged several rendezvous in the French Quarter for sexual encounters in cheap hotels. Mikey became completely attached to Lynn, and it got to the point where he wanted to have a serious conversation about their future together.

They had their talk while sitting on a bench in Jackson Square. Mikey said, "I love you, and I want you to be my wife."

Lynn's response was, "I love you so very much." She reached over and kissed him, saying, "I'm so happy we met and are together."

Mikey had a serious look on his face when he replied, "But we can't live together the way things are. We can't go on like this. I don't want you sleeping with other men. I want you to be mine alone."

"I've always wanted to be yours from the very beginning, but what are we going to do? We've got to get away and find a place of our own. Let's talk about finances."

Mikey offered, "I have a thousand dollars saved."

"I've got a little more than that." This was an outright lie. She had less than a hundred dollars to her name.

"I don't want you using your money." Mikey was a gentleman all the way, but he had made a bad choice in picking her.

Lynn replied, "I guess you'll have to figure out a way of coming up with what we need."

They returned to the brothel and continued playing their roles. She was thirty years old, but had told Mikey she was twenty five. She was unaware that she was very close to the mandatory retirement age Sal invoked. Mikey was little more than a glorified bus boy with little chance of legally accumulating the money he needed. For the first time in his life, he felt trapped. He became desperate.

Fate stepped in when Luke experienced a moment of clumsiness and knocked over a can of paint in her closet. She had forgotten to replace the lid securely, and the contents spilled out on the floor. A couple of pairs of her favorite shoes were ruined. She asked Mikey to clean up the mess.

While working in the closet, he noticed that a jacket was about ready to slip off its coat hanger. When he tried to adjust it properly, he felt several objects in the lining. This aroused his curiosity, and he examined the garment closely. When he opened a zipper, he found a leather pouch packed with something. He opened it up and was shocked to find many pieces of jewelry which he had seen his mother wear. She did not wear them very often; only when she accompanied his father to parties with their friends.

He made a sudden decision. He thought, "Lynn and I are miserable here. We can sell the jewelry. The time is right because it's only the middle of September, and Mom won't wear any of it until Columbus Day."

He hid the pouch underneath dirty linens to be picked up by a laundry service in two days. He quickly arranged to meet with Lynn at a café across from City Park. When she arrived, he excitedly gave her the good news. She said, "That's fantastic! Order me some chicory coffee and beignets."

While they were enjoying the special blend of coffee and powdered sugar snacks, he said in a joyous voice, "We'll sell the jewelry, buy a car and drive somewhere we can start our life together."

She kissed him passionately and then said, "Hey, I've got a better idea. We can make some really big money for ourselves and get away from this trap. I know just where to sell them. I also have a relative close by who can hide them until we get rid of them."

"They'll try to steal them!"

"Not if they're in a locked makeup case. Can you get one right away?"

"Yes," he said. "I'll keep one key, and you'll have the other."

Mikey immediately bought a new beige makeup case, put the jewels in it, handed the case over to Lynn and kept one of the keys. He thought, "It's a perfect plan." He didn't know that she had told him nothing but lies.

The truth was she had no relatives living nearby. She rented a locker at the New Orleans railroad terminal and stored the makeup case there. She also had no idea of where to sell the jewelry. It became a hot potato in her hands.

She decided to sell what looked like the most expensive piece and use the money to get rid of Mikey, head for California and sell the rest of it out there. She told him, "When your mother finds that her jewelry is gone and you and I are no longer around, they're going to put two and two together and call the police. Our only hope is to head for Mexico. They'll think we'll be traveling together, so we'll travel separately. You take a train, I take a bus and we meet in El Paso, Texas. We can just walk across the border to Juarez."

"Your plan is brilliant."

Lynn took an expensive piece of jewelry to a pawn shop in the French Quarter and was disappointed at what she was offered. She decided to try a jewelry store across the street. The owner was behind a counter in the back. She called to him, "I'd like to sell some jewelry. It's a medallion that's supposed to be gold."

"Do you have it with you?"

"Yes, here it is." She handed him a two inch diameter medallion attached to a heavy gold chain. Lynn didn't realize she had walked into quicksand.

The jeweler's name was Giuseppe. He took one look at the eighteen carat gold piece and thought, "I can't believe it! This woman is trying to sell me jewelry I made for Sal Cardinale and his wife Luke." Giuseppe was not only connected to the Mob, he had also purchased several rings from Luke she had won in poker games with her whores. He immediately suspected the woman of having stolen the medallion.

He said to her, "What did you say your name was?"

"I didn't. Why would you need to know?"

"In case I have to write you a check."

"Oh. Well, it's Gwendolyn."

"Gwendolyn, if I were buying this strictly for the gold and stones, I couldn't give you more than five hundred dollars."

"I know. That's what the man at the pawn shop said. Could you do a little better? I could really use the money." She looked at him flirtatiously. "I have a child to take care of."

"You're in luck. It just so happens that I've got a buyer for a medallion and gold chain just like the one you have. I would have to buff off the inscriptions, but I could pay you fifteen hundred dollars for it." Giuseppe's offer was ridiculously high, but Lynn didn't know any better.

She thought, "Fifteen hundred! Wow! That's more than enough to get Mikey to Texas and out of my hair while I go to the West Coast in style." She asked the jeweler, "When can you give me the money?"

"Let's see." He paused for a moment as if he were figuring out the logistics of dealing with the fictitious customer he mentioned, and then he said, "Bring me the medallion at this same time tomorrow. Is there a number I can reach you at?"

"I can't give it out. My boyfriend is very jealous."

"I can understand. Well then, I'll see you tomorrow."

After Lynn walked out of his store, Giuseppe immediately called Luke Cardinale. She answered in her usual husky voice, "Hello. Who's calling?"

"Luke, this is Giuseppe the jeweler."

"How have you been? I have a couple of rings for you. I'll probably stop by next week."

"That's not why I called. Something strange happened just now. A woman came in wanting to sell the medallion and gold chain I made for you and Sal years ago."

"Did you get her name? What did she look like?"

"She said her name was Gwendolyn. She had black hair, blue eyes and a warm smile. She was probably 5' 6" and 130 pounds. I asked her for a phone number, but she said she couldn't give it out because of her jealous boyfriend."

"Well, what you gave me will help a lot. If she comes back, please call me right away. Thanks ever so much, Giuseppe. Give my best to your wife, Donna."

"I will. Tell Sal not to work so hard. Goodbye."

Luke's eyes flashed with anger as she thought, "That bitch Lynn!" She ran to her closet and discovered the leather pouch was missing from the jacket. She thought, "How the hell did she get in my closet? She hasn't been in this room in months. I wore the medallion a couple of weeks ago. Maybe Mikey knows something."

She knew just where he would be. He was busy unloading supplies. She said, "Sweetheart, who's been near my closet other than you?"

"Nobody."

"Are you sure of that?'

"Yes."

He seemed a little nervous and he started to blush. She thought, "He's hiding something." She didn't question him anymore. She went to Sal, and they made their plans on how to handle the situation.

When Lynn showed up at the jeweler's the next day, Giuseppe asked her to go into his back room with him. He said, "The customer wants their merchandise right away and I have to write you a check immediately." As she stepped into the room, both Sal and Luke were there to grab her.

They took her to a nearly empty warehouse and sat her down at a table in a small office. Luke pushed down on her shoulders while Sal grabbed her right arm with his left hand and slammed it on the table. He brandished his Bowie knife in his right hand as he menacingly said, "Tell me who else is involved. If you don't, I'll cut off your index finger." He lightly rubbed the blade along her arm for emphasis.

Lynn had chills and her face turned white. She answered in a very low voice, "Your...your son Mikey put me up to it."

Sal responded, "What was that? I can't hear you."

Her voice became louder, but there was still a tremble to it. "I...I...I said your son Mikey put me up to it."

"Is that so? Why would he do that?"

She began to sob. "He thinks he's in love with me. What are you gonna do to us?"

"Don't worry," said Sal. "You're about ready for retirement, aren't you?"

Lynn answered in a little girl voice, "Yes."

Sal went to the door of the office, turned and said, "I'll be back in a little while."

He returned thirty minutes later with Mikey. His son's face turned chalk white when he saw Lynn. Sal asked, "Who has the jewelry?"

Mikey and Lynn looked at each other before she answered, "I do."

"Is it nearby?"

"It's in a locker at the New Orleans train station."

Sal then said, "Luke is going to drive you there. Bring it back and you'll be all right. If it's not where you say it is, she'll kill you."

Luke and Lynn returned with the makeup case nearly an hour later. When they walked in the warehouse, they saw Mikey's body on the floor. They went close enough to it to see that his throat had been slit. As Lynn let out a piercing scream, Sal came up behind her, grabbed her and slit her throat. After her lifeless form dropped to the ground, he said, "This is what happens when you deal with degenerates. They wanted to be with each other so badly and now they're getting their wishes. They'll be rotting together forever."

Sal and Luke disposed of the bodies by dumping them in the swamp. As they were driving back to the bordello, he asked, "Did you get all your jewelry back?"

"No."

"What's missing?"

Luke became teary eyed before she answered, "The beautiful medallion you gave me. I feel so stupid. I forgot to check Lynn's purse before we dumped it into the swamp with the bodies." He heard her stifle a sob before she said, "I know it's silly, but a love for you has grown in me."

Sal experienced a surge of excitement he had never known before. He thought, "At last I have absolute control over her! She is completely dependent upon me." He stared at Luke in a cold manner and asked, "Do you trust in me as your lord and master?"

She looked him in the eye with amazement, and she managed to keep a straight face when she said, "Yes. Totally."

"Then do not worry. You will always be safe in my hands."

Sal called Giuseppe the very next day. He told the jeweler that the eighteen carat medallion wasn't recovered and that he wanted a duplicate of the original made. When Luke was given the duplicate, she thought, "Double your pleasure, double your fun." The original had been in her possession all along. It was tucked away in her new hiding place; a waste basket with a false bottom that she kept in her bathroom. She had lied to Sal because, "I'd have to be crazy to believe his lord and master crap. I believe in the golden rule; she who has the gold rules. This woman is going to be busy accumulating gold."

DEATH FOLLOWED

When his Mob cronies asked where his sons were, Sal explained by saying, "Kids today are going crazy. My two boys, my pride and joys, begged me to send them to Italy so they could see where their forebears came from. Once they got there, all they did was party and spend money like water. I told them, 'No more *Lira* until you start acting right.' I haven't heard from them since. This has been hard for me because I had such high hopes for them, but it has been even worse for their mother. My poor beloved Luke has been crying all the time. I don't know if she'll ever get used to being without them. If they were to come back and say they're sorry, Luke and I would welcome them with open arms."

When Luke overheard Sal say those things to his underworld associates, she thought, "He is unbelievably amazing. As far as I'm concerned, he has earned an Oscar for his performance."

DEATH FOLLOWED

DEATH FOLLOWED

CHAPTER FOURTEEN

The brothel made Sal wealthy, but he could never get over the fact that he was a minority partner. His cut was only twenty nine percent, while national crime boss Frank Costello received twenty percent, Dandy Phil Kastel received seventeen and a half percent, Carlos Marcello got twelve and a half percent and Dudley Geigerman (Costello's brother in law) was in for twenty one percent. Sal had a dream of one day setting up an operation where he would receive practically all of the profits.

When he heard that the Scientologists had their IRS exemption taken from them in 1967, Sal began to entertain the possibility of starting his own religion. He thought, "Tax exemptions are precious and must be guarded because so many people are willing to donate to churches for charity and tax write offs. Churches operating in poor countries attract donations from do-gooders and bleeding hearts so they can support lazy degenerates who breed like rabbits. What are successful red blooded American males of pure stock to do? They will find a church based on natural law irresistible. They will want to be part of the elite who will be ending wars, eliminating criminals and getting rid of the Flower People, Black Panthers and other scum that are destroying the American way of life. They will see that the natural way is the only way to live. They will be the ones making the decisions on how to maintain the natural order, while the women of pure races will be procreating. If any of the male members choose to have sex with degenerates, vasectomies could be arranged."

Sal arrived at a life altering conclusion when he decided to start his own religion. He would call it the "Church of Naturalism." The idea brought him to such an emotional pitch that the man who had never before freely shared his inner feelings was moved to say aloud, "It is my destiny to maintain the natural order. I was meant to do more than share the fruits of my labor with organized crime. Establishing the Church of Naturalism is my true calling. I didn't ask for this. I was chosen." He knew his church couldn't be based in America, where the Mob controlled all of the vice that made big money. The next question in his mind was, "Where should the world headquarters be?"

His dream started to take form when he recalled Carlos Marcello's troubles with the federal government in 1961. The subject had been brought up at a meeting of underworld associates when they were told, "Marcello has gone into hiding because of what the Feds have done to him."

The mobster telling the story added, "It began when he and the lawyer he kept on retainer reported to the New Orleans immigration office, just as they did every three months. The next thing they knew, Carlos was handcuffed and they were both put on a passenger jet by FBI agents. They were the only passengers on the plane and the minute they were onboard, it took off. He wasn't allowed to call his special immigration attorney or even his wife. Nobody talked to either of them during the special hour and a half nonstop flight. When the plane landed in Guatemala City, the agents dumped the two of them into a jungle."

The other mobsters were shocked at what they were being told, but Sal chuckled inwardly at the thought of two impeccably dressed men in a place where birds shrieked, spider monkeys shook branches, howler monkeys sprang to life with chilling roars and bats whipped by just inches overhead. The man doing the talking also said, "Marcello and his lawyer went through three days of hell. He passed out from exhaustion a couple of times, and then he broke some ribs when he took a fall. It was days before they made it to a small airport. He was lucky that the government down there was willing to make deals. That's how he was able to get back in the country." The story fascinated Sal. He thought, "I wonder just how cooperative the Guatemalan government is?" He tucked it away in the back of his mind until he read the news about the Scientologists. He wanted to find out all he could about Guatemala.

Some of the clientele at his bordello were excellent sources of information. They told him about the involvement of United Fruit and the CIA with Guatemala. They also referred him to some high level CIA officials. This resulted in a visit by a mysterious man from the intelligence agency.

The visitor was 5' 10" and had a close cropped head of curly, rust colored hair. He was conservatively dressed and spoke in quiet, modulated tones. He was also very secretive. He said to Sal, "You can call me Dave Dawson or Double D, but I'll never give you my real name."

Dawson began his comments about Guatemala by saying, "The country offers mineral resources, glorious weather, stable currency, no runaway inflation, no income tax, no perjury laws, no industrial pollution, no drug epidemics and no women's liberation." He added, "The present government in Guatemala is very cooperative. In fact, we've been looking at a location in the highlands as a possible base of operations. It is now owned by a physician who's originally from New Orleans. He runs a coffee plantation, and he built a hospital next to the plantation. The hospital is of great interest to us. He has had offers from United Fruit, but he has no intention of selling."

The man from the CIA gave Sal all the information he had about Dr. Pedro Ordonez, the coffee plantation and Heart to Heart Hospital, and then he left. Sal decided to seize the doctor's plantation and hospital. He sent Bill Sanders down to Guatemala, telling him to do whatever was needed to take over the properties. In the meantime, the whore master began planning the world headquarters of the Church of Naturalism.

A few months later, Sal summoned Dr. Schultz to his suite. When the physician walked in, he took one look at the head of the brothel and thought, "There's something different about him. What is it? I know. Instead of his usual cold, distant look, I can see fire, enthusiasm and actual glee."

Sal said, "Sit down, Doctor." Schultz took a seat in front of Cardinale's desk. He had to look up because of the four inch high platform Sal's desk was positioned on. "I'm going to share my vision with you," Cardinale said. "You already know about the religion I'm establishing."

"That's right, Mr. Cardinale."

"Call me Wisdom. That's my true name."

"Yes, Wisdom, you have already explained the creed of the Church of Naturalism to me. You are amazing, Wisdom. It's been awe inspiring to see you give so much of yourself to rid the world of wars and criminal acts by degenerates."

"Wait until you see where you will be living in the very near future." Sal handed down a large diagram of a planned community. "Those are the plans for the Church of Naturalism's compound in Guatemala. It's going to have a hospital built from brick, and you will be the chief staff physician."

"That's most generous of you, Wisdom."

"You've more than proven yourself, and I reward production. You will be part of what will become the greatest place in the world."

"How much land will it occupy?"

"Twenty thousand acres to start with. I've also been assured that I'll be able to acquire as much as the church might ever need."

"What about security?"

"The church automatically has the best security because all members must take an oath of secrecy. In addition, there is only one way in or out of the compound. It will be completely surrounded by a brick wall. We will take the precaution of having armed guards and guard dogs."

"Where will the members live?"

"We will have a five star hotel. It will be easy for members to visit because there will be a helicopter pad. At a later time, there will be a small airport. If they wish, they could purchase a villa or a home. When the first few villas are built, you will have your pick."

"What else will you offer the members?"

"As you can see on the diagram, there will be a gym. The gym will provide the services of masseuses. There will be a library and swimming pools. There will also be an auditorium. Some of the useful degenerates are good entertainers. Of course, we hope to develop entertainers from pure races who will gain world popularity. I believe that the biggest attraction, though, will be the human sacrifices."

"That could very well be," said the physician.

"That is why the church headquarters must be located in Guatemala. It was the heart of the Mayan civilization which had shedding blood and human sacrifices at its core. This is just the beginning. The good women of pure races will be breeding, and we will be developing young men who will someday achieve the State of Knowing and become gods in their own right. They will need to be educated. I have plans for elementary schools, high schools and even a university."

"What role will Mrs. Cardinale play?"

"Luke will be overseeing the useful degenerates. We've discussed it, and she brought up the point that it would be difficult to deal with the strange names and languages of degenerates from foreign countries. I told her, 'Don't worry about strange, hard to pronounce names. When the degenerates arrive at the compound, they'll be assigned a number. Their number will be tattooed on one of their wrists, and they'll be known by that number for the rest of their lives. As for communicating, I'm fluent in several languages and if that doesn't work, we can resort to making gestures. Besides, there wouldn't be any reason for having long conversations with them. Remember, they're degenerates.'"

"You seem to have everything planned out, Wisdom."

"Yes, it will be the triumph of my life. My destiny will be fulfilled."

For the first time he could remember, Dr. Schultz saw a wistful expression on Sal Cardinale's face.

DEATH FOLLOWED

CHAPTER FIFTEEN

Dave Dawson paid several visits to Sal Cardinale. The man from the intelligence agency expected to be accommodated with Dom Perignon and fine Cuban cigars obtained through the black market, and Cardinale made sure both items were on hand for their chats in his suite. Their most recent conference turned out to be a four cigar meeting for Double D. For the first time, he revealed specific information about what the CIA had in mind. He said, "Most people think that the agency's role is to gather intelligence about threats to our security that may exist in foreign countries. That was true in the past, but now we're in 1969 and out of necessity, we've had to broaden the scope of our activities. The present administration has become concerned about the various groups in this country bent on destroying families, religion, traditions and all government authority."

After lighting his third aromatic Cuban, Dawson continued by saying, "These threats include the Black Panthers, the Hell's Angels, the Weathermen, hippies and many of the groups pushing women's liberation. We need something that will tear away at the core of all these counter culture idiots and get them at each other's throats. We've found what will do the trick. All we have to do is come up with a way to make it affordable and accessible to the masses."

"What is it?"

"Cocaine."

"That's nothing new."

"The drug itself isn't new, but a form of cocaine that is cheap and gives the user a brief high is new. Cheap prices combined with a high that only lasts a few minutes means more addicts, and more addicts mean more turmoil. The government was using Guatemalans as human guinea pigs twenty years ago. From what I know about the Heart to Heart Hospital you'll be taking over, it would be an ideal place to create cheap cocaine."

There was a twinkle in Double D's eye when he added, "Just think of it! We could get practically every black, hippie or lonely, antisocial outcast hooked on the stuff. It'll make them incapable of organizing anything and might even kill them off in a relatively short time. Cocaine turns kids from rich families and people with money to burn into raving drug addicts. It will not allow them to sleep and keeps them from getting hungry, so they don't eat properly. It produces a euphoric state that makes them like zombies. The problem is that it costs too much. We've got to drive the price way down, and we'll do it!"

Sal was grinning like a cat that had eaten a canary. He said to his guest, "I haven't told you about my latest project. You'll love it!"

"What is it?"

"I'm starting a new religion called the Church of Naturalism. It will be based in Guatemala at the coffee plantation and Heart to Heart Hospital. We will work hand in hand."

"You, the man who runs a whore house, is going to be the head of a church?"

"Absolutely. I'm already holding services every Sunday night at a temporary facility." He took a piece of paper from his note pad, wrote down an address a couple of towns over from Gretna and handed it to Dawson, saying, "Why don't you stop by this Sunday?"

"I'll be there. I wouldn't miss it for the world."

DEATH FOLLOWED

CHAPTER SIXTEEN

The Mob was not involved in any way with the Church of Naturalism. Using his own money, Sal took over a house of worship that had fallen on hard times and was unable to keep its doors open. He began searching for members by trolling the customers of his brothel. There was a great deal about the new religion which appealed to men drawn to a culture of indulgence, and they spread the word among their peers who shared a similar persuasion. A movement began that spread like wildfire.

Each Sunday evening service produced a parking lot jammed with new cars. There were Lincolns, Cadillacs, Mercedes Benzes and even a Rolls Royce or two. Some members even flew in from other states. They were lured by the promise of finding paradise on earth at the church's permanent home when it opened in Guatemala.

A banner made from burlap greeted the members as they filed in. The material was intended as a tribute to the highly profitable coffee plantation that would be part of the church's world headquarters. The design on the banner featured an erupting volcano. To the right of the volcano was a drawing of a wild beast's fangs. On the other side was a set of claws. Beneath the three images were the words "Survival of the Fit," which was the religion's mantra. The members greeted each other by interlocking their index fingers in what was referred to as the "trigger finger salute."

Unlike many clergymen, Sal Cardinale avoided pretensions of ornate vestments and sacred vessels made of silver or gold. When asked about his choice of garments, he replied, "Basic black is always best. We don't need frills, bright colors or jewelry. Our members are all intellectuals who strive to achieve the State of Knowing."

From the very beginning, Luke with her wig of long blonde hair was the only female in attendance. All of the members thought she was there to support her husband, but she had a different opinion of his preaching. She thought, "You'd have to be nuts to believe this load of lies and BS he's spreading." She was wrong, though. The most dangerous thing about Sal Cardinale was that he believed every word he told his members. The religion he created had taken over his life by consuming his every waking moment and dominating dreams he had every night. He loved every aspect of his calling.

In his very first sermon he said to the gathering, "You know me as Sal Cardinale, but my real name is Wisdom. I am one of a higher order of human being. I have no mother or father, for I came from nature. I was spawned in the sea and as I grew, I achieved the State of Knowing. I am the equal of Socrates, Plato, Aristotle, Einstein, Dharma, Lao tzu, Gautama, Moses, Jesus Christ and all gods. Since you are all members of pure races, I can guide you to achieve the State of Knowing and become gods. Being a god carries with it enormous responsibility; the duty of maintaining the natural order."

He continued by saying, "The answer to all of life's questions can be found in nature. Since the dawn of civilization, mankind has been faced with social ills and warfare. None of this was necessary. All wars were caused by the desire of one group to impose their rules of conduct on all other groups. This was wrong because there is only one set of rules, and that is natural law. If we all lived according to natural law, wars would be eliminated. Crime is at the root of all social ills. The definition of crime is 'the unlawful taking of something that belongs to another.' It could be their money, their property or their life. In most instances, crime is committed by degenerates. Even though all of them are in a constant state of being half asleep, they are destructive people. They do senseless things repetitively. They fail to take care of their possessions and once they destroy what is theirs, they replace what they had by taking what belongs to someone else. If degenerates were eliminated in accordance with the natural law, crime would practically vanish."

Cardinale elaborated on this theory when he said, "Complete extermination of degenerates is not necessary, though. A great many of them could be useful. They must be guided and if they were treated with consideration by the higher order of humans providing for their needs, this would undoubtedly draw out their awe and reverence toward us. Once that is accomplished, they can be led to function in ways that will promote the natural order. This is a worthy goal which will greatly enhance society and bring peace to the world."

On the night Dave Dawson was in attendance, the man from the CIA could tell by the look in the eyes of the congregation that Cardinale had them in the palm of his hand. Before the service, Sal had mentioned to Double D, "I'm the only man on earth with the guts to tell them the absolute truth."

During that night's sermon, he said, "If despite showing them consideration, certain degenerates fail to be useful in maintaining the natural order, they must be eliminated. This means they must be killed. Do not misunderstand me. Killing a degenerate is not murder. True, it is the taking of a human life, but it is done in accordance with natural law. We must remember that the essence of nature is to kill or be killed. Nature never intended for every living thing to thrive and survive. Only the fit do. For the strong to survive, they must feed off the species they dominate. Proof may be seen in man's ability to hunt, to fish and to farm with the use of beasts of burden. To kill a useless degenerate is a laudatory act which benefits society as a whole. To kill the sick or weak is an act of mercy. Killing is not always murder, and we of the Church of Naturalism condone killing in the interest of maintaining the natural order. Once each of you have attained the State of Knowing and are gods, you will be just like me. You will have the power to decide who lives and who dies. Guatemala is the perfect place for us. Our church is in keeping with the Mayan tradition of human sacrifice that existed there for centuries."

Sal Cardinale, a man who had reinvented himself more than once, had performed magic. He had stood before a large group of wealthy, powerful men, reached into the cores of their being and lifted their imaginations to new levels.

Luke thought, "They're hanging on his every word. They actually think they'll find happiness following him. This is getting to be really scary. How can I escape having to go to Guatemala?"

The man who preferred being called Wisdom then said to his congregation, "The mission of the Church of Naturalism is to maintain the natural order. This includes providing the male offspring of the pure races a moral compass by teaching them right and wrong. Once they are grown, they are to be guided toward achieving the State of Knowing and becoming gods."

He added, "When we talk about the roles of men and women, we must remember that the man is the master because he is the dominant gender. The woman's purpose is to give birth to children, and she can't do that without male sperm. The woman has no choice but to obey her master; to mend his socks, prepare his food and bear him children. A good woman from a pure race must slave for her master during the day, but at night she must try to be a plaything, a sweet little plaything with which the man can amuse himself and forget his worries. Our playthings provide us with strength from the joy they give, so I call them our 'Strength through Joy Girls.'"

That brought the congregation to its feet. As Dave Dawson watched all the men stand and applaud, images came into his head that were as vivid as if he were watching a movie reel. He thought, "The whore master pulled it off. He's on to something. They'll be killing degenerates as human sacrifices in Guatemala, and we'll be getting every loser addicted to cocaine. America will be safe at last."

DEATH FOLLOWED

DEATH FOLLOWED

CHAPTER SEVENTEEN

When Matt Logan arrived at the Gretna address Bill Sanders had given him, he found that it was a nondescript warehouse. The front door had been left unlocked. It was obvious that he was expected.

He had a sour feeling in the pit of his stomach, and he sensed that his life was about to be profoundly changed for better or for worse. It would be suicide to take on Sal Cardinale, who had the weight of the Mob behind him. The easiest thing for him to do would have been to turn and walk away. After all, who was Nathalie Ordonez to him? He thought, "I'm trying to make her into the daughter I never had. Sal did terrible things to her, but why should I be the one to take on the evil in the world?" He hesitated for a moment and then he thought, "It's really not about Nathalie. It's about me and my wife. I tried to escape from myself after the war, not accepting the fact that I could run but never hide. I never want to put her through that again. I'd rather die first."

He opened the door and entered. No one appeared to be there, and the place was so empty that the sound of Matt's wing tip shoes on the cement floor echoed throughout the structure. A single light bulb was burning. It provided just enough illumination for him to see that that the place wasn't large as warehouses went, more like an overgrown shed. He started walking toward the most well lighted spot.

He didn't quite make it before he felt a strong hand on his shoulder. He was spun around and came face to face with Sal Cardinale.

His old sergeant said, "We meet again. You're not going to like this, but I'm going to love it. I'm going to do what I should have done a long time ago. The world needs to be rid of those who dishonor their race."

Logan thought, "I've been set up! I don't know what Cardinale is babbling about, but I was a fool to listen to Sanders."

Sal unleashed a straight right hand blow that put the lawyer on the floor. Matt had been known to have a good chin during his boxing days and he still knew how to roll with a punch. His teeth were still intact and when he put his fingers to his mouth, he didn't feel any blood.

"Get up, you miserable excuse for a man!" Sal scowled at him. His eyes were cold and deadly. "I'm going to kill you and savor it like a sumptuous feast. I'm going to take my time about it because I want to hear you beg me to finish you off."

Cardinale used both hands to grab Matt by his suit coat and yank him to his feet. When Logan was upright, Sal swung his right hand and landed a blow just below the lawyer's breast bone. When it bent Matt over, the whore monger raked his fist up along Logan's chest and over his chin and mouth. The technique was known in the fight game as a "two for one punch." The powerful blow did not stop until a ring Sal was wearing tore off the tip of Matt's nose. Logan's eyes watered and he screamed and moaned from the excruciating pain. He fell hard on the cement floor.

Sal then began kicking his victim in the ribs. The first kick landed solidly, but before Cardinale could launch another, there was a blast of gunfire. A bullet went into Sal's back and through his heart. All he said before he dropped to the ground was, "What the hell?"

A husky voice Matt recognized said, "Now you'll know what it will look like. You were headed there all your life." Matt focused his eyes and confirmed that Bill Sanders had done the deed. He was holding a .38 Smith and Wesson snub nose and smoke was curling from the barrel. Sanders calmly walked closer to Sal's corpse and emptied the remaining four bullets into the head, just to make sure. He looked at Matt and said, "Surprise, surprise."

The lawyer was dumfounded. All he could say was, "I don't understand. What's going on?"

Sanders tucked the pistol away into a shoulder holster and said, "I'll tell you everything, but you've got to understand that things aren't always what they seem. I'm not going to say anything more until I show you something."

Bill took off his fedora, his suit coat, his shoulder holster and continued removing his clothing until he had stripped naked except for his socks and loafers. The truth about Bill Sanders was revealed. "He" was a "she" whose breasts were strapped down with ace bandages and was just like any other woman. She said, "My name is really Lucretia, but you can call me Luke."

Matt was amazed at how comfortable the woman with the buzz cut was about being naked in front of a man. It was as though they were both males in a locker room. He felt completely under her control. He thought, "She wanted to make me helpless. That's why she let Sal beat me up so badly. I have no choice but to listen to her."

Luke said, "I was married to Sal strictly out of convenience. I've always been a lesbian." She pulled a pack of Camels from the suit coat and lit one before telling Matt the whole story.

She told him about her being second in command of the brothel. She also told him about the church Sal had started and all about the diabolical scheme her husband had cooked up with a high ranking official in the CIA. She revealed how Sal had masterminded the death of Nathalie's parents.

Luke said, "I handled that myself with two men. We broke into their home, injected them with lethal doses of morphine, put the bodies in their car, sent it over a cliff and then set it on fire."

The broad shouldered lesbian with the large hands and feet gave him all the details of the plot to kidnap Nathalie. She admitted every part she had played, including her murdering Solomon Garcia and the two prostitutes. She then said, "Sal thought your friend was soft and could be frightened into signing over the coffee plantation and Heart to Heart Hospital. They would be turned into the headquarters of the Church of Naturalism, and the CIA would also be there. When the stupid Indians in Guatemala screwed things up, Sal got impatient. The CIA was pushing him to have things ready by a certain time. He decided to kill Nathalie himself two weeks from now. She wouldn't have stood a chance. I never want to set foot in that country again, so I had to act. That's when I called you. You were a helluva decoy. There was something about you that always pushed his buttons." After she finished, she went back to the suit jacket, pulled out the revolver and a reloading device and inserted five new bullets. Matt was still in pain and his shirt had become soaked with blood, but he was able to ask her, "What's going to happen next?"

"That's up to you. I've got some pills to help with your pain, and I'll get you to a hospital after we're done. First, I want you to help me drag this body to the loading dock, put it in the car parked there and drive to a swamp where I've got an air boat all ready to go. We'll ride further out into the swamp and feed Sal to the alligators. It's poetic justice, because he's been doing the same thing to his aging whores for years. If you do that with me, we'll get along just fine. Otherwise, I'll have to shoot your ass and feed two bodies to the gators. It'll be a little harder, but I never mind hard work. "

Matt had a wary look in his eyes. Luke could tell that he needed more of an explanation to close the deal. She said, "I never wanted to go to Guatemala. I wanted to take over the brothel from the greedy bastard. You know, he never gave me any cash. Oh, he'd let me use his cars and ride on his yacht. He gave me clothes and jewelry, but not enough cash that I could accumulate a nest egg. I was living well, but I was still one of his slaves. He was the most evil man who ever lived. He didn't like sex, and the only thing that got him off was killing people. Look at it this way, Sal Cardinale wasn't human. Why should he be treated like one?"

She looked at Matt with a knowing smile and then continued. "I want to be a madam, and I'll be in heaven. I love the touch of a woman, and I love touching them. The only thing a man is good for is pointing out where the good looking women are. I can't get enough of having sex with women. I can satisfy any of them... including yours... better than any man can. My fingers, hands and mouth never fail."

She dropped her cigarette on the floor and crushed it with the sole of her loafer. She then said, "After we get rid of Sal, we go our separate ways. I don't bother you or your friend Nathalie. You don't bother me. Live and let live. Agreed?"

Matt was an attorney; an officer of the court. If he went along with what Luke proposed, he would be an accessory to murder. For a moment, he asked himself, "Do two wrongs make a right?" Then he remembered his Janet. He thought, "There has always been evil in the world, and that will never change. The only hope is to give myself to the woman I truly love. I'll have to live in order to do that." Matt had a steely eyed look on his face when he said, "Agreed."

DEATH FOLLOWED

DEATH FOLLOWED

CHAPTER EIGHTEEN

Giuseppe Bertolani answered the phone in his jewelry store and found that Luke Cardinale was on the line. She was in tears and sounded distressed. He had never heard her in such a state before. Sal's wife blurted, "They're... they're dead! All of them are dead!" She sounded inconsolable.

"Who's dead?"

"My Sal, my Steve, my Mike. They've all been taken."

"Who took them?"

"God took them. A priest in Mexico called and told me."

"Why would somebody in Mexico be calling you? What do they know?"

"Father Mendoza is a wonderful man. We've known him for years. We've helped him do his charity work, and he has helped us to raise our sons with morals and standards. Sal and I were so happy a couple of weeks ago when Steve and Mike called him and told him that they wanted to make things right, just like the prodigal son the priests told us about. He and the boys met in San Pedro, Mexico. It's near big caves, and Steve and Mike love to explore them. Sal knows all about them from what he did during the war. It was something that gave so much pleasure to all of them, and he looked forward to this trip. I was so worried, but when he held me in his arms and kissed me, he said, 'We will be careful. You don't have to worry.' I believed him, and now..." Her voice cracked and she broke down sobbing again.

Giuseppe was shocked. He didn't know what to say. After a moment, he told her, "Donna and I will be right over." He thought, "My wife will know what to do. After all, a woman always knows what another woman wants."

Within an hour, the jeweler entered the brothel alone. His wife waited in their car because he would never want her setting foot in such a place. He was surprised to find that the whores who were around acted as though everything were normal. When Giuseppe was approached by a mulatto maid, he said, "I'm here to see Luke. She's expecting me."

The maid led him to the door of Mrs. Cardinale's suite. She knocked and said, "Miss Luke, a man is here to see you."

Luke answered through the door in her husky voice. "Who is he?"

"Luke, it's me, Giuseppe the jeweler."

They could hear the door being unlocked. When Luke opened it, she appeared calm. Giuseppe thought, "I'm glad she stopped crying, poor woman. She's probably putting up a brave front."

After telling the maid to go back to her regular work, Luke closed the door, locked it, turned to the jeweler and said, "Giuseppe, I don't know what to do. My Sal... my sons... they're... they're dead. Can't you hear me? They're dead!" She began sobbing again.

DEATH FOLLOWED

She was trembling, and he helped her to sit on a chair. Giuseppe thought, "All of us in the business know that Sal and Luke had something special. They were inseparable, and they were devoted to their sons. Now it has all been taken from her."

After she calmed down, he asked, "Do you want to tell me what happened?"

Luke nodded and said, "Father Mendoza called me. He told me that three bodies were found in a cave. They had been there for days. By the time they got them to San Pedro, they were rotting and had to be buried to keep from spreading disease. Father Mendoza said there was no doubt it was my Sal, my Steve and my Mike."

Giuseppe looked at her with deep sympathy and said, "You're coming home with me and Donna. You can't stay here."

She nodded and then replied, "I've to get my things together. Giuseppe, please go down and ask Roxanne to see me." Roxanne was Luke's current bed partner. She was a raven haired Cajun beauty with hazel eyes. The madam trusted her to handle things during any of her absences because the courtesan from the bayou country had become enraptured with her. When they had sex the first time, Roxanne gushed, "Luke, you are the woman I dreamed about when I was a kid. It's so exciting when you hold me and press my body against yours." It was strictly a one sided love affair, however. Luke exploited the woman's devotion to her. Roxanne's capacity for judgment had been washed out of her head, and she obeyed every command unquestioningly.

When she reported to Luke, the madam told her, "I'll be gone for a few days, dear. You know what to do."

Roxanne had taken over for Luke several times. Only two weeks before, the madam had told her devoted lover that she was going out of town, but didn't say where.

Luke had taken a trip to San Pedro, Mexico to meet with Father Alexis Mendoza, the priest who had been so helpful in arranging for Sal and her to adopt their two boys. She knew he could be counted on to come through once more.

When she arrived, she discovered that the twenty years since her last visit had been kind to the priest. Gray hair was the only visible sign of his age. He welcomed her with open arms because she and her husband had been most generous whenever they paid him a visit. Of course, they only came to see him when they needed something.

After Luke was escorted to Father Al's office, he greeted her with a hearty, "It's so wonderful to see you again. It has been much too long. It's a shame your husband didn't join us."

"That's what I've come to you about, Father." She became teary eyed and began to sob. "I don't know what to do. You are the only one who can help."

"What seems to be the problem?"

"My Sal and my two sons have disappeared in a cave near here. They wanted to visit their home country again, and they love to explore caves. He called me from the village where they were staying just before they went to the cave. When I didn't hear from them, I called their hotel. They said they hadn't checked out, but no one had seen them for days. I got on a plane right away but when I got to the village, nobody could help me."

"What village was this?"

"The name of it is Garcia."

"I'm familiar with it."

"Father, the thought of never seeing Sal or my sons again is horrible. What also saddens me is that I can't honor Sal's last wishes unless I have proof of his death."

"What do you mean?"

"My husband took out a life insurance policy with a double indemnity clause some time ago. If he dies because of a crime or an accident, it pays double. He made me the beneficiary, but he was so grateful for you helping us adopt our sons that he told me, 'If anything happens to me, give Father Al what the policy pays.'"

The priest's ears perked up. "M...M...May I ask you how much is that?"

"One hundred thousand pesos but with double indemnity, it comes to two hundred thousand pesos. I like to keep things simple, so I took the liberty of advancing the money to you from my own funds." She placed a thick manila clasp envelope on the priest's desk. He opened it and saw that it was crammed with Mexican currency. It was all he could do to keep from salivating.

Father Mendoza smiled and said, "Mrs. Cardinale, you have suffered a great tragedy, but this is also a time of blessings. Your appearance here today is a miracle, and miracles beget miracles. I see your situation as a case of confusion about which village has jurisdiction over vital information. Permit me time to consult with a servant of the public here in San Pedro. We will meet again tomorrow at this time. By then, I should have everything worked out. Will you be staying at the El Conquistador Hotel?"

"Yes."

"Fine, I know how to reach you if things move quicker."

Father Al had a private meeting with Ruben Gonzales, the mayor of San Pedro. He listened patiently to the priest's tale and when it was over, Father Mendoza placed a thick envelope on the mayor's desk. After taking a quick peek inside, Gonzales exclaimed, "The most amazing thing has happened, Father! You have miraculously solved our problem of identifying three unclaimed bodies we recently buried in an unmarked grave."

Father Al replied, "Take me there so I can bless them. It is the right thing to do." The next day, Luke met with the priest and was given death certificates for her departed husband and sons. Before leaving, she said, "Could I ask you to have three crosses placed on their graves so they may rest in peace? Just send me the bill."

"Consider it done, Mrs. Cardinale."

DEATH FOLLOWED

As she walked out of his office, she thought, "Father Mendoza is a true miracle worker. He brought the two adopted bastards back to life so they could finally be useful and helped get way more out of Sal dead than I could when he was alive."

The four days Luke spent with Giuseppe and Donna forced her to go cold turkey from her lesbian activities, but she and Roxanne more than made up for it when she got back to the pleasures of her circular bed.

After making up for lost time, she took the Mexican death certificates to a funeral home and made arrangements. All of the caskets would be closed. Stevie and Mikey's were empty and had small wreaths of white roses placed on them. Sal's was draped in an American flag because he was buried with full military honors. Luke had all the trophies of his victims, his trademark hat that he loved and his Bowie knives put into his casket because she didn't want them around anymore. She told everyone, "He wanted to be buried with his war souvenirs, and this is the best I can do under the circumstances."

The service was held at St. Joseph's Roman Catholic Church in Gretna. Hundreds of mourners packed the church. Rosaries were flying, and there were lots of Kleenex and handkerchiefs needed to dry all the tears. Everyone was dressed in black out of respect. The saddest of the men in attendance were members of the Church of Naturalism. Their dream of a Guatemalan utopia had died along with Sal.

Many who attended had underworld ties, and eight of them served as pallbearers. They loved Sal so much that they didn't mind their relationship to him being put on public display. All of the whores from Sal's brothel paid their respects. Luke had told them, "If you show how sad you are at losing him, I'll wipe out whatever you owe me." To a woman, they seized upon that once in a lifetime opportunity and bawled their eyes out. Roxanne put on the most dramatic performance. She nearly became hysterical and had to be gently escorted from the church. After the long funeral procession made its way to the cemetery, Sal was given a big sendoff. Seven members of the U.S. Army fired three volleys with M1 rifles, and a bugler blew Taps. Luke thought, "They should have thrown Bowie knives into the air."

After a band played When the Saints Go Marching In, Luke was given a chance to say something. She read a poem written for her by Roxanne. It was the crowning act in the madam's performance.

DEATH FOLLOWED

I have cried more tears

Than there are stars in the sky.

How I miss you.

When will you come back?

When will I see you again?

You have been buried

In this large hole,

A cold hole under the ground!

What a chilling way to leave me!

You are now in eternal silence,

Silence of silences without an echo.

I will miss you forever.

The madam's current lover hoped that her poem would be appreciated as much as Mercedes' had been. Luke thought, "I might give her a piece of jewelry for what she has done during this funeral but on second thought, I don't think I will. I'm beginning to get a little tired of her." Luke and Roxanne lived in a world where people were easily discarded.

The three caskets were placed in the same plot. Sal had the largest and most elaborate of the headstones. The inscription on his read, "Salvatore Cardinale. Born 1922. Died 1969. Warrior, Husband, Father."

The funeral was talked about for years by the New Orleans underworld. Even though they had downplayed their involvement with the brothel, the Mob was determined to see that Sal was never forgotten, and they paid for a bronze statue of him which occupied a place of honor in the bordello. Luke thought, "They insist on putting it in the front room, and it will be a big dust magnet. If it were up to me, I would have put it outside and let the birds crap all over it. Maybe I'll do that at a later time."

DEATH FOLLOWED

Book Three
The Aftermath
Love Conquers All,
Evildoers Self Destruct

The Aftermath

Chapter One

On the day before their church wedding, Alfredo hugged Nathalie and brought her close to his body. He whispered in her ear, "Since the time I spent in my mother's womb, I have been drifting toward you," and then he kissed her passionately.

Their second marriage ceremony was conducted at the La Merced Roman Catholic church in Antigua. It was a candlelight service which began at seven thirty in the evening. Police had been assigned to hold back the curious who always seemed to crowd around lavish weddings.

A light pink runner extended along the entire length of the aisle to the altar. It had a border of rose petals on each side. The petals were from white, pink and yellow roses. A heart had been painted by an artist in the middle of the fabric. He had used a fuchsia instead of the color red to match the total color scheme. The heart was inscribed with "A and N Milla" in black letters.

The lights inside the church had been dimmed to better illuminate the altar. A kneeler had been placed there so that Nathalie and Alfredo could recite their vows before God. Lighted candles had been positioned in candelabras on both sides of the altar. Each of the candelabras held twelve candles, and both were adorned with different shades of roses and mint greenery. Massive arrangements of pink roses, yellow roses, white roses and wide ribbons in the colors of whisper pink, light mint green and light yellow had been placed next to the candles. All of the arrangements were contained in tall marble stands.

The pews had been decorated with small arrangements of various pink roses and baby breaths. The flowers were accented by light yellow, light mint green and light pink ribbons.

A classical guitarist played *Romance Anonimo* as those attending the ceremony entered the church. Everyone was given a five inch high pink candle to hold. As soon as Nathalie arrived in a white Lincoln limousine, it was announced, "Please stand so that ushers may light your candles." The congregation was also asked to blow their candles out once the bride reached the altar. Practically everyone in attendance kept their candles as souvenirs.

The priest led Alfredo and his cousin Marcel, who was the best man, from the sacristy to the altar. Marcel wore a black tuxedo, white shirt and a black bow tie. There were no groomsmen. A trio of three women, a harpist, a violinist and a cellist, played Johann Pachelbel's Canon in D Major as the men took their places. Alfredo stood with great confidence.

By then, Tisha, who acted as both maid of honor and ring bearer, and the five bridesmaids had arrived in their limousines. Matt Logan had recovered from his serious injuries, and he was on hand to assist Nathalie out of her vehicle. Tisha took a few minutes to rearrange the bridal gown so that it would fall gracefully on the carpet.

Nathalie wore a striking wedding gown. The upper part of her dress was a very light pink organza with a layer of brocade ending in soft scallops forming a "V" midway down her back. Along her waistline in the back was a cascade of light pink roses made with silk Dupioni in a shade darker than the rest of her garment. Material below her waist had been gathered in towards the back to form a bustle, and part of the cascade of roses fell between that material. The remaining portions of the dress were a whisper soft pink. The organza was lighter in color than her cascade of pink roses in order to emphasize the flowers. Fine mesh netting had been sewn underneath the whisper soft pink organza and Dupioni in the same shade of pink as the cascade.

She wore her hair upswept with curls falling to the back of her neck. Five small roses adorned the top of her hair. These crowning roses were the same shade of pink and made of the same material as the cascade down the back of her gown. A whisper soft pink veil fell to within four inches of the roses around her waistline.

Her shoes matched the color of the gown. She wore a platinum necklace with a heart shaped five carat diamond that Alfredo had given her as a wedding gift. She carried a cascading orchid bouquet with flowers of various shades of pink.

Tisha and the five bridesmaids all wore long gowns of whisper yellow. Their dresses had three quarter sleeves, scalloped necklines and three ribbons of different colors at the waists. They were a three inch pink ribbon, a two inch mint green ribbon and a one inch pastel yellow ribbon. The ribbons were partially sewn at the waistline to allow them to flow halfway down the gowns. They wore small light yellow veils that came down six inches from the crowns of their heads. Large pink dahlias were centered on top of their veils. They each held a bouquet of light pink and light yellow roses. Their shoes matched the color of their gowns.

Tisha carried the four carat heart shaped diamond wedding ring on a heart shaped pillow of pink satin. When she reached the altar, she would transfer the ring to the priest.

As Nathalie entered the church on Matt's arm, the three female musicians were joined by a brass section flown in from New Orleans. They performed Felix Mendelssohn's Wedding March while the bride walked down the aisle. She could see Alfredo waiting for her at the altar. He was very handsome in his black tails, and a pink carnation in his lapel matched his bride's gown. His black hair was closely trimmed. He smiled at her and gave her a sexy wink. Nathalie felt a tingling sensation and thought, "Shortly, I will be Mrs. Milla. The love Alfredo and I have for each other will last until the end of our lives." As she walked along the forty foot runner, she noticed how the soft light from all the candles gave an attractive glow to Alfredo's face. He glanced at her with loving eyes that melted her heart with every step she took. She felt the eyes of all the guests on her, but she was only watching the love of her life.

The many guests in attendance let out a collective sigh at the sight of her. Some of them became teary eyed, and tissues popped out of purses to wipe away tears of joy. Matt Logan began to choke up as he walked Nathalie down the aisle. His wife Janet became teary eyed. She always did that whenever she attended a wedding.

Nathalie looked toward Matt and whispered, "I'm so happy that this day is here. I love him so much."

He had regained his composure and replied, "He adores you. You two were meant for each other."

When Nathalie and Matt reached the front of the altar, she looked lovingly at Alfredo. She smiled with contentment. Alfredo looked at her and said, "You are beautiful."

The priest began the ceremony by saying, "And love was born between Alfredo and Nathalie."

They exchanged their vows, kissed and left the church. Everyone headed for the reception at the Hotel Antigua.

Chapter Two

The Aftermath

A large guest book bound in pink leather on a pedestal stood at the entrance of the hotel's banquet hall. The cover bore a drawing of a heart containing the initials of the bride and the groom.

The reception for five hundred was held in a large oval room that could have held even more guests. Brightly lit Austrian crystal chandeliers hung from the ceiling.

The room was lushly decorated. Between each window, a large gorgeous flower arrangement perched on a pedestal held blooms of various colors. As the guests entered, they were immediately drawn to the wedding cake. It was a five tier yellow cake with pineapple filling and light pink frosting. Since the cake was five tiers tall, no cake stand was needed. It had taken two days to prepare the cake and two hours to assemble it in the banquet room.

Rather than the traditional likeness of the bride and groom, the cake topper consisted of a decorative cardboard heart covered in pink frosting two shades darker than the frosting on the cake. The cardboard heart bore the couple's monogram initials and the date; "A and N, 1970." There was lattice work all the way around each of the tiers. Each tier was decorated in a distinct way, but still incorporating an overall theme. The top tier featured gum paste flowers of the same color as the floral arrangements in the room. The second highest tier had two large gum paste doves kissing. A gum paste bouquet had been placed in the middle of the third highest tier. Its colors also matched those of the floral arrangements. A gum paste dove in flight was placed at each side of the bouquet. The tier next to the bottom had a gum paste heart the same color as the cake topper. It bore a message in white lettering, "My love forever." The bottom tier had gum paste doves in various positions of flight. Two three foot high slender artificial trees bracketed the cake. They were secured to a wooden cake board that was covered in the same pink frosting as the cake. A ceramic dove crafted with real white bird feathers was mounted at the tip of each artificial tree. The two doves supported a mint green banner with light brown letters which read, "And love was born."

An open bar bordered a twenty by twenty foot wooden dance floor at the back of the room. There was an area behind the dance floor reserved for musicians. This allowed the dancers to make requests. Three violinists walked around the room playing romantic music while the guests dined.

Alfredo had loaned the hotel a large stained glass ceiling display from his villa to be used for the reception. He had paid two hundred thousand dollars for the thirty foot by thirty foot glasswork. It was lit from the ceiling, and its colors covered the entire dance floor. The stained glass contained the image of a giant heart with the name Milla inscribed in red letters. The heart was surrounded by a variety of flowers. At the bottom of the heart was inscribed "And Love Was Born." Nathalie and Alfredo intended to pass it on to their heirs.

The guests were seated at round tables of eight, covered in medium pink damask. The center of each table was occupied by a smaller version of the flower arrangements that

had been placed on pedestals underneath each window. Every table arrangement had a lighted candle in the center. Rose petals of various colors were scattered across each table cloth. The napkins and chair coverings were a light yellow that made for an attractive contrast with the pink tablecloths. The chairs were also decorated with large pink bows. Pink hearts hung down the chair backs from each bow.

Unusual favors were set at each place setting. They were small heart shaped crystal containers that could be used as jewelry cases. Each container was engraved in gold letters which read, "And love was born between Alfredo and Nathalie, 1970." Little marzipan hearts were inside the containers. Some of them bore the initial "A" for Alfredo and others had "N" for Nathalie.

All waiters and waitresses were dressed in white shirts, black trousers and pink cumberbunds. Special bread was served that had been baked in the shape of doves. Pure unsalted butter formed into heart shaped pats accompanied the bread loaves that resembled doves.

Hor d'oeuvres consisted of shrimp puffs, escargot, anchovies, mushrooms, lobster, dates stuffed with pecans, caviar and tidbits of assorted cheeses. The dinner menu was tossed salad with hearts of palm, prime filet mignon, asparagus and oven baked small potatoes. Water was served, and so was wine. Dom Perignon was served at the bride's table.

Champagne was served to all the guests after the meal. Several toasts were made to the bride and groom, and then there was a toast by all. Following the toasts, many of the guests gathered around the bride and groom and watched them share the first slice of their wedding cake. The top tier of the cake was saved for the christening of Nathalie and Alfredo's first child.

Then it was dance time. Alfredo and Nathalie had the first dance. They danced to their song, A Woman in Love. After that, whoever wanted to dance joined in. At the conclusion of the evening, each man was presented with a red carnation and each woman was given a pink rose.

After a long but joyous day, the newlyweds were awakened from their marriage bed at five in the morning by firecrackers and a serenade. Alfredo said, "I arranged this, my love. I wanted you to have the serenade that your father took away from you when you were a young woman."

Chapter Three

The situation at the brothel changed drastically after Luke Cardinale took over. The whores were no longer retired at the age of thirty. Luke didn't want to eliminate them the way Sal had. She decided, "They signed employment contracts, so why can't I just fire them. It's

less messy than killing them." She gave the oldest prostitutes their pink slips and handed each of them five hundred dollars severance pay. They all complained, and this came to the attention of the Mob. They thought, "Why are we having these problems now? This never happened when Sal was around." The bordello was still bringing in big money, so the issue was swept under the rug and Luke continued running things.

She lacked the presence and cunning Sal had possessed, and it didn't take long for the whores to fool her. They could manipulate and trick her by covering for each other. Luke made the mistake of keeping Dr. Schultz around, and he became an ally of the prostitutes because he enjoyed having sex with them. Roxanne was ostracized because they knew she was in love with the boss and would rat them out in a heartbeat.

Luke knew she could control Roxanne, but wasn't sure about the others. She sensed that there was a lot of "palace intrigue" going on, and she became paranoid. She worried about defending herself without Sal around, so she set up a gun range in the wooded area behind the brothel. She spent a good deal of time sharpening her aim with her .38 snub nosed revolver, and sometimes even fired at the targets from a window in her suite. Whenever the whores heard the shots, they would say, "There goes the coo coo bird again!"

One night, a Cajun named Rusty came to the brothel. His real name was Antoine, but he had acquired his nickname because of his dark red hair. He was rugged, but a large gap in his upper front teeth spoiled his looks. He was surprised to find his old flame Roxanne working there. From the time they were kids, Rusty had an insane infatuation with her. He would have done anything for the raven haired beauty, but she couldn't stand him. Even when she told him she was a lesbian, it didn't make any difference. He said, "You could learn to love me and we could have a great life together."

It didn't bother her a bit when he hired her for the night. She thought, "His money spends as much as anyone else's. Maybe he'll finally get the message and figure out how little I care for him." When they finished having sex, he started saying such things as "Why are you doing this? You've got to get out of here!" He pressed a slip of paper with his phone number into her hand and said, "If you ever need anything, just call me." She was about to throw the number away after he left, but for some strange reason slipped it into her address book.

Luke was the love of her life, and it seemed that everything was beginning to take shape. The madam of the brothel was relying more and more on her. She was even allowed to use any of the seven cars Luke had inherited from Sal. It made Roxanne feel domesticated to run errands for Luke, and she enjoyed being part of every little thing about her.

The Cajun woman's world was blasted apart when Luke dumped her in favor of a redhead named Velma, who was a new addition to the brothel. She was informed of the change when Luke said, "We're not going to be using the same bed for a while. I want to make sure the new girl understands how to please the men. It's just for a little while, and it doesn't really mean anything. You're still the most important one in my life." Luke tried to appease her with a kiss, but Roxanne was devastated.

The Aftermath

She thought, "I allowed her to dominate me because I love her. We find so much enjoyment in each other, so why doesn't she love me? I feel used. She thinks she can bring me back to her bed and then send me away whenever she wants."

Roxanne became depressed at first, but then felt scorned. The hazel eyed courtesan began to plot against her former lover.

She decided to take the most valuable pieces of jewelry which Luke had hidden in the false bottom of the wastebasket in her bathroom. Roxanne had known about the hiding place, but had kept it quiet out of love. Now that her heart had been broken, she would take what mattered most from the cold hearted woman who valued diamonds, rubies, emeralds and sapphires far more than people.

Her plans wouldn't work unless she had help, so she found the phone number Rusty had given her and dialed it. When he answered, she told him, "I want to get together with you. I need your help. Can you meet me in front of my cousin's house tomorrow morning at ten? You've been there. It's the place in Metairie."

"You can count on me. I love you, and I will be there." She could hear the excitement in his voice.

They sat and talked inside the cab of his pickup truck. She said, "I've been thinking about us, and I've decided it's time for me to get out of that life and make a real life for myself. I really like you."

He held her tenderly and said, "I'm so happy to hear those words from you. You know I love you, and you have been the only one in my life."

"I'm glad you feel that way about me. I love you too."

They kissed, and then she asked, "How are we going to do this. It takes money."

"I've got five thousand dollars saved. We can buy a home, and I know a nice one that's for sale. Remember the place down the road from where you lived?"

"I've got something different in mind. If you help me, we can get some big money."

"What are you talking about?"

"The woman who runs the brothel has been collecting jewelry for years. I know her hiding place. It will be a breeze to take it. Then we can go far away and live a great life together."

"How much are we talking about?"

"She trusts me, and she once told me she had over fifty thousand dollars in jewelry. She has diamonds, rubies, sapphires and emeralds."

He thought, "Man, we could really be living good." He asked her, "What do you want me to do?"

She answered, "If you help me get the jewels, I'll go away with you." She figured she could ditch him somewhere along the way.

Rusty said, "We'll need some help. I know two brothers; Travis and Beau. Travis is the best I know with a gun, and Beau has one of the fastest Chevys around. Will there be enough to cut them in?" Roxanne assured him there was.

The plan was for the three men to arrive at the brothel at one in the afternoon when

Luke would be busy at one of the companies which supplied many of the brothel's toiletries. After she had taken over, she had become tight fisted and often had lengthy meetings with her suppliers to haggle with them and fight for bargain prices. She had often said to Roxanne, "Every penny I save means more in my pocket." Rusty, Travis and Beau would all be in suits and ties and have their hair cut so they would look like businessmen in the market for afternoon delights. Roxanne waited until the queen of the brothel mentioned she would probably be tied up most of the following afternoon. The raven haired Cajun thought, "Now's the time to take our shot."

She immediately called Rusty. "Hi, lover boy, will you and the other two be ready to go for a one o'clock appointment tomorrow afternoon."

"We'll be there."

Luke left at twelve fifteen and as soon as Roxanne saw her pull away, she went into the madam's bathroom, unfastened the false bottom from the wastebasket, took all the jewelry out and spread it on the circular bed. She only wanted to take the most valuable pieces. They would be placed in a jewelry pouch she had purchased beforehand that could be slipped into her bra.

Beau and Rusty hung out in the front room of the brothel. Travis was supposed to stand guard outside Luke's suite but after he arrived, he became engrossed with one of the prostitutes. Temptation got the best of him, and he went to the whore's room for some action. As he began to undress, the prostitute noticed the .45 automatic he carried in his shoulder holster. She insisted, "Put your gun on the night table. It makes me nervous." He figured he could still grab it quickly, so he said, "Sure, no problem," and went along with her.

Luke returned much earlier than expected. She came in through a back entrance and went straight to her suite. When she walked in, Roxanne had already taken what she wanted and had slipped the pouch into her bra. The rest of the jewelry had been put back into the false bottom, but the hiding place had not been reattached to the wastebasket. When Luke saw the false bottom on the counter of her bathroom, she shouted, "WHAT ARE YOU DOING?"

Roxanne's face was filled with panic. She stammered, "I... I... just wanted to look at your beautiful jewelry and hold it for a little while."

Luke screamed, "THIEVING BITCH! FOR THIS YOU DIE!"

She pulled her .38 snub nose out of the shoulder holster under her jacket. Roxanne was petrified with fear and unable to move a muscle. Luke shoved the barrel of the revolver against the Cajun woman's breast, less than an inch away from her heart. The madam pulled the trigger, and blood spattered the front of her pants suit.

When Travis heard the shot, he bolted out of bed, grabbed his pistol and trousers and ran to the sound of the gunfire. He took a few moments to pull his pants on before storming into Luke's suite just in time to see her coming out of the bathroom. There was blood all over her from firing at close range. She pointed her revolver at him, but he fired first and put three bullets into her; hitting her head, her heart and her lungs. She died instantly. By then, Rusty and Beau had entered the suite.

When Rusty saw Roxanne's lifeless body, he became distraught. He hugged her to his chest and sobbed. "You're a good woman, and I'll always love you." Rusty wept while Travis and Beau gathered up all the jewelry they could find. Once they had it, they said, "We've got to get outta here! You can't help her now." They had to struggle with him before he let go of the woman he loved so much and they finally got him on his feet. There was blood on the front of him. Beau slapped him in the face to bring him to his senses, and then all three bolted out of the brothel. Beau revved up his Chevy with three deuces and a four speed and barreled out of parking area with the tires smoking. Travis muttered nervously, "Cops'll be here any second."

Chapter Four

Velma ran to Luke's suite when she heard the shots. She made it there in time to see the three men dash out of her lover's quarters. The door was left open, and she entered. When she saw the bodies, she froze for a moment, then placed her hand against her lips and said aloud, "My God, what's happened!"

She walked closer to the corpses, making sure they were no longer alive. Once she was sure they both were dead, she ran to the door and locked it from the inside. Velma was not at all like Roxanne. She was a cold hearted opportunist. She began looking through Luke's purse for anything of value.

She found a manila envelope that contained some rings. It was addressed "Giuseppe Bertolani," and a phone number was written on the right hand side. She knew enough about Luke's business to recognize the name of the jeweler in the French Quarter. She was about to pick up the phone and call him when someone knocked on the door. They said in a loud voice, "We heard shooting. Is anything wrong?"

"Who is it?" asked Velma.

"It's Tina." She was another of the whores. She hadn't been working there very long, and Velma hardly knew her.

Velma went to the door and replied in a low voice, "No, it was just Luke taking target practice. She's taking a shower, and you really don't want to see her right now. She's in a foul mood, and I'm having real trouble putting up with her demands." After she heard Tina walk away, Velma went to the phone and dialed the jeweler's number. Giuseppe picked it up on the third ring.

"Hello."

"Mr. Bertolani, you don't know me, but Luke asked me to call you." Velma was working herself up into a highly emotional state. She was able to make her voice crack and force herself to shed tears. "She... she's dead!"

"Who are you? Where are you?"

"My name is Velma. I'm in her bedroom. She was shot by people stealing her jewelry. She died in my arms. She told me to call you. She trusted me and told me where to find your number."

"Have you told anyone else?"

"No, she said you would know what to do. I'm shaking all over. I can't think right. This is horrible."

"Stay where you are. Don't let anyone in the room. I'll be right there."

Within a half hour, the jeweler was at the door to the suite. After Velma let him in, he quickly assessed the carnage. He said to her, "Don't let anyone in here. I'll be back with help. Stay by the phone."

"Mr. Bertolani?"

"Yes."

"Luke told me to give this to you." She handed him the manila envelope. He looked inside, spread the ten rings it contained on the bed and then put them back into the envelope. Velma said, "Luke told me you'd give me money for them."

"We'll worry about that later. Here's some walk around money." He pulled out a thick wad of cash, then peeled off two twenties and handed them to her.

An hour and a half later, Giuseppe returned, accompanied by three men. He introduced them to Velma. "This is Dante, Vito and Tommy. Boys, meet Velma." They each smiled at her and shook her hand. She thought, "This is all going along better than I expected."

The jeweler began giving orders. "Tommy, you clean up all the blood. Vito and Dante, bring up the body bags and moving boxes; the ones marked fragile." The two of them left the brothel and went to the moving van that they and Tommy had arrived in.

When Vito and Dante returned with the bags and boxes, they put the bodies of the two women into the bags. After they had closed the bags, they put each corpse into a cardboard box. The two men made two trips to carry both boxes out to the van. No one paid any attention to Vito, Dante and the boxes that were marked "Fragile China." After the bodies were in the van, Giuseppe said, "Good work, boys. Tommy and I are going to finish up here. Dante, you drive the van. Vito, please take Velma to my home. Use Luke's car. Velma just gave me the keys. Unfortunately, Donna is out of town today and tomorrow. You know where the guest room is in my place, right?"

"Right, boss."

"Make her comfortable. She needs to sleep soundly tonight." Vito had a knowing look and he nodded to Giuseppe.

Velma was given time to pack a bag, and then she and Vito went to the brothel's garage, got into Luke's burgundy Lincoln with a black vinyl roof and then drove off. They crossed the Mississippi and drove for some distance. Velma asked, "How far do we have to go?"

"Not much farther. We're almost there. Giuseppe likes living in the boondocks where he and his wife have privacy."

They pulled into the driveway of a large home. After they got out and Vito took Velma's luggage out of the trunk, he carried the bag and led her around to a back entrance. Velma noticed a tennis court in the back yard and thought, "I can get used to living here pretty quick."

He unlocked the door, led her into a bedroom and placed the bag on the bed. He said, "Well, we're here. Relax. I'm sure you'll sleep like an angel tonight."

She said, "I think I will. The bed looks very comfortable. Thank you for all your help."

"You're welcome."

She was holding her purse in her right hand, with her elbow bent. He suddenly grabbed the elbow with his left hand and spun her around. He made his right hand as narrow as possible and then slid the hand underneath her jaw until her neck was placed exactly where he wanted it; in the "V" formed by his right forearm and bicep. He placed his left hand on the back of her head and firmly grasped his left bicep with his right hand. She was in a choke hold, and it all happened so fast that she couldn't fight back.

When Vito pulled his shoulders back, the resulting pressure on the arteries along the sides and back of her neck cut off the blood to her head. She started to moan, but quickly became unconscious. He kept the pressure on until her body went limp. He had killed her with a martial arts technique known as the "sleeper hold," or *mataleon*. Vito thought, "This is my thirty eighth kill! *Macho*!" He had permanently sealed Velma's lips.

He rolled her body into a blanket, dragged it to the Lincoln and dumped it in the trunk. He then drove to the incinerator in Algiers, Louisiana, where he met up with Dante. They put all three corpses into the intense flames. As all the evidence went up in smoke, they shook hands in celebration of a job well done. Vito said, "I worked up an appetite. How does some Cajun cooking and beer sound?"

"Good idea."

As Vito followed his accomplice in the Lincoln, he thought, "This is a great road car. It's a shame it has to be chopped up, but that's part of the business."

Vito called Giuseppe from the restaurant and assured him that "All the laundry has been done." The jeweler thanked him and then hung up. He thought, "No one will ever know about these killings. It's strange how problems sometimes have a way of working themselves out. The brothel was making money, but not quite as much as it used to. Luke was showing signs of becoming unstable, and a decision had to be made whether to let her keep running things. The way it turned out, the decision was made for us. The way it happened was a blessing. Best of all, the Mob's involvement is still hushed up."

The only remaining loose end was the jewelry that Rusty, Travis and Beau had stolen. Word was spread throughout the underground network that if the three thieves tried to sell the merchandise, they were to be sent to Giuseppe's shop. "The Dago in the French Quarter needs some of the pieces really bad and is willing to pay big."

After the message was given to them by a cigar chomping pawn shop owner in Slidell, all three made a bee line to Giuseppe's store. He was happy to see them, and offered fifty grand for the whole lot. They were too dumb to realize how unrealistic the offer was. He said, "Come into the back with me and I'll write you a check." As they stepped into the back office, Vito, Dante and Tommy overpowered them. The Cajun and his redneck buddies ended up in the same incinerator as the two whores and the madam.

The Mob placed one of their men in charge of the brothel. It wasn't the same as when Sal ran it, and it eventually became too much of a headache to continue operating. When it closed, an underworld associate of the whore master took the bronze statue that had been on display in the front room. He wanted to keep it in the recreation room of his home, but his wife refused to go along with that. She said, "It's either me or the statue. Take that damn hunk of bronze out of here!" The commissioned likeness in tribute to Sal Cardinale ended up in the mobster's backyard, where it was decorated with bird droppings, just as Luke had wanted.

Chapter Five

Alfredo and Nathalie could have lived anywhere. Both the coffee plantation and Heart to Heart Hospital were thriving, but they chose to settle in Antigua because they considered it the most beautiful place in the world. Nathalie told her husband, "I'm amazed that it is like spring all the year around." A little more than a year after they settled in, they had their first child, a son. Nathalie insisted, "We will name him Alfredo Milla II after the most wonderful man in the world." Each time Alfredo looked at his little boy, he thought, "I am so happy about the life I have with my family." He was a concrete example of a well-adjusted man who found contentment being a husband and a father.

The husband and wife's desire for each other had not diminished in the least. If anything, it had become stronger with the birth of Alfredo II. When they would retire for the evening, Nathalie often gave the love of her life a coquettish look that left no doubt about what she wanted. When that happened, Alfredo thought, "She is undressing me with her beautiful eyes from the top of my head to my shoulders to my manhood, and she continues all the way to the bottom of my feet. How wonderful it feels for her to want me in such an exciting way!" After leaving the bathroom, he would walk towards Nathalie, who was waiting for him in bed. He thought, "I can see clear through her green eyes all the way into the goodness of her heart and soul. She is so transparent in how she loves me. Her eyes melt me like a flame melts a candle."

Matt and Janet Logan paid Alfredo and Nathalie a visit after they had been married a couple of years. Alfredo II was a year old and had taken his first steps. He could walk a little bit with the help of his mother or father. When Janet saw the child, she said, "Oh, Alfredo, he looks just like you."

During the visit, Matt spent some time revealing the entire story of what Sal and Lucretia Cardinale had tried to do to the Millas. When he finished, Nathalie looked at him in awe and said, "You were a gallant cavalier who came to my aid at a time of great need." The plaudit lifted the tall lawyer's spirits, and he felt redeemed. He was finally free of the battle fatigue that had haunted him for too many years. It was a priceless moment he had to share with his spouse. He reached out to Janet, brought her close to him and kissed her sweetly on the lips. He said to his hosts, "This is the woman who kept my inner being alive for so many years. Without her, I would have been an empty shell. Her belief in me gave me the strength to do the right thing when I had to." Alfredo and Matt were friends who shared a common bond. Both of them had taken the time and put in the effort to build peaceful relationships with the women they truly loved. Each had reaped the rewards of fulfillment and happiness.

The night after Matt and Janet left for New Orleans, Alfredo found a letter on his pillow. It read,

Dear husband, companion and my lover,

I want to thank you for the most wonderful life you have provided for me. You have taken me to another level of love. You have treated me with such kindness and gentleness. I know I am the happiest woman walking on this earth.

I compare you with Rudolph Valentino. He was a man who loved only one woman, as you love me. I often wonder in my quiet moments why most other men can't be like you; loyal and tender and thoughtful in every way. Think of how many women would be happy in this world. Treating women properly would mean more rewards that men could reap. What a simple equation! You are among the few men who understand this.

The son we have because of our love is a beautiful duplication of you. I truly believe he will be just like his father, and you have been exceptional as a man, a husband and a father. I am looking forward in the future to having our little girl.

I will close this letter by saying my love for you will never die. The flame that you ignited inside me will last for all eternity.

Yours forever,

Suquita

Alfredo and Nathalie lived for love and found true love. Sal and Luke lived by violence and died by violence. There is no paradise for depraved people who believe that evil is good and good is evil. Wrongdoers eventually turn on each other, while true love will never die. So it was that when love was born, death followed

The End

The Aftermath

www.ingramcontent.com/pod-product-compliance
Lightning Source LLC
Chambersburg PA
CBHW060539260626
47161CB00003B/972

* 9 7 8 0 6 9 2 3 7 4 6 4 1 *